Serpent's Wake

Based in Queensland, Australia and Rhode Island, USA, Lauren Elise Daniels launched her career with Ziff-Davis Publishing in Boston after attaining her BA in Creative Writing from Fairfield University. She completed her MFA at Emerson College with Andre Dubus III, Sam Cornish and M.G. Stephens. A senior editor, Lauren has edited over 70 titles of fiction and non-fiction, developing the work of celebrated international authors. Her writing has appeared in commercial and literary sources since 1987, commencing with first prize in the Newport Poetry Contest. Lauren has served as a literary panelist, judge and mentor and directs the Brisbane Writers Workshop.

This manuscript shortlisted with the international Half the World Global Literati Award 2016, ranking 4th in the top 40 for the People's Choice Award. *Serpent's Wake* is her first novel.

Interactive Press
Brisbane

Photo credit: Dean Holland

Serpent's Wake:

A Tale for the Bitten

L. E. Daniels

Interactive Press
an imprint of IP (Interactive Publications Pty Ltd)
Treetop Studio • 9 Kuhler Court
Carindale, Queensland, Australia 4152
sales@ipoz.biz
http://ipoz.biz/

© 2018, IP and L. E. Daniels.

All rights reserved. Without limiting the rights under copyright reserved above, no part of this publication may be reproduced, stored in or introduced into a retrieval system, or transmitted, in any form or by any means (electronic, mechanical, photocopying, recording or otherwise), without the prior written permission of the copyright owner and the publisher of this book.

Printed in 12 pt Cochin on 14 pt Avenir Next.

National Library of Australia Cataloguing-in-Publication data:

Author:	Daniels, L. E., author.
Title:	Serpent's wake : a tale for the bitten / L. E. Daniels (Lauren Elise)
Publisher:	Carindale, Qld. : Interactive Publications, 2018.
ISBN:	9781925231694 (paper)
	9781925231700 (eBk)
Subjects:	Fiction.
	Magical realism.
	Childhood trauma.
	Redemption tales.

*For those
who forget
and want to remember;
For those who remember
and want to forget;
And for
those swallowed whole,
but who
survived
even thrived
in the serpent's wake.*

Acknowledgments

There are so many people to thank and not all of them are mentioned here. Stories like these are always born from the love and will of many.

Dr. David Reiter, Publisher, IP, for believing in my work, and thank you, Annabelle, Anna, Joshua, Geneve, Karina, Selina, Hans, Lisa, Siobhan for your editorial and creative expertise. Angela, Troy, Rosemary, Jasmine for your medical review and tropical medicine insights.

Trev, William, Amelia, for driving this story in spirited flesh; that life insists upon life in spite of, and perhaps because of, what preceded it.

My parents and our *Leeward*. Lee, Christiaan, JC, Steve, Nicole, Jen, Tania, Julia, Leighann and Michelle for your support.

Stephen King, for answering my letter via typed index card precisely thirty years ago when I was seventeen: 'Take as much criticism as you can stand. READ READ READ and write every day.'

Fairfield University and Emerson College. Sam Cornish, M.G. Stephens, Andre Dubus III, the most challenging, gracious mentors I could have hoped to encounter.

Richard Hoffman, for *Half the House,* your warmth and knowing.

St. Francis House Homeless Shelter of Boston, for lessons about life rising from the cracks.

Drs. Judith Lewis Herman, Bruce Paley, for the compass and map.

Dr. Clarissa Pinkola Estés, for answering my email in '92. Your books are lighthouses.

Dr. Sheldon Cashdan, for the exquisitely written *The Witch Must Die.*

Dr. Bruno Bettleheim, for pointing to a tale for the inner children of adults.

The *Hereford Mappa Mundi* for such visions.

Horace Beck's *Folklore and the Sea,* a talisman.

Wise men, Dr. Neil Robertson and Medicine Crow.

The ancestors and spirits when I got stuck in the mud showed me the roots buried there.

A special thank you to all those I met along this journey, who retained their compassion, held fast to the present, and shone brightly in their humanity despite all that tested them. Infinite blessings upon each one.

Contents

Part I: A Sea Of Night   1

Part II: Will This Fever Pass?   31

Part III: An Octopus Has Three Hearts   81

Part IV: Blood & Fire   175

Part V: Prayer Labyrinth   201

Author's Note

Serpent's Wake is a recovery story written purposely for our inner children: the ones who are always there, listening, waiting to emerge when it's safe.

In this tale, confrontations reflect familiar emotional landscapes and events embody milestones encountered as we heal from trauma. While recovery itself is not linear, *Serpent's Wake* articulates the concentric rings into a path of metaphors. For those who know them, these signposts include feeling again after prolonged numbness; re-experiencing trauma when life finally appears inviting again; the trap of creating a closed circuit; and the cost of being pushed to heal too quickly, among others.

Just as in a dream or a fairy tale, the characters of this story each embody aspects of one mind. In short, we are the captain. We are the bar pig. We are the poet, etc. And we are even what becomes of the snake. All of the characters in this story seek some form of redemption and finally, integration. True to the fairy and folktales that inspired this novel, major characters have their counterparts [the hunter has the captain; the father, the doctor, etc.] to balance their traits as they light the arduous climb toward wholeness.

Lastly, the unnamed coastlines, nationalities and blurred ethnic markers are deliberate. While the details texture a traceable geographical journey, a softening of labels reflects the deeply universal experience of trauma and recovery and the resulting story intends to be what readers bring to its shores. It is drawn from the shared experience that is the courageous, determined and expansive emergence from trauma.

Serpent's Wake is a story for the bitten. It's the story I wanted to read when I was feeling my way through the darkest of the dark, when some part deep within me trusted this journey eventually opened to a point of light.

Serpent's Wake:

A Tale for the Bitten

PART I: A SEA OF NIGHT

Part I: A Sea of Night

I know you are brave: you of the many faces and the one; you who have crossed mountains and seas in the search that always follows the bite.

Your story is ready now: steeped in brine and dried upon stones, its many parts sung together again for you.

Hear it like wolves calling down the moon, like waves caressing a ship on a fine day. See it like a table repaired, each leg guided back into its joint and a place set for all.

Believe in a sacred place that's yours, waiting to receive all that you have set out to become.

§

One afternoon, just outside a village quite like this, a child was swallowed whole by a serpent. The young girl's parents were unaware, mere paces from where she played, of what slid through their budding orchard. While her father stacked wood near the barn and while her mother kneaded dough in the kitchen, the unthinkable happened to their only child.

The snake, enormous and black, had been roused from a deep, century-old slumber. It woke to the tremor of silver charms sewn into the hem of the little girl's dress and nosed up, up, up through a crevice, urged by a terrible hunger to eat that song. It curled against a sunbaked stone in the orchard, and waited. Still as a fallen tree, the serpent watched. Tiny, twin reflections of the child hovered on the polished night of those eyes.

Of course, the child had been warned about many dangers in the woods. By the time she was seven, her father had schooled her on snares and how to read the land. Her mother gathered wild herbs and showed her which caused illness, which cured them, and how often the two grew side by side. At school, the teachers taught that wolves were for shooting and never to speak to hunters she didn't know.

But no one discussed great serpents. No one had ever seen anything more than a rat snake lolling in the barn or a corn snake in the orchard, its pattern so ornate, it may have been mistaken for a discarded bracelet; snakes so harmless, even horses ignored them. No one worried about big snakes here. They lived far away, in godless,

Serpent's Wake

forbidden places; in unforgiving deserts or alien swamps. Anywhere but here.

Squatting with her dress pinched between her knees, the little girl sang. She wasn't particularly gifted but she kept a tune and breathed her music in that faraway voice a child has when she thinks she's all alone. She swept her long, dark hair behind her ears and drew shapes in the dirt as the serpent, still as a slab of granite half-buried in the earth, watched.

Balanced on her heels, she kept her dusty fingers far from her hem. Her mother had made the dress for tomorrow's spring festival—when all the children her age walked from church to a bandstand and a feast in the town square. The dress was adorned with tiny silver bells her father had scored and looped on his workbench, making extra so his horses also jingled with each step.

The girl badgered her mother for days to let her wear that dress, touching the little rosewood box that stored baker's yeast. A pattern of roses and thorns curled around the lid.

'Not yet,' was the answer, the scent of rosemary drifted from a chopping board. Fat, braided loaves cooled all over the kitchen.

'Aww, Mama.' Then, 'Is this really magic?' The girl opened the rosewood box and poked the cotton sack inside it.

'Makes dough rise like the sun,' her mother said, sifting. 'Always, anywhere.'

'Anywhere?'

'Yes. It's very old. It never dies. Your great-grandmother said we will never run out.'

'Can it make dough rise in a wind?'

'Mm-hm.' Her mother poured flour in a great circle.

'On a boat?'

'Mm-hm.'

'Can I please wear the dress now?'

'No.'

In her room, the girl slipped into the dress.

As her mother pulled loaves from the oven, the girl appeared. 'It's so beautiful, Mama!' A tinkle of footfalls: outside, swallows answered.

'Oh, all right.' Her mother smiled. 'But keep it spotless and don't let me catch you hanging from a tree.'

'I promise.'

'Gimmie kiss.' Her mother bent to offer a cheek and the child planted a wet kiss.

The woman touched her face. 'Is it sparkling?'

'It's sparkling,' her daughter laughed in spinning turns. 'My dress is sparkling too!'

So through the trees, where apple blossoms hung in clutches of white, the girl heard her father stacking wood and her mother clapping flour from her hands. She drew in the soil with her fingers—a man with a cap, a woman with hair to her feet, a barking dog, a leaping horse, a ship like the one on the postcard her father tacked to a beam in the barn. The sun warmed her hair and the birds sang and she was thinking that of all the seasons, she loved spring the most.

But, in the orchard, when the birds fell silent, the girl's song ceased. A dank scent swept across the ground. Stillness unfolded as a great shadow rose, obscuring the sun. She looked up into a face of terrible symmetry, its eyes inhaling the light from all around them.

In the distance, thunder rumbled.

She opened her mouth and felt her breath pulled from her like a fine thread spun and stolen from her lips. Her arms went numb as her fingers held star-points in the soil. The hem of her dress slid into the dirt.

She could not move. She stared into lacquer and saw twin selves reflected in those eyes, insects adrift in dark liquor.

Then, a stroke of lightning!

The snake lashed once, knocking her sideways. Her chest flooded with heat. Her heart scrambled: so fast, it felt slow; so hard, it churned into liquid. Flames spread, searing everything. Dust swarmed her mouth, speckled her eyes. Her breath startled the air in thin washes. Askew on the ground, she no longer saw the serpent but felt its cold heat. The sky shimmered—light on oil. A light rain surprised her.

In a moment, the beast seized her. It looped her expertly in its coils and swallowed her whole.

Very much alive, the girl drifted and watched as if from some distance. Sometimes she peered from behind one of the apple trees at this thing, as it happened to someone else. Then a curtain parted and pain speared her again.

Serpent's Wake

She waited for it to be over.
A rippling blackness enclosed her.
A warm stasis followed.
She was gone.
And back for a stammering heartbeat.
And gone once again.

§

Rushing water woke her.
The child's cheeks were wet. Water poured. She coughed. Assessing her condition, she was in the dark and pulled along by this darkness as if carried by some mean current.
Then, a heave of memory.
She realized she was curled up inside the snake, her dress clinging about her, silver bells stabbing her face. She tried to right herself but her body was limp, swept up in a tide turning against its own private moon.
She could not move, could not weep: the darkness absolute.
She wondered: *Do the dead think they're dead?*
God save me! she cried.
Nothing.
This close, sticky dark held her taut as wet rope.

§

A shudder.
She gasped.
Her parents. She heard them. She heard horses. Bells sang on a bridle. She heard the engine of a truck. She imagined flour on her mother's apron; sawdust on her father's sleeves. She strained to turn her head, an exhausting effort. Her torso was in flames.
She heard them again: her father, angry; her mother, frantic.
Their voices drew closer, coupled with another sound she hadn't noticed before.
Tha-dump.
It confused her.
Tha-dump.

Then she knew.

Tha-dump.

The serpent's heart beat deep and resonant as a timepiece rooted in the earth.

Sickened, she strained. She pushed against this place. Pain swept her body, her chest a thundering axis. She tried to yell but her words hardly left her mouth, their voices fading.

With a final fit, she tore at the closeness but the great serpent absorbed every blow. The beast raised its head for a yawn—she saw a flash of light—and sank back into its coils.

§

Over time, her tears dried and again she wondered. She had seen light. Sometimes it pulsed through the flesh of her confines with such measure that she knew the serpent was sunning itself. Though poison soaked her being, she could see her hands in that subdued light and she knew she was alive. The pain in her chest also changed. The devouring heat cooled into sluggish ice.

Through a slurry of time, she adjusted, no matter how crookedly. She no longer pounded the walls. She did not weep to be found. She understood she had escaped being killed outright and was caught: her dress snagged above her head and bound her in this congested void.

Once, in the dark of night, she touched her wound: a swollen score; tight, cleaver-sharp. She balled her hands under her chin and listened.

§

Slowly, she uncurled as best as she could inside the serpent's gullet. Her eyes attuned; her ears grew keen; and when she strained for the world beyond the serpent, she found it.

She listened through the painfully long sleeps of the creature, herself drifting in strange places. When the snake traveled, she read the terrain. When animals fled, she felt their panic. When the snake wound around trees, she felt it compensate for her weight. She warmed as it warmed, the sun bringing a welcome light to her eyes.

When the serpent drank, delicious blooms of the river lettuce and watercress rushed over her. She drank and washed. She gorged. She

Serpent's Wake

crunched on little snails. She rinsed the fabric of her dress and packed it with lettuce and felt the thrum of a waterfall in her bones.

Pine needles crackled as the snake entered the water. The serpent glided to and fro and as it rocked, she imagined herself as a speck of pollen, departing a dark horizon. She would listen, eat when she could, and, one day, she determined, she would go home.

§

Although the girl noticed that the serpent seldom fed, she knew when it was hunting. She felt its body twitch as it set to tracking. She felt it curl for the ambush with more patience than she had ever known.

In a burst, it lunged.

Sometimes it missed and the prey fled.

And sometimes, it struck.

The first time was the most painful for the girl. She twisted away from the carcass of a hare, big as a farm dog. It came at her snowshoe feet first, ankles hooked in repose, head lolling as it slipped past her in a torture of contractions.

She held fast and understood that the serpent had fixed upon her as well and a profound grief entangled her anew. She ran her fingers over the remaining silver bells of her dress, silent and caked with sludge. She remembered the festival. Did the church bells ring that morning? She wondered at her god.

Where are you?

Darkness.

Do you see?

Silence.

She drifted in her nowhere, sleeping away the days as though at the edge of a cliff.

§

Breath.

The whistle of a clotty nose.

Breath called her back the present and the present called her back to her mind. She opened her eyes and felt her fists under her chin. The present was something she had, even if everything else was gone.

Part I: A Sea of Night

There, she could begin again.

So she did.

She felt the serpent hunt and saw she was one among many. Some escaped. Some didn't. Days grew warmer then colder and nights turned bitter then balmy again. The world turned. And unlike the other, atrophied creatures that slid past her, she lived.

Wake, a voice that was not a voice moved within her.

She felt.

Both alone.

And not alone.

Is someone here?

She knew she could choose.

Wake.

And first it was water. At the falls, she imagined water bronze with algae in the heat. Then, she saw birds. Pheasants lofted over scrub, shouting. Fat doves cooed overhead. Swallows chittered as they skimmed an open field for insects. When deer bolted, she saw hooves leave the ground. When a hare thumped its foot, a flurry of golden pollen hovered over dry grass.

But above all others, the wolves showed her the most. Before, when she heard them from her cottage, they had terrified her. 'Are they close?' she asked her father. He shook his head but stepped outside to fire a shot. Villains, they grinned from storybooks and the stories at church called them wicked. But hearing them now—a raucous family reaching into her isolation—wolves spoke of salvation.

When the serpent sidled along wolf territory, she heard growling. About a dozen wolves nipped and clawed the beast. As they tugged its tail, she felt fear in her captor. When she threw her weight against the walls, she knocked the snake off-balance but the animal recovered and succeeded in its retreat.

She shivered with excitement and as the wolves sang of victory, she rose like vapor. She slipped like a cloud-shadow over mountains, a ghost of the wilderness.

She listened to their cascading howls. *You are ours*, they sang. *We are we.*

§

Serpent's Wake

The snake hissed. It leaned hard into trees, fumbling through the forest as though blind, rubbing against stones. It bumped into fallen branches and spat. It dragged its body through tangled places until it came to a crack between stones and began a long, cool descent.

Down, down, down it went.

And down further still.

The world darkened and her sight of things beyond the serpent faded. She no longer heard birds, or water, or the creak of branches. As they descended, even the sensation of roots retracted.

The creature continued with a patience the girl now believed only serpents truly possessed. As the muscles of the snake arched against cool earth, the girl strained for a sense of direction but only felt down.

As the snake came to rest, sliding its body into concentric rings, the girl closed her eyes, thinking that maybe her journey had finally come to an end. She surrendered and both the snake and the girl fell into the deepest of sleep.

§

Something woke her.

She listened.

Silence. Had the serpent's heartbeat stopped?

Tha-dump.

No, but nearly.

She stretched. A little further here; a little further there.

She climbed.

She pulled on the remaining tatters of her dress and carefully, with a bit of twisting and a bit of turning, she found herself reaching the back of the serpent's mouth. With her fingers, she felt teeth, twin rows of curved blades.

Tha-dump.

In the darkness to which she had grown so accustomed, she felt the serpent's thick tongue: a crossroads at midnight.

She paused.

Don't think said that voice that was not a voice.

With something more brazen than courage, she pushed against the roof of the beast's mouth, listening for that barely beating heart, feeling every fiber of muscle for the slightest awareness.

Nothing.

Again she pushed and the jaw was a stiff, unoiled hinge but slowly, it gave. Her arms trembled. And, every few minutes, *tha-dump* went that cold, cold heart.

With a heave, the girl slid between sheathed fangs. She fell to the ground with a thud, tearing away the last remnant of her dress.

She felt earth on her hands.

Darkness.

But as she moved, something was caught. Her head was not free. She touched the base of her skull and pulled. Her hair trailed behind her, right back to the lips of the sleeping beast. She shuddered, thinking at any moment, the serpent would snatch her up again, with finality this time.

But it didn't.

Instead, she felt the occasional, reptilian wash of the sleeping serpent's breath roll across the ground like fog. The girl blinked, lighting up her own dark now.

Both hands on her hair, she turned and even in that blackness, she sensed it: an immense face shining; the trail of her hair cascading from its mouth like a tongue.

She began to crawl, feeling her way one inch at a time, away from the beast. Head down. Neck and shoulders tight. Pulling her hair free.

Her hair slid from the creature's mouth with each pull: another inch, another foot, another yard. Her hair sizzled across scaly lips. Kneeling, she turned to free the last strands but they were stuck. She yanked them from her scalp.

And with that, there was movement.

She listened, hands tented on the ground.

She heard the serpent's head crackle and rise with a sigh.

She held her breath.

She heard it gag. Its great fangs flexed in a yawn and a silver bell threw a spark.

She heard the tongue flick once as the great serpent returned to its repose.

The girl pulled the trail of her hair toward her and wrapped it about her body again and again. She trembled, but not from cold.

Serpent's Wake

She tucked the damp ends of her hair beneath an arm and she rested, nose to the soil. She flexed her fingers into the earth, pressed her face into it, and steadied herself.

She crept, following a draft, and climbed a trail she believed led to the light.

With longer limbs than she remembered, she pulled herself along a narrow passageway. She rested, placing her cheek on the ground, and heard crows.

Something crackled under her palms and she found the papery end of the serpent's discarded skin. She coiled it into a ball as she crawled and it drew her closer to the crows.

Up, up, up. Until tree roots bumped her shoulders. She felt them with her hands and smelled them with her face as she listened with dreadful care back along the cavern.

Stillness.

No heartbeat but her own.

A dizzying sensation.

The girl fixed on the crows and crawled toward light. Tiny winter moths twirled about her, startling her. She rested, plucking spider webs from her lips, and continued again. With the mouth of the cavern in view, she rested again in changing light. She rubbed four filthy fingers hard against a stony wall, leaving a grimy tidal ripple of snake.

When she met the mouth of the cave it was banked with a snowdrift, backlit and too bright. She punctured the crust and wriggled a hand in open air.

Light crumbled through snow in a whitewash. She winced. She thrashed a passage with her arms and stepped barefoot into snow. Cold whirled against her, singing of the wide open, of excess after all that humid scarcity.

She had always felt the cold and remembered blankets piled high in her bed. *Before*.

She marveled now that she felt no sting in her feet and no ache in her chest as she pulled ravenous breaths. She watched through watery slits as each exhalation barreled into sunlight.

With the snakeskin in her arms, she strained to see through the wires of her lashes: a dazzling winter's day. Everything shimmered with prisms—the trees, snow drifts coated in diamonds. The sky ached unbearable blue.

She squeezed her eyes shut before trying to take it in again.

When she could crack her eyes, she put a handful of snow to her mouth and examined her body. She was skinny. And filthy. And covered in sores. Her crusty fingers were long like her mother's. She saw how long her hair was: it wound around her body a dozen times; the once black hair shimmered a starlit indigo.

Past the snakeskin, she saw blurry toes in the snow, far away.

She blinked at the white country and focused hard upon an immense solitary oak at the edge of the wood. Her father had taught her to spot an oak and she willed her eyes to behold its expanse, opening her heart to its endurance.

A pulsing thumped through her feet, a novel sensation: first at a distance, it intensified. The sound spread, stirring the air. Figures descended a bluff, toward her.

Closer now. A man and a horse. A shout.

She turned away from him, turned back to the cavern.

Woolly arms cast around her.

She crumpled.

'Got you!' a voice split her ear.

Stony thighs pushed under hers. Arms hugged her, a strange sensation. She smelled smoke. His words sizzled her ear; the snakeskin whispered in her arms.

When words took shape, she heard, '...wild thing...no shoes!'

She craned to meet this muscle, to gape into the face; close now, he was handsome and crude as a new mountain. A black beard darkened his cheeks, a swathe of black wool encased him. She remembered her village. This was a hunter.

'Where did you come from?' He reeked of a foul tooth. The serpent taught her about creatures with something sick inside them.

The hunter pulled on a rope with his free arm. The horse snorted, as far back as the rope allowed, lips flapping.

The girl wheezed.

As she coughed, he shook her. 'What a hack! You gotta be on something, out here like this. What have you got in your arms?'

She coughed again and he clapped her back with fingerless gloves. 'Cough it up. Maybe it's a hairball.'

Serpent's Wake

Her skin moved against his touch like paper over fire.

He slapped spider webs from her skin. 'All these spider webs! And your wild hair! Looks like I found an abandoned showgirl!' He leaned to look into the cavern then he smelled her in a gust. 'You came out of there? You smell worse than the mattress of a whorehouse!' He tilted her with ease to look into her eyes. 'Bloodshot as disaster! Come on, what are you on? Give me some!'

She hissed, 'Let me go.'

'It speaks! No. You'll run to your death.'

She shook her head. She couldn't run but fostered the impression of choice.

His fingertips clasped her jaw. 'Bet I could knock you down with my boot.' He looked at her body, limp. 'What you been living on out here? Rabbit crap and icicles?'

'Blanket.' She was suddenly aware of her arms wasted to broomsticks, her knuckles knobby under grime. 'Blanket.'

The hunter took a step toward his horse and fished into a saddle pack. The horse jerked its head, ears flat. Nostrils blown, it flashed ochre teeth and told the girl: *I'll kick you to death.*

The hunter laughed. 'Old boy doesn't like your godawful stink.' He handed her a rough wad.

Snakeskin under her arm, she found the blanket coarse and full of horsehair but she held it to her face. It smelled like *before.* Like hay and stacked wood.

'Ah, easy to please,' he said.

She fixed her eyes to the ground as she wound the blanket over those coils of hair. The horse glared and though she tried not to feel anything, she felt like a monster.

The hunter looked at her dirty feet in the snow, 'Opium, right? Or that new stuff they got in town? Wouldn't notice if your toes fell off.' In one motion, he swung her onto his horse.

'My dogs weigh more than you,' he said, then inspected her feet. 'Happy to say you still got all your toes. All warm too. Lucky lady.'

Under her weight, the horse kicked up snow and screamed the way only horses can, burning the girl's ears. The animal bucked, aiming to cast her to the ground until the hunter punched its shoulder. The horse shook its flanks until the hunter torqued the rope, drawing the horse's head to a crude angle. The animal hung its head and licked its lips.

And like this, the hunter took her away, looking back at the mouth of the cave, the shoulder of snowdrift beside the spread of the great denuded oak; wrapped in the horse blanket, snakeskin in her arms, hair pulled around her body.

She saw a ridge and mountains. A fuzzy horizon looked like a woman lying on her back—snowy belly, one breast, a smooth rise of chin and a face gazing into the arch of blue. The girl strained for the way home.

Which way?

But the mountain just smiled.

§

The girl sat before an ailing campfire. Darkness fell between the trees in cold spears. The snakeskin crunched in her arms and the horse bellowed as the hunter tied it to a tree. A pair of scabby dogs poked their noses from a bank of hay and whined.

'I know, she stinks!' the hunter said. He broke a skin of ice in a bucket and dunked a rag. He flung it in her direction and she heard the slap. 'Wash yourself, would you?'

She didn't move.

He kicked the coals of his campfire into an orange spray and fed it bark and pine needles; she startled at the curling colors.

Heat touched her face. She pulled the snakeskin tight to her chest, parted her lips, and warmed her front teeth. She felt ancient. She was caked in dirt with a head of dark, twisting hair as if she had crept out of the ground a thousand years ago. She looked into the fire and saw the phantoms of ancestors, of wise women hunched over stones. She saw curtains of smoke carried off into the night air: prayers to the gods who remain.

Warmth rushed through her, a lit fuse, and she felt the scar on her chest heave under the tourniquet of hair. She was still human. First the crows told her, then the oak. Now the fire said it was true. The serpent couldn't swallow this, the fire said, kissing every cell of her being. She listened and the fire moved like a forgotten face. Calm spiraled within her.

Serpent's Wake

The hunter, snapping sticks, saw her face change and called out, 'Like fire, huh?' He leaned on a sledge and untied a flap of canvas. He unpacked a biscuit of hay and the horse tore at it.

As she sat before the fire, she began to search. This hunter was strong and he aimed to hurt her and he was taking his time, just like the snake. And like the snake, he would bite and not let go.

The girl saw that the sledge was dense with frozen carcasses. The icy air smelled of iron. He was a good hunter, she observed, and good hunters were hard to shake.

He added logs to his fire, sending up sparks. He positioned a pot over the flames. Occasionally, he stirred it with a knife. He looked at her as he licked the blade then drove it into the snow.

He caught the girl looking at the knife and said, 'Dare ya.'

Leaning on his sledge, he rolled a cigarette. She stole glances at his campsite. Beside him, a pair of huge, winter-white hare skins were stretched on a frame.

Holding his cigarette, he approached and scooped the ball from her arms saying, 'Looks like snakeskin...' She screamed a sound so ugly, snow fell from the overhead branches. He let go.

He pulled a bottle from his sled and opened it. 'Want some?' He pointed the neck of the bottle at her. 'Might sweeten that voice.' He took a swig and placed it on a stone near the fire.

He squatted to stir the pot again then threw a dollop to the dogs. They savaged the hay for every morsel and sneered for more. The hunter flung another lump at them and they turned on one another with a roar of hide and teeth. He threw a spoonful of stew into a bowl and dropped it before the girl. 'Eat up.'

She looked at the soggy gray meat and waited, touching the calm again that the fire caressed within her. She went still as she would in the serpent, slowing her breathing; listening as the fire made things clear.

Feed me, it said.

The girl knelt in the snow and unwrapped the blanket from her body. She began to unwind her hair, stiff as old rope. Coil after violet coil fell into thick, shining rings against her palm. Her ghostly form emerged in the firelight.

'Well now, wild thing, must be my outdoorsy charm.' He swigged his liquor and rested the bottle again by the fire.

Part I: A Sea of Night

The hunter looked down to loosen his belt, and the girl measured out an arm's length of hair. It was heavy. She tightened her grip, then heaved it onto the coals, knocking the bottle along with it.

She hunched.

Steeped in tides of the serpent's venom, the hair sizzled. It cast a bright purple flame. The girl heard the hunter's surprise as the fantastic hue shone over the snow all around them.

Glass broke and the coils exploded.

The girl peeked under her arm as a shower of coals swelled from the ground and the hunter fell backwards in the wave. The hare skins cartwheeled.

The hunter—boots up and laces dangling—was out cold. Snow fell against the lapping fire, while the dogs sprang against their ropes and the horse shrieked.

The girl sank the smoking ends of her hair—shoulder-length now—into the snow and stood to wrap herself in the horse blanket. Everything was easier without those yards of hair.

She walked to the hunter's body and touched his face with her foot. She peered at him, her eyes stinging from smoke. He was peppered in soot. Where glass had nicked his nose and cheeks, little red globes swelled and ran. She stooped to see that he was indeed handsome, if only in a cruel way. His mouth was open. A dollop of snow melted on his tongue.

She looked down at his open trousers, at the pale patch of belly and a line of black hair. His hands, palms up on both sides of him, were flowers in their fingerless gloves, floating in the snow. She was sorry, in that moment, that she hurt him.

As she turned, she saw the knife planted beside him. She stepped over the hunter's legs and plucked it from the ground. A dimpled horn handle rested in her palm; the blade winked.

She turned to the dogs and cut their ropes but they didn't move, trying with all their might to dissolve into the hay. She walked to the horse, thinking she would cut its rope as well, but it lunged, teeth exposed.

She tucked the knife into her blanket, took up her snakeskin and left the hunter's camp.

Serpent's Wake

§

In the dark, she listened to the night noises. Eyes wide under a full moon, she twinkled with snow dust. She straightened her spine with a crackle. Had she grown another inch this minute?

Which way?

She closed her eyes.

An answer: *This way.*

She listened.

The stars were many. The moonlight was kind to her eyes. Long ago, *before,* she would have been afraid at night, out walking all alone. But not this night. Not under these stars and this moon, so hard earned, so desperately hers. This night was holy; a word that now surpassed anything she ever thought she knew about it.

Holy.

The sky was gracious. A sea of night shimmered a cosmic welcome so intimate, she trusted that so long as she kept walking, she would find home.

Holy.

Every step she took, she stretched and grew a little more.

Holy.

So long since she'd seen such stars: she spun to meet infinity and walked as if led by the hand.

I'm in the dark again, she thought, *and what a beautiful dark this is.*

She wasn't worried about the hunter coming after her. She wasn't worried about losing her way or freezing to death. She wasn't even cold.

I am life in all this darkness.

And life itself was surrounded by more. The frosted trees cast sober glances. The great owl spoke in the pines. Icicles held fast in stillness. Once, there was only silence and it frightened her but now, silence had a multitude of voices.

You, without a face, speak to me through dirt and fire.

She thought of how she grieved her god; how she mistook silence for absence. And through that voice that was not a voice, she heard: *I bear all.*

That's when she heard it: one wolf, then a pair, then a choir. A whole pack burst the night and she was not afraid.

Part I: A Sea of Night

She knew their voices: *You are ours. We are we.*

She walked; each step, lighter. Filled with night, she had mountains of treasure after such a season of want. She slipped across the snow like a spirit, listening to the wolves until they faded. She moved across the hills, following an arch of stars that pulled her homeward.

When she found a lake, memory kindled: her father's ice saw cut holes to catch fish, his horses breathing fog. She crossed it consciously. Behind her, the glass reflected only moonlight; snow dust spiraled like spirits.

When she felt tired, she sat on a stone near a copse of trees. She inspected her feet, wiggling her toes in her hand: they were crusty but warm. Standing to walk, she heard a sharp cry.

She froze.

A pleading whine melted through a thicket.

She spun away from the trees, her feet jerking over frozen ground. She stumbled then half-ran across the snow, away from a trap into which she could fall again and in her running, she slipped and fell in a heap.

As she lay there, she felt eyes upon her. She wiped snow from her cheek and listened.

Another cry drifted across the cold ground, desperate, like a baby. *Come back.*

She rolled onto her back and faced the adorned sky.

It called again.

She turned toward the trees, peering into the thicket. A set of eyes flickered, white gold, low to the ground.

Crawling, she circled the thicket; the smell of dog and blood heavy in the air.

She gaped between tangled trunks and thorny briers.

Within a hollow lit by the moon, she found a pale creature slumped on a shoulder. One hind leg was pulled high, suspended by wire. A young wolf's face, white as snow, was aimed at her with an expression of abandonment; his limbs lanky and ears too large. A torn rabbit drooped out of reach.

Her father once told her about snared animals and she retreated again, but the wolf whimpered just as she stepped backwards.

Beneath the strung leg, the girl saw the black oil of bloody snow.

She placed her snakeskin on the ground and pulled the hunter's blade from the blanket with shaking fingers. The wolf tracked her.

She traced the wire away from the animal's bound foot to the trunk of a springy sapling. When the trigger was tripped, the tree must have flung the pup with it. She searched for the anchor, remembering her father kicking snare spikes from the ground, cursing as he pocketed them.

There. Beneath the snow was the end of the line at the animal's shoulder.

She knelt. She reached with the blade to expose the anchor but her hands trembled wildly. She withdrew them. She calmed herself, banishing thoughts of what this animal could do to her. The wolf stared.

She prayed, not with words but images. Behind her eyelids, she saw the pack, this wolf returning to leaping smiles under the moon. Tails exuberant.

You are ours.
We are we.

Again she reached for the anchor, hands steady, but it wouldn't budge from the frozen ground. She found a stone and slid it under the wire closest to the anchor. She slowly pressed her weight upon the knife handle; the wire crunched. The wolf's body jerked, its strung leg shuddered into her waiting hand.

She traced the wire, noosed into the dark pads of the ivory paw. She packed snow along the wound, calm as the moon as if watching from afar. She fed the wire toward the wound and it loosened. The loop gave with a metallic zip and the young wolf sprang to its feet, one paw dangling. It showered the girl with snow and was gone.

The girl felt the blade of the hunter's knife with her finger; the wire had knocked a kink from its perfect edge.

Shame, she imagined her father saying.

The girl sat on her feet. The light was changing again. Dawn crested over the landscape. Wolf blood shined on her fingers and she could see its color in the new light. She touched the crimson slick to her forehead, her cheeks.

'Never touch an animal in a snare,' her father once told her. 'Well-intentioned people get killed every day.'

But not that day.

She took up her snakeskin, hid the knife back in her blanket, and resumed her journey toward the sunrise. When she smelled another campfire, she stopped.

A gutted deer hung upside down from a tree. The rungs of its ribs glinted with frost over a churn of frozen red slush. Overhead, dawn-lit icicles encircled the camp.

She scanned the site, hugging the snakeskin. Then she saw him sitting by the fire. Fair ringlets of curls framed a gentle face under a hunting cap.

The man stood. 'Good morning!'

But as he took in the sight of her, his voice shifted. 'Are you alone? How...' He pointed at her feet. 'You can't survive out here...in what? A blanket? You know this is the coldest winter in a hundred years!'

She touched the knife in her blanket.

'Get by the fire! Get warm. Don't rub your feet!' He trotted toward her, flushed cheeks round as a schoolboy's.

She winced at his litter of words, tightening her grip on the knife. The ice in her hair slid across her shoulders with a hiss.

'Wait. I know you...'

She didn't move. Memory was not something she called up; rather, it called her.

'It's you, isn't it?'

Her eyes fixed on his.

'It's you! I know your parents. Oh how we prayed for you that first year. We all prayed...and we still pray every year on the anniversary and our prayers have been answered!'

Anniversary? The word pricked.

The man extended his hands, 'You're skin and bones! Where have you been? We were both children...you were just a child when we lost you!'

She stiffened. Something grew in familiarity about this hunter. She searched his face but her eyes burned in the welling light.

'Oh don't cry. We'll get you home, but...' he pointed at the snakeskin, 'what is that?'

She looked into her arms. It was too soon to tell this story.

'It is you, isn't it...' He examined her. 'Incredible. I see your mother's eyes. But your hair! It's purple!' He removed his cap. 'You don't know me anymore, do you? No matter.'

Serpent's Wake

She watched as he replaced his cap, curls catching the morning sun.

He rubbed his hands. 'Come on then. Sit. Get to the fire and warm up. I'll make a cup of tea for you.'

'I want to go home.' Her voice still surprised her.

'I'll take you there but we need to check those feet.' He touched her shoulder. She flinched.

'Which way?' she searched the rising sun.

'I'll take you. The authorities will want to know everything. You know, some people said you ran away. Some blamed the storm and the flood that came up fast that day.'

The girl thought of her parents.

'So what happened?' he asked.

She shrank from him.

'Seven-year-old girl in her spring festival dress gone!' He clapped his hands, startling her. 'No trail, no nothing. People will want answers.'

The girl remembered just before the bite, the pictures she drew in the dirt. She asked, 'No trail?'

'None. There was a storm and flooding—didn't you see it? We were all caught by surprise. The day before the festival and everything was washed out. And you. Everything stopped. I was your age...'

The girl felt dizzy.

'Please, rest.' He sat her by the fire and poured tea from a kettle. He handed it to her, casting another glance at that snakeskin. He threw a blanket around her feet and looked at her, 'Your hair,' he said again. 'Is that blood on your face?'

The cup tingled her fingers with heat. 'I want to go home.'

'Someone's coming tomorrow to help me get my gear. I can't see how another day will make a difference.'

'It does.'

'I have a dozen snares to check,' he sipped his tea, 'and I'd hoped to take another deer.' He looked at his inverted quarry.

'How long,' she clenched her fingers around the mug, 'has it been?'

He inhaled sharply. 'Years.'

'How many?'

His eyes flickered and she saw he was afraid to tell her. She pressed him. 'How many?'

Part I: A Sea of Night

His face twitched. 'We'll get it all sorted out back in town. I don't know how you're alive out here. You're so thin. And dirty!' he trailed off. 'No matter. The dear Lord has led you to me. Show me your feet.'

She lifted one.

'Warm? No frostbite? How about the other?'

She lifted it.

'I don't understand. Please. Is this a trick?' He shivered. 'You couldn't have been walking long. In minutes, the flesh is hard as ice. Wrap them up. Have that tea. Get warm.'

His blanket felt soft to the touch, unlike the one she was wearing. Still, she let it slip to the ground. She lowered the mug and got to her feet.

He followed. 'I don't understand. Are you all right?'

The world blurred with dawn as she stepped from the fire. 'Home.'

'Tomorrow. I promise.'

The snakeskin crinkled in her arms when she set foot into something soft. Fur gave to her flesh. She leaned for a look. Reached a hand.

A thick gray pelt lay at her feet. Several more were drying on pine branches, pink side up, veiny as maps. Beside them, she saw the colors first, that unmistakable crimson and white of three skinned beasts, carcasses supine in pink snow. She saw the blurred riot of their faces in the ripening morning light: a trio of wolfish grins. Beside them, spools of wire, long iron spikes, a mallet, and wire cutters.

A terrible sound spilled from her mouth. She thought of the snare she broke, and the young wolf's face, the brightness of it.

'Are you all right?' the trapper repeated, too close.

Her words jumbled. She gagged.

'Sit down. No harm will come to you. Sit by the fire and regain your strength. Sit.'

She turned. Heat flushed, a forked temper rose. 'Don't know who you are,' her voice climbed, 'but you talk too much!'

Behind them, a growl erupted. A gray wolf stood on a snowdrift, gaze leveled at the trapper.

He pulled the girl aside, nearly knocking her down. 'You just wait a second. Wait one second!' He muttered, 'Devil...the devil wants my

Serpent's Wake

deer...' He grabbed a fistful of rounds and swiped at his rifle. He pulled the bolt back; an empty shell clinked on the icy ground. He loaded it.

The girl put her hands up, waving the animal from the camp. The wolf watched like a king.

The trapper swung the rifle to his shoulder, aimed.

The girl flew at him, knocking him off balance.

The wolf disappeared behind the drift.

He shouted: 'What is wrong with you? Never do that to a man with a gun! It's a wolf! It won't hesitate to kill you! That is, if I don't shoot you by accident! Get back by that fire!'

She didn't move.

The trapper scanned his camp, muttering. 'Never seen one so bold. They always avoid me. God in heaven, what's gotten into them?'

Another growl broke near the deer. The trapper swung the barrel toward a pair of wolves under the carcass. With a swat, the deer was sent swinging. Hooves clattered against the trunk, a haunted, unnatural sound. The rope squealed. A shatter of icicles rained and wolves bounded from the trees.

The man barked: 'Get off!'

The girl tried to yell, to scare off the wolves, but instead a garbled caw flew from her lips. She yowled, arms out, and rushed them.

The trapper was terrified now, his face crimson. 'They'll kill you! They will!'

But she wasn't afraid. She saw they had no intention of harming her. She saw it in the way their bodies moved, in the way they grinned and leapt. They wanted his quarry, to eat his kill, and drive the man with the snares from their territory.

A wolf urinated beneath the deer. *Mine.*

At that, the girl stood between the trapper and the wolves and laughed, a hideous sound. He lunged for her arm. She slipped and fell. Her blanket dropped, exposing her body.

He stepped over her, saying, 'Cover yourself!' and tried for another shot. She heard the chime of rounds; the bolt ground metal against metal. The trapper aimed at the closest wolf. She dived for his legs but he kicked at her. She tripped him and he fell.

More faces shined from the trees. He scrambled to his feet. The girl crawled naked on all fours, shouting nonsense. One wolf looked at her and blinked.

She sat on her feet, listening.

Go home, the wolf said and looked toward sunrise.

She snatched her blanket. Behind her, ropes creaked. Frozen hooves danced. More snow and icicles poured to the ground. Rifle shots rang, hitting nothing.

The girl slid down a drift.

More shots and a terrible yelp clawed the wood.

Another shot. Silence.

The girl sank into the trees.

Don't run.

Which way?

Her eyes were hazy. She faced the rising sun.

This way.

Worry skittered: *I could die guessing the way.*

An answer: *Death took care of that.*

Her feet sank into snow melting over pine needles and she hoped the man wouldn't follow.

She looked into the pines. She knew the slope of the land and carpet of needles and followed the sun through the forest. Through her soles, she felt water moving underground, beyond the frozen earth, and by midday when the sun was high and slush churned to her ankles, the girl reached the river. In the distance, a waterfall burned white.

Hours from home.

Sculpted by drifting ice and melting snow, the falls made everything smell clean as sunlight. She loosened the blanket and wanted to be clean too. She closed her eyes to see that golden pink she remembered from *before:* a sun star cloaked by a child's eyelids. She felt the thrum of the water, telling her right where she was, as it had for so long.

How long?

He said years.

The length of her limbs said years.

Approaching the water's edge, she saw that the river was swift with sledges of ice. She bent to the river's edge and drank. Her throat tightened at the cold; at the indulgence of making decisions; and at the calm of following a whisper. Her fingers drilled into the muddy bank and creation dripped from her chin.

Serpent's Wake

She leaned back. She had to cross the river to get home.

Several boulders created a narrow, but eventually, she would get wet. She climbed the rocks and they took her as far as they could. On the last stone, she took off her blanket, wrapped the knife and held it over her head with the snakeskin.

She slid into the wash.

The shock of cold ransacked her; the current belted her with ice. Gasping, she dug in her heels. Layer upon layer of dirt loosened from her skin and whirled away in spirals. Pain followed.

She had felt no cold before and now she nearly drowned in the agony of it. She fixed on crossing and took another step.

Her heart contracted in a heave.

She moved diagonally across the river, her toes gripping the pebbled bed like hands. All the while, grime lifted away from her, peppering the churn.

The blanket, knife and snakeskin stayed aloft while water bubbled over her chest, tightening the old wound. It ached bitterly and the breadth of the scar surprised her when she looked at the hardened flesh—pink, white, even gray leather.

She clenched her teeth. She dipped her head underwater and screamed herself alive. She swallowed a mouthful, rose and shook out her hair.

Chattering, she climbed onto a warm slab of slate on the shore. She dropped the snakeskin and hid the knife in the blanket, just in case. Crouching and listening, she could see everything from that rock. Slowly, she reclined, the knife a horned bump in the blanket under her hand. She stretched over the stone and examined her body.

She touched her scar, quiet again as it warmed, and ran her hands over her clean skin. She was pecked by bruises and sores but still, somehow, she was a woman. Chubby wrists had lengthened. Her legs were tendrils. She had even discovered the suggestion of breasts framing that scar as she rested in the forgiveness of sunlight. She dozed and twitched until she found herself wide awake, already standing.

She wrapped herself in the blanket, tucked the knife, took up her snakeskin and followed the path along a trail she knew led her home.

With her first step into melting snow, to her surprise, the cold stung. She retreated to the warm stones, confused. She tried again, and found herself back on the stones.

She eyed the snakeskin. She tried to tear strips from it with her fingers, then teeth, and though it felt papery enough, the skin barely stretched. With the hunter's knife, she punctured it and cut long strips and wound them around her feet. In the wet of the slush, the snakeskin shrunk to fit and blocked the cold.

Again she walked through the melting snow and by dusk, the woods grew familiar. The girl knew this sleeping orchard, though the branches were thicker and higher than memory.

The mud grew crisp against her heels and she climbed over a crumbling wall she once watched her father repair. Her father shifted rocks while she, light as a bird-child in the branches, tasted the first apples of the season. She gazed at the remains of that tree.

She took another step and saw where her mother had showed her vines that caused a blistering rash: stripped of their leaves, they were still potent in winter. Beside them, the twiggy, flattened stems of jewelweed, the perfect salve for the rash, leaned in a clot over frozen ground.

And there, in the distance, was the cottage.

Smoke ribboned from the chimney. Light shone in the window.

So close now. She swooned. But what would she find? And what would they?

She touched her face. What did she look like? The hunter said terrible things but the trapper recognized her. Would they?

She touched her arms. Bony.

The ends of her hair. Burnt. And what of its color?

She pressed her face against an apple tree. A sensation of filth rose all about her, as if she had never washed in the river at all. She felt ruined. She wanted to run; to crawl off and die in the woods.

The sound of distant shuffling startled her. A crackle of icy ground. The surprise of tobacco smoke. Light flickered through the trees. A lantern swung, heading her way.

Another hunter. An old one. Silver hair shone under a woolen cap. His shoulders were broad but hunched. A rifle rested on his arm. A cigarette glowed.

She curled around the tree, into the shadows.

As the old hunter walked, his lantern rocked light through the trees and a black dog snuffled the earth beside him. She saw a string of

Serpent's Wake

rabbits over his shoulder. Then the dog caught a scent and veered away from the man. It had picked up her trail.

The man whistled but the dog ignored him.

The girl watched the way the dog pricked its ears, its muzzle stabbing the frozen leaves where she had walked.

She had to be quick.

Softly, she let the snakeskin roll to the ground. They'd find it, marvel, and she'd be on the steps of the cottage before they even moved.

On her toes, she stepped into the dark, silently at first, then pressed into a crooked run. Her hips stabbed; knees ached. She looked over her shoulder to see the lantern resting on the ground.

She loped home. She slipped and fell into frozen mud, churning the splintered ground up to her wrists. She bled. She scrabbled to her feet and kept running, wiping her hands on the blanket.

She saw the barn. The cottage. The light. The sagging eaves and roof. Everything looked weathered, even in the dark. Shingles were missing and a gutter dangled like a limb.

She peered into the barn, expecting to see her father's horses but found empty stalls and an oily silence lit by a single lamp. Wads of leaves were banked against walls.

She turned toward the cottage and climbed sunken steps, the wood marred by a spray of hard winters and wet springs she couldn't count. Her parents were always so house proud, she wondered if they were gone, but no, the trapper said...

She pushed on the door, trying to control the painful slices of her breathing.

An old woman was fast asleep in a chair by the stove. A radio twinkled with static. The woman's white braid hung over a knitted shawl. In her lap was an orange, half-stuck with cloves with the rest in a twiggy pile on her skirt. The girl took in the kitchen. The same. A rosewood box sat dusty on a pantry shelf.

She took a step.

Mama.

The girl watched her mother's face crumpled in sleep. Deep furrows had replaced the bloom. Her brows were still dark but her hair was white as all those miles of snow.

Part I: A Sea of Night

The woman stirred at the draft. The shawl slipped. The orange rolled. Cloves scattered. She opened her eyes and stared at the girl. No words, just a sharp stab of breath before a sob moved the very stones of the walls.

'I knew!' Her hands reached. 'I knew...I knew...I knew...'

'Love, look what I found,' a man's voice poured through the open door as he kicked muddy snow from his boots. 'Look at the size...' He and his black dog emerged, the snakeskin unraveled.

The girl and her mother were kneeling on the floor.

The old man and his dog fixed on them. 'Twelve years! Twelve godforsaken years!' he choked. 'My daughter!'

Her mother wept. 'Next week is your birthday,' she said. 'The first one that won't tear us to pieces.'

The girl did not weep.

Her father buried his face in her shoulder, his sobs terrifying.

When they gathered at the kitchen table, the girl told them as much as she could. Even to her, it sounded like lies: preposterous in this world of glowing kitchens and dogs lying upon braided rugs. Still, she told them, though her words were like gravel.

Her parents held their heads. They touched her pale arms, shying from the sores on her skin, and listened.

PART II: WILL THIS FEVER PASS?

Part II: Will This Fever Pass?

Later that night, the girl watched her mother stoop to draw a bath. In each of her mother's aged, painful movements, the girl saw the joy of her return splinter in every direction.

Still as frost on the window, she watched her mother pour crushed oatmeal into a stocking, knot the end, drop it into the tub and knead it, turning the water white as milk. She said, 'For your skin.'

The girl, still wrapped in the hunter's blanket, sat on the floor to peel damp snakeskin from her feet.

Her mother folded fresh towels and hung one of her own cotton nightgowns and a bathrobe on a hook. She rested her hand on the door, waiting for something, and when the old hinges squeaked, the girl startled, her eyes black as a night animal's.

'Oh! I'm sorry,' the girl's mother said. 'This door…' She approached her child slowly, hands out as if to a new foal, then stopped and said, tears brimming, 'Gimmie kiss.'

The girl didn't move.

'Remember?' The woman pointed to her cheek. 'Gimmie kiss.'

The girl stared, lost, then a glimmer. With a jerk, she clambered toward her mother's face.

'Is it sparklin?' Her mother touched where the kiss had scratched.

'Yes,' the girl whispered, retreating, 'it's sparklin.'

Alone before the steaming bath, the girl heard her mother stifle a sob in the kitchen. Every time her parents wept, she felt her own eyes grow drier. She came home to wreckage; all of them, casualties. She unwound the blanket and stashed the knife within it. She wanted to protect her parents, if only from the sharpest teeth of what she brought home.

She slipped into the tub.

She closed her eyes, listening as her mother turned one of her father's rabbits into stew. She smelled butter and onion dancing on hot iron and heard the zing of peeling carrots, potatoes, parsnips. She heard her mother clip stalks from the hanging herbs in her kitchen and smelled them when they hit the pan—parsley, basil, thyme. The sensation of chopping and frying was at once both familiar and sad.

Serpent's Wake

All those missed meals. Sundays after church. Birthdays. Drummed against the cutting board.

But the girl found no appetite.

The rabbit. How could she explain that she couldn't eat what she'd seen? She slipped further into the water, her breath rippling the surface.

Her father's baritone rumbled under the frying, though she could tell he was trying to whisper. She caught every word: 'Why is her hair that color? I'm going to drive into town now. He told me to get him. Day or night. Get her to eat. She looks like a corpse. Oh love...'

His boots hammered the stairs and his truck fired up with a wheeze.

She didn't know who her father was going to get. In the whiteout of tub water, memory steeped. Then she remembered a doctor.

The girl remembered how her mother told the story again and again; how, in the middle of a cold, late winter's night, the doctor caught her. 'I dreamt of the sea,' her mother always began, 'just before you were born. A wild, stormy sea and I've never been to the sea. When I woke, you were crowning.' Her mother, much older than most new mothers, had long since accepted childlessness when one simply appeared. The birth was swift and awkward and her mother was unable to have any more but the doctor saw the family back to health. 'And I was happy. And you were happy. So happy, you sparkled.'

All those years ago, the doctor had helped her into the world. Now, she sensed her parents hoped he'd do it all over again. She stepped out of the tub, sank her face into a towel and got dressed, though she needed help with the buttons. She held the nightgown tightly to conceal the scar as her mother buttoned three little pearls.

With the rumble of her father's truck, the men arrived just before midnight. The doctor wore a severe expression over his coat, a satchel in his hand. His face was creased from his pillow but when he saw the grown girl, all traces of sleep evaporated.

Her mother asked her daughter again, 'Are you sure you won't eat anything?' before offering the doctor a haggard smile. 'A little broth?'

The girl shook her head, staring at the doctor. Like her parents, the doctor had also aged. Something had happened; she read it in the way he removed his coat, in the curve of his shoulders. His once dark brown beard was ivory and his now thick glasses gave him an acutely attentive look.

Part II: Will This Fever Pass?

Her mother offered tea.

The doctor nodded then said to the girl, 'Your father told me, but I'd like to hear it from you.' Four mugs steamed on the table as he continued, 'This might be easier, if you give us some time.'

'We've only...' her father began but his wife led him to their bedroom. He coughed fitfully behind the door between the murmurs of her mother's reassurances.

The doctor sat. 'Please pardon me. I was asleep. We can talk or,' he looked at the table, 'we can just drink four cups of tea.'

The girl held the silence as long as she liked. The doctor waited, trying to appear relaxed. He took out a notepad. She wanted to help him but didn't know how. First she thought she should start with the start, with the last day she was a little girl in sunlight but her heart wilted and nausea crawled. She would have to work up to that. She had said so little to her parents, she realized, and still it felt like too much.

It would be easier to work backwards, she thought, to start with her escape.

Then she pondered everything in between and the world felt syrupy. She knew her parents were listening. Her mouth went dry.

She looked to the doctor who blinked, pen poised, and began to speak.

She told him everything she could with words that broke off and fell from dry lips. She began with the river, the trapper then the hunter—he made a face as he wrote; he knew them both. She re-entered the cave and traced the snakeskin back to her escape. She stopped at the beginning: where the weight of her story loomed.

He scribbled then waited.

And she told him more, flushed with heat and trembling uncontrollably, of the bite that did not kill her.

She held her breath, trying to steady herself, and wondered how much her parents heard, and if she was hurting them all over again. She drank cold tea. And it stayed down. She drank a second cup.

The doctor's eyes shimmered. He cleared his throat and adjusted his glasses. He rubbed his beard.

Her story hung in the silence like a wrinkle in the air. It did not feel better to have it out; it felt like the monster was coiled around the room. It was suffocating to hold that space. But she held it. She held it

Serpent's Wake

by remembering every single thing she did to get herself seated at that table.

The doctor laced his fingers.

The girl waited and decided she would never tell her story again.

She reached for a third cup of tea, sipping it more slowly, trying to focus anywhere else.

The doctor leaned on his elbows. 'I realize this may be exceptionally difficult, but would you please show me the scar?'

Her hands darted to her chest. She looked at the collar of her mother's nightgown, a frilly edging that looked preposterous. Those little buttons. Her face flushed. She knew she must or none of it was real for him. So she lost herself a little. With puppety fingers, she loosened the robe and there in the light of hearth, she watched herself struggle with the pearls. The doctor reached to help. She flinched. A gulf expanded between herself and her body as his fingers revealed the scar. It shined like a rip patched with spare material.

She hoped he wouldn't touch it. If he did, she was wound so tightly, she'd strike the ceiling.

But he only looked. His face gave nothing away. 'Does it hurt?'

A whisper: 'Sometimes.'

'Flesh and bone were punctured,' he gestured. 'The inflammation was so severe it left all this scar tissue.'

The girl found her fingers and secured her mother's robe over open buttons.

'Are you all right?'

She felt herself returning.

'Years ago, as part of my medical training,' he said, 'I spent time in the tropics. It was there I met my wife. Do you remember her?'

The girl blinked and began to breathe. His wife. 'She painted,' she said, 'the sea.'

'You remember.'

'Birds?'

The doctor laughed. 'Oh yes, a painting was never finished without the seagulls.'

The girl wondered at him. She read again the misty loss that traveled with him and wondered if his wife had died.

'She doesn't paint anymore...' He paused and the girl saw that sorrow before the shade lowered. 'She does canning now. Preserving things. Jams, pickles. She keeps bees too. Speaking of which,' he reached into his bag, 'this is for you.' He opened the jar and pushed it toward the girl. She leaned in with her fingers ready. He said, 'Let me get you a spoon.'

She retracted her hand, asking, 'Why did she only paint the sea?'

'Each was a visit to her island. She left paradise for me.' He handed her a spoon. 'But then, paradise has serpents.' He reached for the last cup of tea.

The girl pulled the spoon away from the jar, honey a golden cord. She twirled it, salivating.

The doctor watched her. 'It's been a long time. Go easy.'

She touched it to her tongue and the sweetness exploded. She coughed.

The doctor poured water into a mug.

She drank it all.

He rifled through the kitchen and found alfalfa sprouts growing in a window box, which he trimmed with a knife. 'Eat what you know first.'

She shoved a fistful into her mouth.

He clipped another bunch, sat and folded his hands. 'I saw many snakebites in the tropics. I saw scars, amputees, death. I also saw something I would not have believed if I did not see it for myself.' He described a peculiar group of people on his wife's island, 'They were utterly beyond the bounds of my science. It was like this: if any of them were bitten—and they had some of the most venomous vipers in the world—they did not die. Never a single recorded death. They said they had a divine arrangement and declined all interference from outsiders.'

The girl tried the honey again, coughed and dropped the spoon on the floor.

The doctor said he was permitted to visit the tribe with an interpreter, '...on the condition that I keep my medicine—my witchcraft, as he called it—to myself. His niece had been bitten on the thigh and I was allowed to watch her treatment: strange herbs smoked into mush and applied to the wound. I thought she'd be dead in hours, but within a week, she was wearing hibiscus in her hair, grinding taro with her mother.' He shook his head. 'One of the most humbling experiences of my life.

Serpent's Wake

I took great care not to offend them as I was so utterly curious about them.' He smiled a little. 'You know, they loved chocolate. I brought chocolate in a rucksack on the advice of the sea captain who took me there.'

The girl licked honey from her fingers.

'Mind you,' he continued, 'they didn't encourage a bite then claim an act of divine mercy when they survived. It was taboo to interfere with a snake, but quite different if the snake interfered with you.'

He scratched his beard while the girl stood and silently pawed the window box. 'Throughout my time there, I saw people who should have been killed by the chemistry that savaged their bodies—toxins all perfectly evolved to halt and dissolve living beings into paste, but they lived. I was baffled. Just as I'm baffled tonight. I've never seen a bite so close to the heart!' he tapped his chest. 'You should have been dead twelve years ago but here you are.'

The girl had consumed the rest of her mother's alfalfa sprouts as he spoke, leaving only a box of churned dirt. She chewed soil from her ragged fingernails.

The doctor said, 'The sores and bruises will heal with good food but your mother's well-intentioned stew is too much. I'll speak with her.'

He dug into his bag and placed a small paper bag on the table. 'This is for parasites, which you must have.' He also produced a small set of scissors. 'May I have a snip of your hair?' She tilted her head toward him.

Later, by the door, the doctor stood with the girl's parents while she tried several times to screw the lid back onto the honey. 'Let's keep it quiet. Just tell people she's back after a terrible ordeal and we're working on it. I'll talk to the police on my way home. If people find out about this—if they see that snakeskin—they'll lose their minds.'

Just before dawn, the family retired to bed. As the girl lay in hers, her feet touched the footboard. She stared at the ceiling and listened to her parents' murmurs. They were both crying as quietly as they could. She sank into herself.

Under the strange weight of a homemade quilt, she ran her fingers over her ribs. The dusty room made her eyes itch. Her nose ran. She scratched then closed her burning eyes. When she opened them, a face loomed: a great shining face in the darkness, inches from hers. Its breath rolled over the bedspread.

I want my skin.

And she was up, wild with the bedclothes as she aimed to blind the beast with them. But she hit the cold floor with a thud.

'Are you all right, dear?' Her mother was in the doorway.

'Yes,' she gasped.

'Are you sure?'

'Yes.'

'All right then.'

And she heard her father whisper, 'He warned us. It's to be expected.'

In the morning, the girl woke beneath the bed, curled into the quilt, tracking a square of sunlight on the floorboards. She heard breakfast. She smelled bread.

She pushed out from under the bed. The horse blanket was still folded on the nightstand where she left it, the knife inside it. The blade glinted in her hand. She belly-crawled back under her bed and stuffed it between the wooden slats.

She worked at those pearls until her nightgown was done up to her neck and paused at her bedroom door to look back at the horse blanket; it would be gone by the afternoon. She knew her mother would be anxious to get rid of it.

'He's a good friend,' her father said about the doctor, bent over his plate of toast and eggs. 'He's right. We'll keep things quiet.' He leaned against the table with a creak and threw a piece of toast to his dog.

'I've asked you. Not from the table.' The girl's mother wore a lilac shift, white hair neatly braided. She placed toast in front of the girl, the butter and jam smeared together. 'Try to eat.'

'Five years ago, he lost his son, his oldest,' her father began, cutlery poised, 'while you were,' he measured his words, '...gone.'

Her mother glared. 'Do you really think...?'

'Yes, I do,' he raised his voice, 'I do think she can handle it. She can handle more than we know. I want her to know we trust him. That we grieved our children together,' her father's voice wavered.

Her mother sat at the table, spatula folded into her arms.

The girl tore her toast and wished it plain.

Serpent's Wake

Her father coughed that wet cough again. 'His son got into medical school. Only just started, then he was gone. Your mother thinks it was the pressure, or maybe he had a harder time because of his background.' He looked at his wife for agreement but she ignored him. 'I don't know. People accept more than they used to, but maybe that's just how it looks when it's not happening to you.'

The girl didn't know what he meant.

'No staring,' her mother pointed her spatula at the dog; the dog then looked to the wall. 'See what happens when you feed him from the table?'

'Don't worry about it,' her father said to his eggs. 'His other son. Now he has his head on straight. Works with his hands. Helps me around here.' He placed his hand near, but not touching, his daughter's. 'Listen. They've had their share. They're the only people who remotely understand.'

She nodded. Her toast was torn to pieces, fingers smeared with butter and jam.

'Good. Because everything is going to settle down. We just need time.' He poked at his eggs. A yolk collapsed. 'It's a small town.'

He sputtered into a coughing fit that wouldn't stop. He pushed himself from the table, the wood crackling. 'Excuse me.' His chair scraped the floor and his cutlery scattered. He stumbled down the steps; the dog behind him. Within seconds, tobacco smoke curled under the door.

Her mother collected the cutlery and went to the sink. 'Be patient with him.' She drew in a sharp breath. 'You have no idea what these years have been like. How he looked for you and barely said a word. We had help at first but people move on.'

She touched her daughter's arm, slipping a tangle of alfalfa sprouts onto the table. 'He couldn't talk about it. So we each bore it alone in a way and each spring, we died all over again. Your father and I clung for dear life. People told us to grieve. We didn't. We just stopped where we stood. Our only child! When you were born, you were such a surprise, you grew our hearts so big. And when you were gone, they stopped.'

Then the sound of running water lit the room, her mother back at the sink, looked over her shoulder at her. 'It kills us that you had to do this all by yourself.'

The girl stared at the sprouts, a hundred little suggestions.

A pan clanged and the girl flinched. Water steamed. Her mother sank the cutlery with a complicated shatter.

After a time, when it was safer, the girl asked, 'The horses, Mama. Where are the horses?'

'Oh,' her mother shook a dishtowel. 'A sickness came through years ago. Many horses got sick. People died too. Everybody shot them and your father never wanted to go through that again.'

Picking at the alfalfa, the girl smelled more tobacco smoke leaking into the room.

'I can't just feed you sprouts,' her mother said. 'I didn't know a girl could walk and talk and still look like you do. Do you just want plain bread?' She tore off a hunk and replaced the plate. 'I'll make you anything you want. Anything.'

The girl looked around the kitchen and saw a wooden bowl of brown-skinned pears.

Her mother followed her gaze. 'Stewed pears? They were the first solid thing you ate at four months.' She began peeling.

The girl noticed the orange pierced with cloves was hanging from a peg in the sunlit window. As the sunlight warmed it, the scent wafted. 'That's nice,' she pointed.

Her mother leaned on the sink to sniff, the braid slipping over her shoulder. 'Helps me cope with his smoking.'

'I don't remember smoking.'

'It started when the horses died. He didn't keep hay in the barn anymore and he started smoking in there. No amount of complaining can stop it.'

After a moment, the girl asked, 'Where's my snakeskin?'

'Put away,' her mother wiped her hands. 'Let it lie. No one needs to see that right now.'

§

But someone did.

Someone indeed did see.

Despite what the girl and her mother and her father and the doctor decided about keeping things quiet, someone watched from the darkness as the men went into the barn last night, trailing that monstrous skin under shimmering lamplight. And someone watched them roll it up and hide it at the bottom of a great wooden chest, under a splay of rags and rusty tools.

And after her father drove the doctor home, that very same someone stole into the barn without a sound, rifled through the chest and took the snakeskin.

And so, despite their efforts to keep things quiet and tell a simple story of 'little girl lost, now found,' word got out. Then late one Sunday night, not long after the girl's return, the red curtains in the windows of the town pub pinched closed and the snakeskin appeared. Unrolled along the bar—which comfortably sat over thirty burly farmers and tradesmen—it hung generously off both ends. About a dozen men, one barmaid and the pub's resident pig saw the skin and swore oaths at it, but not one of them was sober enough to offer details on who had stolen it.

When the girl's father heard the rumor and went digging in the barn, he found the snakeskin gone. He didn't say a word.

§

A tap at her door. The girl quickly covered a scaly rash that had broken out along her collarbone.

The door opened and her mother said, 'It's your birthday.' She held another bowl of stewed pears, a single candle burning, her hand cupping the tiny flame. 'I added custard this time.'

'Mama...'

Her mother sat on the bed, handing her daughter a spoon and touching her hair. 'You look better every day.'

The girl blew out the candle and took a bite.

'You're nineteen today. Nineteen.'

The pear fell apart on her tongue. A hint of vanilla clouded the notion of years.

Her mother smoothed the bedspread. 'Can I ask you something?'

The girl looked up from her spoon.

'Have you, has your body started to bleed yet?'

'I don't think I bleed at all.'

Part II: Will This Fever Pass?

Her mother persevered. 'There is a book I'd like you to read. Maybe the stress of everything, maybe it delayed things.'

The girl scraped the bowl, indifferent, then looked up to see water spill from her mother's eyes.

'We are women,' she told her daughter. 'Survivors. We birth; we bury. We're here when the rest are gone. My mother, your grandmother, told me we are blood and fire. Don't ever forget that. You've proven your strength a thousand times over with whatever happened and you don't even know it.' Her mother held her tightly and the girl relaxed in her arms. 'Happy birthday. I mean it. There's been enough of the rest.'

That night, the girl sat on the edge of her bed, watching the darkness through the window. She listened to her parents fret in bed and didn't move until she was sure she heard their sleeping sounds.

Then, light as ash, she slipped down the hall, past her father's books. The dog followed and she thought it better to take him than risk his bark upon her return.

She went outside, sinking her fingers into the dog's dark coat as he walked beside her. The girl crunched across a film of snow in her mother's thick socks and stopped at the orchard, where she heard the stars speak. Her breath rose to them. She closed her eyes, listening, holding her first birthday home.

§

The following week—the week of the anniversary—after everyone went to bed, the girl heard her father say, 'We've got to end this. She's got some meat on her bones. Get a dress on her and a hat for that hair. We're going to church Sunday. It's the spring service, goddammit. We're going.'

'Are you sure? But tomorrow is...' her mother didn't say the word.

'We don't worry about that anymore.'

'You know what it's like in town. And her hair—what about that?'

'Like I said, a hat. You two need to leave the house. Stop the goddamn nonsense.'

Silence. Then, 'I leave the house.'

'The garden doesn't count. I can't believe what I'm hearing in town. You know they did the same thing when the doc's son died.

Serpent's Wake

Rumors and lies. So we go in there and act like a normal family and we stare right back and that's that. Besides, they can't crucify her in church, can they?'

'This Sunday?' her mother whispered. 'Nothing fits her. She still only eats fruit and weeds, for heaven's sake. I only managed to get her to drink milk this week and eat a walnut. A walnut! And she made that last an hour. I nearly lost my mind! All she does is read your books and reject my food. And you want me to put her in a dress and take her to town? Oh what will she wear?'

'You're good at these things. You'll figure it out. And you're right: she needs to do more around here. I'll give her jobs, build up her strength.' He began to cough a cough that squeaked the bed.

Her mother sighed. 'Oh would you ever stop smoking? Listen to yourself. Wet cement in your chest! She's finally home and you're going to drop dead!'

In the next room, the girl chewed her blanket. She remembered the spring festival and the dress with the little silver bells. The memory struck like fire and the old wound ached.

Anniversary.

She listened as her mother got him a drink of water.

Part of her said that the worst was behind her; another part howled that the worst was breeding a cellar of rats.

Her mother returned to bed.

The girl heard a tearing sound. Thread spilled from her mouth like hair.

In the morning, no one mentioned the anniversary. Her parents called her to join them in the garden but she again hid in her father's books.

§

That blustery Sunday morning, the family stepped from the truck onto icy church grounds. The spring festival was slated for the same Sunday after the first full moon of spring, but this year, the weather had not warmed. Every step crunched. Fallen branches, shed by the relentless wind, littered the churchyard like bones.

Her parents wore their Sunday best under a layer of wool. The girl clung to a borrowed hat—hair tucked beneath it. Her coat flapped in the wind. She wore her mother's boots and slid with every step.

Her mother asked, 'Warm enough, dear?'

'No, Mama,' she said, but her words were stolen by another squall.

'All right then.'

Climbing the steps to the wooden doors, the girl slipped on a patch of ice. Both parents took an arm, but she wished she could have fallen for good. Fallen hard.

She looked at her father. 'Please…'

He placed her hand on the railing and went ahead of her, scuffing the steps with his boot. His eyes were bagged, lined, and a little crazy. He muttered, 'Need more salt and sand on these…' Above him, swallows huddled in the eaves.

Her father pushed on a door, stepped into the church and dished out a look to those who turned, clutching their coats against the draught. Jaw set, he flattened his hair against his scalp and dared their gossip.

No one said a word.

Though the church was creaking and cold, she drowned in heat. She didn't pray. Didn't sing. Didn't look up from her hands. Rivaling the songs of rebirth, a gale howled. Occasionally, the notes of the organ were swallowed by a rush of wind and a strange excitement washed through her.

A whisper rose from her heart, beneath the hymns. *Come to the window,* it said.

She ignored it.

A window popped open and the wind swelled down the aisle and brushed the girl's cheek. A man pushed on the rusty hinges until the window slammed shut and her mother pulled the girl by a coat sleeve to stand.

The organ pumped and the lights flickered. The wind thumped the roof and pushed on the walls, dousing the candle flames.

When a young man relit them, he peered at the girl and she saw the trapper of wolves. Her heart knotted. Sweat beaded under her nose. The hat itched. The pews were too close now; she bumped her knees. The air felt pregnant with the bodies of the congregation.

Her mother produced a handkerchief. 'Dear,' she nudged the girl to dry her face. She tried to unbutton her daughter's coat but the girl swatted away her effort.

Serpent's Wake

Just as the priest began his final blessing, the wind rocked the church. Again, the lights went out. A torrent threw open one of the doors and with it, a flurry of snow danced over the aisle, but it was what stood just beyond the doors that made the old women gasp.

On the top step, a lanky white wolf with big ears looked into the church, a pup really, frozen except for the wind that ruffled his coat.

The trapper lurched up the aisle, wielding a brass candlesnuffer.

The girl clambered over her father to reach for him and watched as the wolf sprang from the steps. It limped across the graveyard and disappeared.

The trapper threw himself against the door and stared at the girl. She let her father push her firmly back into place beside her mother as the priest resumed his blessing.

When the service ended, people piled out of pews and crowded toward the door, many peering out the windows, claiming, 'It was just a dog.' Conversation swelled and people laughed as they wound their scarves. Some were off to the pub; others to a feast that lasted all day. There was music and dancing in town, despite the cold.

A few people approached her parents, who flanked the girl closely. Her father dealt firm handshakes and led his family toward the door.

'Was that a friend of yours?' The trapper's voice was warm but his eyes were cold. 'He won't last long in town.' He extended his hand.

Her mother nudged, 'Be polite,' but the girl searched the floor.

'No matter,' he said in a way that sounded like everything mattered to him. He said, 'It's a blessing to see you home with your family,' and returned to his duties.

Parishioners surrounded the family and her parents slipped ahead in the crush. They approached the priest who stood at the door, one hand keeping his vestments from flapping in the wind. So close to the open door, the girl finally dropped her shoulders and sank her nose into her coat. The cold wind ploughed up the aisle, a relief. She eyed the trees where the wolf disappeared, giddy at the thought.

When a darkness moved against her, however, she faltered. It leaned into her, pressed in on her backside, her eyes on the smiling priest. She knew who it was without turning her head.

Thick fingers tugged a lock of her hair out from under her hat. A growl rolled into her ear: 'Gonna leave marks on you.' Wet wool. A bad tooth. Everything swirled; the church a cartwheel of rabbit skins.

When she turned, the smear of that dark woolen coat disappeared as the hunter retracted into the milling congregation.

§

The family sat at the kitchen table. Her father cut into a steaming roast. 'That wasn't so bad, was it?'

Silence hung.

'They should get the wiring fixed though,' he said. 'The flickering lights were a little dramatic.' Blood pooled on the platter.

The girl curled her fingers into fists on the tabletop. 'Please don't ask me to go back.'

His wife spilled peas across her daughter's plate.

Her father inhaled for a lecture but began to cough.

'Please don't ask me to go back.'

He blinked as if waking, looking down a long while at the splayed roast, then continued slicing.

His wife couldn't help herself. 'Stubborn as you, dear.'

He said nothing and cut far more roast than he and his wife could eat. Lunch was a brittle affair.

The dog broke the silence occasionally, scratching and thumping the floor with his heel. Her mother said, 'He has fleas. I'll give him a rosemary bath this afternoon.'

After lunch, her father said, 'Come with me,' and led her down the cottage steps into the barn. Inside, he leaned against the wall near the truck and rolled a cigarette. 'You can't do this without faith.'

'I have faith.'

'But you don't want to go to church.'

'Different things.'

Her father struck a match and looked hard at her. 'Do you still believe?'

'Believe,' she breathed the word. She wondered how she could ask her father to see what she earned in darkness. 'Do I have to believe in breath to breathe?' she asked, knowing there was a time when she did.

'Your mother wants me to leave you alone on this subject. Wants me to let you be.'

The girl didn't remember hearing that conversation.

Serpent's Wake

'But I know what I need to get by. I know what we taught you and I hope you still have something of it. Godlessness. It's dangerous.'

She stepped out of the line of his cigarette smoke, searching for a way to reach him. 'Your books. You read them to me when I was little. They told me things. Now, when I look at them, they say more.'

'You've grown. But the church can hold you. In the good and bad. It's steady. We all need something steady.' Her father fiddled with his cigarette. Ash fell on his shirt. 'Your mother and I are getting old and we're worried about you.'

'You read to me about churches in your books. Someone builds a church from bones and blood and someone else burns it to rubble.'

He blew smoke at the rafters. 'The way of the world.'

'Well,' the girl took another chance, 'people are always surprised when it's their church that burns.'

He rolled his shoulders and shook his head.

'My church burned,' she said. 'What was once only inside it, is everywhere.' She stopped. If she spoke too much, her father would call the doctor again. Finally, she said, 'I can't just go to church to make you happy.'

The father flicked his cigarette to the ground and stepped on it. He opened a cabinet beside the truck and drew out a shotgun. 'You know how to use one of these?'

She drew away from him.

'Look.' He loaded the magazine. 'Five shells. Five shots.' He pumped it once. 'Look down the barrel and squeeze the trigger.' He aimed it at the barn wall.

'Why...?'

'If you live in an age of burning churches, you need to know how to protect yourself.' He unloaded it and handed her the shells. 'Show me.'

She mimicked his behavior. Loaded. Pumped it. Aimed at the barn wall. 'I'm shaking. Are you happy?'

'No, I'm not happy,' he looked at the barn wall. 'I'm afraid. Go help your mother. And while I want to see you reading those books, I also want to see you working around here too.'

§

A couple of weeks later, the weather warmed and there was a wild hunt. Small children were told frightful stories about snakes: giant beasts slipping into banana crates and craned onto ships in jungle ports and creeping toward mountain villages. Men hung onto trucks in hunting packs. Keg beer flowed, axes thwacked, rifles rang, and the pub became the auxiliary town hall.

One particularly warm Saturday, the mayor addressed his constituent in front of the pub. When he opened his mouth, however, he was shouted down by a gang of alcohol-fueled hunters. The one the girl met in the woods, all those weeks ago, was right at the front—spent cigarette on his lip, his face pocked from his encounter with her. 'You know,' he jeered, 'you really should go back to your desk until it's over.'

The crowd howled.

The mayor quietly told the police chief, 'Lock up that jackass,' but no matter how many hunters spent the night in the drunk tank, they had no control over them. So with the mayor holed up in his office, all manner of snakes were killed and hung in the town square like grotesque streamers: not one of them big enough to swallow much more than a rat.

§

That same day, the girl and her mother took the truck into town to pick up items for the pantry. When they heard shouting and looked out the shopfront window toward the pub, they saw the exchange between the hunters and the mayor and the girl saw him, at the front, flick his cigarette at the mayor's feet.

Her mother gasped, 'The mayor! Look at them all! All liquored up...with guns!'

'Let's go, Mama,' the girl said, carrying bags of sugar and flour and venison for her father.

'This is bad.' She allowed her daughter to lead her away from the pub. 'It's not safe! We're not safe!'

Though they'd avoided the town square on their way to the shops, they saw it now: carcasses of all those snakes hanging and bloating in the sun, just as the breeze shifted, lifting the dense, uncurling stench across their path. Her mother buried her nose in a handkerchief. 'Oh! Don't look! Has the whole world gone mad?'

Serpent's Wake

As the girl steered her mother, she couldn't rend her eyes from the sight. She pushed through an alley alive with flies and packed with garbage. Her mother's feet slipped in the juice of deflating vegetables but the girl caught her arm. 'I'm sorry, Mama. I'm sorry.'

'It is certainly warming up, isn't it? The smell!' Her mother dabbed her face with a handkerchief.

'We're going the wrong way. Where did we put the truck?' the girl searched. 'Wait…'

Another loud rumble from the hunters. Closer now.

'Oh dear…'

The girl and her mother were so turned around that they were at the pub's backdoor.

'Mama, we need to go back…'

Suddenly, a face framed by tapered, drooping ears nosed from a pile of trash. A pig shouldered its way between broken crates and snorted at the women.

A door flew open in a brick alcove, a woman's voice scolding, 'Dammit, girl! She'll cut your throat if she finds you out here again!'

The pig grunted and shuffled toward the steps. The woman squatted, saying, 'Your face!' and wiped the animal's snout. 'That's better. Now get inside.'

The pig clipped along through the door as the woman looked up to see mother and daughter. 'Hey, I know you.'

The girl's mother snapped, 'Leave us alone!'

'Don't worry,' the blonde descended the steps. 'It's only me.' To make a path, she lifted a sack of garbage by its neck and swung it onto a pile; she leaned against the wall and cleared her throat, a manly sound. Her once white shirt was unbuttoned past her cleavage. 'We're doing a roaring trade because of you.'

The girl's mother sighed brutally.

The barmaid was familiar, though the girl recalled a less scalded version. Under thick eye pencil and red lipstick, behind the wrinkles around her mouth, the girl saw a schoolyard face.

'Tell you the truth,' the barmaid yawned, 'I'm exhausted.' She wiped her hands on her skirt. 'We haven't stopped with this snake hunt.' She drew a flask from a pocket and swigged. 'Hunting always brings out the devil in them.'

Part II: Will This Fever Pass?

'You're drinking!' The girl's mother slipped in the sludge. 'At this hour?'

She motioned toward the town square. 'Ah, everyone is. Pig's got the munchies. Whole town's trashed.'

'It's two in the afternoon!'

'Bit early to be staggering around my alley, don't you think?'

'I do not drink.'

'You should. God, if anyone should, you should. I know your story. And yours.' The barmaid contemplated the girl. 'Don't remember me? From school. So what was it? Drugs? Rape? Giant snake, huh? I heard your hair is blue under that hat. Can I see it?'

The girl saw through the make-up. She saw the barmaid twelve years ago and felt ill at the swift passage of time.

'Come on, you remember me.'

'Yes.' Before she thought it through, she asked, 'What happened to you?'

'To me?' The barmaid laughed. 'What happened to you?'

The crowd roared again. The girl's mother was losing patience. 'Let's go!'

'You know,' the barmaid ignored her, 'you really upset my boyfriend when you knocked him out with a bottle. He got frostbite, lying there in the snow. Knowing him though, he had it coming.' She slipped her flask into her pocket.

'Is he...all right?'

'He was never all right.'

'Boyfriend? I don't want to know.' The girl's mother hissed, 'Let's go.'

The barmaid put a hand out, 'Hold up, Mama,' her breasts peeking. 'Yes, my boyfriend. Best hunter in town. The hunter that everyone hates but let's face it, without him, we don't eat.'

'We eat just fine, thank you,' the woman answered.

'Oh really? Your bag's got his venison in it.'

Her mother swished the barmaid away from their bags but she wasn't deterred. 'Let's make time for catch-ups and weird alley confessions. Come on, what's the truth? When you disappeared, this whole place went crazy. I was your age and scared to death. Did someone just steal that crazy snakeskin from a circus?'

Serpent's Wake

The girl felt her mother's hand tighten on her arm.

'I saw it and I mean,' she held her arms out as wide as she could, 'it was gigantic.'

The girl pulled away from her mother. 'You saw it? Where?'

'Someone brought it to the pub. It must have been twice as long as the bar! Sunday was our slowest night but that was before the goddamned circus came to town. I can't wait to see the clowns. When do they show up, huh, Mama?' The barmaid leaned over and tapped the woman.

'How dare you!'

'Go ahead, dare me,' the barmaid winked. 'You wouldn't believe what I do on a dare.'

'For heaven's sake, your breasts are hanging out! Where's your dignity?'

The barmaid drew closer. 'I lost my dignity so long ago, I don't even miss it.'

The girl asked, 'Who has the snakeskin?'

'Never name names. If there's one thing we've both learned, it's how to keep our mouths shut.'

'Crude.' The girl's mother pulled on her daughter's arm. 'Trash.'

The barmaid scoffed, 'Yeah, Mama, try not to break your hip in it!'

'Wait,' the girl said but her mother tugged. She looked back at the barmaid, who was now resigned to a look of pity as she leaned against the wall.

The girl and her mother slipped through the alley muck, all the while the barmaid shouting, 'Come on, you can tell me!' They heard the pig snort. 'I won't tell a soul!'

They rounded the alley and emerged onto a side street hugged by a sloping stone wall. Three hunters and a police officer were leaning on the wall, all holding pints from the pub.

The girl's mother whimpered, 'I can't take much more of this.'

The glasses lowered to the street. 'Hey!' one of the hunters shouted.

The officer turned a corner. The three approached mother and daughter, toothy, with an air of gunpowder and heat.

One said: 'Hey, what's the story?'

Another said: 'Where is it? All we got is a dead end.'

The third said nothing but his face was sinister. They slowed, closer now, confident as lions.

The first said, 'You can't just drag this shit into our town and then hide. Get in that pub and draw us a map! I'll drag you in there if I have to.' He reached for her.

The woman pushed in front of her daughter. 'Where did that officer go?' her voice trembled. 'Where did he go?'

The men laughed. The first persisted, 'Come on, lady, we got a job to do.'

'Don't you lady me.'

He reached for the woman's wrist, 'You can come, too.'

She raised her fist. 'Don't you touch me or my daughter. I know you. And you,' she pointed to the silent one. 'I know your parents. How would they feel about you threatening us in the street?'

'Threatening?' the second said. 'Look, we just want to kill the thing.'

And that's when they heard a whistle. Down the road, the barmaid hung out of a pub window, shouting, 'Happy hour, boys! Bring back my glasses or I'll sick the pig on you!'

The girl and her mother hurried back to the truck, the girl looking over her shoulder at the barmaid who waved a dishtowel. They didn't speak again until they were clear of town.

'Well, that was a surprise.' Her mother shoved the truck into gear.

They rode quietly, retreating into the safety of the woods. 'Someone took the snakeskin.'

'It doesn't prove anything.'

The girl was surprised by her mother's words.

'I'm glad you didn't tell that awful girl anything,' her mother continued. 'You never have to tell anyone. Ever. Leave it behind you. Wash your face and move on. Soon enough, we'll get you back in school. In another town maybe. When it's safe.'

The girl scratched at her neck. If she could just wash her face and start over, she would. But she had no face to wash. At least not the kind her mother was talking about. The serpent swallowed it and she was still trying to make a new one.

She turned her thoughts back to the town square. She considered the ease at which life was pinched to a close around her, the sum of a day's violence bloating in the sun. The girl scratched again just as her mother reached over from the wheel to bend the collar of her daughter's top. Welts had climbed above the neckline. The truck weaved on the dirt road.

'Your skin.' Her mother's voice was softer now. She stopped the truck and gathered a big bunch of jewelweed, the waxy stems trickling with juice, the yellow star-shaped flowers bobbing in her arms. 'Hold these,' she told her daughter, climbing back behind the wheel.

Back in the kitchen, her mother boiled the cuttings into a tea that smelled a little like hops and impatiens.

The girl spied again the rosewood box of yeast on the shelf as her mother poked a wooden spoon into the pot of boiling jewelweed.

'Is it really magical like you said?' She touched an ancient fingerprint of dough on the lid.

'Magical?' her mother looked up from the simmering pot.

'You said this yeast was ageless; it was from my great-grandmother. That it's why you won prizes for best braided bread. That it makes dough rise anywhere and that you'll never run out.'

She took the pot off the stove. Finally she said, 'You remember.'

After the broth cooled, the compress was applied in silence and the girl skipped dinner and went to her room. When the girl heard her father ask at the kitchen table, 'What the hell's the matter?' she heard nothing in response.

And as the night crawled from one dark hour to the next, the heat hung like iron. The girl heard her parents talking but could no longer make out their words. She sweated and tried not to scratch. Then she stilled her mind as she would in the serpent and let her eyes film. She slowed her breathing and sleep finally carried her through the bars of the night.

§

It seemed to the girl and her parents that there had been no spring that year. Heat oppressed the village as soon as the snow had melted and never abated. Rain came and went without relief. Humidity stained everything and conjured mold. Over the weeks, the villagers grew irritable and suspicious of the weather. Farmers worried over their crops, rotting in the fields; their young plants decimated by fungal

Part II: Will This Fever Pass?

infestations they couldn't control. Conversations were repetitive: 'First the harshest winter in a hundred years, then the hottest, wettest summer on record. What next?'

By late summer, the extermination of the snakes in early spring caused an explosion of vermin across every farm in the territory. Any meagre harvest that managed to escape molding in the field was fouled by rodents. When farmers opened their storehouses, waves of rats and mice and feces spilled out in squeaking tides.

Fearing a plague, people brought in crates of cats but there were far too many rodents and the cats disappeared. They then resorted to poison but most food stores were already ruined and several hunting dogs that gobbled up bait were lost in the campaign. Imported goods were shipped in from the coast, a few hours away, and the price of everything doubled. Tempers rose. Snakes were declared protected animals by the mayor and some of the townspeople, furious at the ordeal, blamed the girl for everything.

'Did you notice when all this started?'
'Any ideas how much this giant snake has cost us?'
'What's with that purple hair?'
'She just wants attention. Don't give her any.'

There was always talk of expense at the pub. Business, during this time of heat, rot and pest, was down for everyone except the pub owner, who grew rounder in the bust and belly while everyone else grew lean. To secure her clientele during that oppressive summer, she installed a ceiling fan and offered salty cheap food with her pints: home fries and sausages.

Spinning in rickety circles over a mist of grease, the fan only added to the dank atmosphere, but people lined up anyway. Farmers, tradesmen, even the local school master on summer break, all in damp shirts, got drunk and the pub owner kept the lights low to obscure the bitterness on every face. Even the pig turned out to be an asset in this time.

'Put her hat on and give her another beer,' a farmer said. 'God's sake, I had to kill all mine today.'

'Only one more,' the barmaid said. 'She's tits-up as it is.'

And everyone laughed as the barmaid slipped a fascinator onto the pig—red with white silk flowers from an ancient horse racing carnival—

and the pig held up her head to clasp a bottle in her long mouth, drained it, belched, and slumped onto her side.

'Just like my wife,' the farmer said.

About this time, the hunter, a daily patron of the pub, told stories of how the girl aimed to seduce him in the snowy woods. Taking out his bag of tobacco, he wiped sweat from his face and said the girl stunk, '...and I worked in a slaughterhouse when I was twelve.' He pinched a rolling paper. 'I say she worked the streets in some other town until she decided to walk home, and now she's got everyone in an uproar.'

The barmaid swiped the silk off the sleeping pig. 'So what about that snakeskin?' she slapped the sticky bar top. 'We all saw it when you brought it in here!'

'Off a ship to keep her story going. The doc's been to the tropics. Maybe it's from him and his savage wife.'

'Why bother?' the barmaid looked up at the wobbling ceiling fan. She turned to the pub owner who was hunched over the grill. 'You know, it looks like it's going to come down and take off our heads.'

The pub owner swore at her.

The barmaid turned back to the hunter, 'I want to know why they would go to all this trouble.'

The hunter said, 'Because their daughter is a whore and unlike your parents, they don't want everyone to know.'

The barmaid withdrew, asking, 'Why am I even with you?'

A few of the patrons were leaning on their elbows, smirking over their beers, but the hunter continued: 'I'm out two good hunting dogs. Rat poison. Puked themselves to death.'

The pub owner wiped the sweat from her face with her palm. Her hair was a burned cactus roiling under a dishrag; her t-shirt stuffed to the collar with bosom. 'I can't stand it.' She pointed a greasy pair of tongs at him. 'You probably never even met that girl in the woods. You're so full of it, your eyes are brown.'

'My eyes are brown,' the hunter squinted. 'Those were good dogs.'

'And I say you're full of it.' Short as she was, the pub owner huffed onto a step she kept behind the bar. Bosom on the bartop, she leaned toward the hunter's face. 'You kicked those mangy dogs up and down the street. Skinny as fences, scabby pair of them. Good hunting dogs? Ha! They were thick and lazy and if the poison hadn't killed them, you'd have done it yourself. At least it was quick.'

'What do you know about quick death?' the hunter looked at the pig; the pale trotters twitched.

'Ah, that pig's a whole lot happier than you are.'

He held up his hands, showing the marbled tips, gone to frostbite. 'These. Are from that damn girl.'

The barmaid was filing her nails now. 'Any excuse to whip those out.'

A couple of men chuckled. The hunter swept a gnarled finger across the pockmarks on his cheeks. 'Only a whore throws glass in a man's face.'

'Let me tell you about your face,' the pub owner said, her eyes wild from the heat. 'You're off it and you're killing the mood in here.' The fan squeaked, a sausage spat and the pig farted. 'Eat something before I kick you out.' Sweat coursed down her face as her eyes drilled into the hunter.

He pushed back from the bar and crossed his arms. 'The hard sell, is it now? I butchered that pig for you. Gimmie one on the house.'

She stepped from her box, plucked a sausage from the heat and slapped it onto buttered bread. She dropped a dollop of greasy home fries on a plate and told the barmaid: 'The fan isn't going to behead anybody. The heat's so much worse without it.'

The barmaid pointed her nail file at her boss. 'You really think so? You're sweating like a horse!'

A troupe of sweat-soaked farmers pushed through the door and the pub owner sent the barmaid away with: 'You got customers.' She climbed back onto her box and looked at the hunter, his mouth full. 'Better?' She dabbed sweat from her thick neck with a kitchen rag then began polishing a glass with it.

He nodded.

'Tell me. What are you doing with that little sliver when you can have the whole pie?'

The hunter paused in his chewing. He gave her a wide grin and said, 'Clear my tab.'

'It's terribly high...'

As sweltering day moved into sweltering night, even the pub owner bent her rules around staff drinking and the pub blurred, lit from end to end. The night moved like a salamander from a burning log.

Serpent's Wake

Well into the night, a farmer leaned into the street from the front door and said, 'Anybody smell that?'

'Smell what?' the schoolmaster finished his scotch and spun the ice in his glass.

'Something's burning...'

A slather of drunks gathered at the door.

'What is it?'

'The church! The church is burning!'

Bells rang.

§

The girl's father threw open his daughter's bedroom door to find her sitting on her bed, a book of fables over her knees. A drawing of an eagle flying into the sun shined from a page.

'The church is on fire!' he said. His wife appeared at his shoulder and he told her, 'I'm going to help. Stay here.'

When he returned late that night, reeking of smoke, his wife said, 'They aren't saying what caused it. What happened?'

'They don't know,' he said, looking in on his daughter who pretended to sleep. 'They don't know but it was razed to the ground.'

'Oh my, was anyone hurt?'

'No. Everyone helped. Bad times, my love, and people are looking at us. Why are they looking at us?'

§

That Sunday, the village gathered under a borrowed tent; the rubble a perch for sparrows. The altar—a donated card table—stood over grass thick with buttercups. Parents refused to take the limited folding chairs, took off their shoes, and sat on the grass with their children. Old women fanned themselves in their seats and watched butterflies wing through the tent. Despite everything, the mood was light.

Just as the priest rose from his chair to give the final blessing, the trapper took the podium—borrowed from the schoolmaster—saying, 'Can I have your attention please?'

To those perceptive enough to see, the priest startled, as the young man always adhered to their strict routine without prompts. Several members noticed the priest, standing now and clasping his hands. Everyone knew that since the girl's disappearance years ago, the priest had looked after the trapper and that he trained the seven year-old as an altar server because he couldn't get rid of him.

'I'm sorry, Father, but this must be said. I prayed long and hard on this and considering recent events,' he looked toward the rubble, 'I must confess what I saw.'

The priest had delivered a multitude of sermons on charity since her return but a tide far stronger than he was rising.

'When that girl came upon me in the woods,' the trapper's voice rose and shook, 'I witnessed things that defied natural law. Barefoot, exposed in the coldest winter in a hundred years, but her feet, in all that ice and snow, were warm. I offered her food and drink but she rejected it. She was getting her sustenance some other way.'

Someone coughed.

'It's in our scripture: these signs of evil at work.'

The priest winced, 'A heavy word to bandy about in my church...'

The trapper corrected, 'Our church! Even if it is burned to the ground!'

'Well, yes—'

'The girl carried something with her. A snakeskin, a skin so large it could go around this place six times. It's even visited the pub! Have you seen it, Father?'

The priest shook his head.

'And there's one more thing I can't forget. The girl—was accompanied by wolves!'

Someone laughed.

The priest approached the podium. 'Now...'

'She knew my business and wolves came with her to attack my camp! Never have I seen such a thing. They arrived with her and left with her! She tried to knock the rifle out of my hands when I was protecting myself! She spoke in terrible tongues!'

The priest gripped the podium. 'You're demonizing a fellow human being who was kidnapped as a child and suffered terrible abuse. You should be ashamed of yourself.'

'Open your eyes! Look around! What did you teach us? Consider the fruit? Look at the fruit rotting all over the ground! Who burned the church?'

The priest's face flared red against his white robe. 'The wiring was ancient! I put off replacing it...if it was anyone's fault it was mine!'

'That girl has brought a destructive spirit to us and that destructive spirit should be exorcized!' He looked at the parishioners, sweat rolling like triumph.

Someone said, 'Amen, brother!'

With a nod from the priest, the organist strummed a note on a guitar and directed the choir to launch into the closing hymn. Some of the angrier church members, however, nodded at the trapper. The hunter, leaning against a tree, smiled.

Under the cover of the hymn, the priest took the trapper's arm, saying, 'You'll set them upon her! Is that what you want?'

'Of course not!'

The priest left the podium, circled the tent, and caught the hunter making his exit. 'Good morning! I haven't seen you...'

'I know, Father.'

'I hope this means you'll be...'

'Good bye, Father.'

§

Summer faded into autumn. The girl helped her parents harvest the apples for auction in town but when the buyers saw whose apples they were, no one bid on them. Her father returned his heavy truck to the barn and smoked ceaselessly.

The following morning, the girl watched from her bedroom window as the doctor's antique car bounced up the drive; engine bubbling, burgundy paint sharp against the yellowing orchard. The doctor and his son looked through the barn doors at the laden truck. Her father looked rumpled in yesterday's clothes.

While the doctor wrote into a notebook, his son, hands in his jeans, looked up at the girl. She backed away from the window.

'Where are they going?' she asked her mother in the kitchen.

'To sell the apples.'

'Where?'

'Far,' she said, to a shipping company on the coast where the doctor had made arrangements and thought the sea air would do her father some good.

'Why didn't you go? You always wanted to see the ocean.'

Her mother shook her head and pushed in a chair.

With the doctor's help, her father sold the whole truckload to a produce shipping company. The trip perked her father up for a time but once again, he receded into himself. Holding another of his books, the girl watched him disappear nightly into the barn.

In the kitchen, her mother peeled apples at the sink. 'It was like this when you were gone,' she said. 'We drifted.'

§

Autumn turned, once again, to winter and the cold hit her parents hard. With the growing angst of the village, the girl's aging parents suffered without conclusion. They took ill that winter following her twentieth birthday, and one after the other, they died.

Her father went first. His cough grew junkier until, one morning, he dropped his axe in the snow. He groped along the side of the barn and fell, taking half the woodpile with him. The doctor arrived as quickly as he could, his car skidding on frozen gravel. Holding his friend on the ground, he asked, 'Is there no end?'

A month after her father was buried, her mother complained of the cold and took to her bed. Her legs swelled as she slept and upon waking, she spoke only of household chores. She asked the girl if the garlic was spread across tables in the barn to dry. 'Dry it right or it will rot.'

'I did it weeks ago, Mama.'

She then asked if the garden had been turned.

'Not yet. After the thaw, Mama.'

She asked if herbs were hung. 'Don't forget the rosemary.'

When the girl tried to feed her, all her mother wanted was ginger tea. 'Everything repulses me. Is this what happened to you? Let the chickens go.'

'We don't have chickens, Mama.'

'Oh. If we did, I'd ask you to let them go. I don't want to take anymore.'

'OK, Mama.'

'And the yeast. It's yours. It's still good. Always good. You never run out.'

'OK, Mama.'

The doctor gave her something for the pain. Most of her body thinned while her legs filled like water pipes; her behavior grew erratic with the medicine, punctuated with longer, deeper sleep. 'Something's bothering the horses. Go see what's bothering the horses.'

'The horses are OK, Mama.'

Soon she failed to recognize her daughter, sometimes for long, awful spells.

'Why is your hair that color? I had a beautiful little girl once. A long time ago. But I don't want to talk about it.'

'You don't have to talk about it,' her daughter said.

'Can I have some water, please?' Her mother turned her cheek into the pillow to sip.

The doctor's wife surprised the girl with a hug and said, 'Why don't you take a walk? You need to eat and sleep, too.' The woman pinned up her hair and rolled her sleeves. 'There's food on the kitchen table. I'll look after her.'

The girl reached for the pile of soiled linens but the doctor's wife shooed her. 'Those are mine.'

'But the smell.'

'Go.'

The girl went as far as the cottage steps. The dog sat, leaning against her; the touch of his animal shoulder a blessing. A slice of warm bread sat in her lap, streaked with strawberry preserves. She gave half to the dog, which he hardly tasted. She stared into the trees but her eyes could find nowhere to rest in those tangled branches.

She took a bite of the bread and the strawberries were so joyous, she coughed. There was love in this food.

She heard her mother wake, her voice a creaking door. The doctor's wife answered but the girl realized as she got to her feet, she could no longer make out the words.

§

Early one morning, the girl braided her mother's hair, which had grown as long as it was thin. The woman opened her eyes. 'There's more to life than bitterness,' she whispered. 'You know what your father says about you?'

'No, Mama,' the girl choked. Her mother, asleep for days, suddenly burned back like a bright flame.

'Your dad says you're deadly. Says you can go anywhere. Do anything. Don't stay. World's bigger than this. I still remember. It's beautiful. Gimmie kiss.'

The girl kissed her mother's cheek.

'Is it sparklin?'

'Yes. It's sparklin.'

The girl hugged her mother's waist and heard her whisper: 'You were the best part of my story.'

Her mother slept for three days as the girl sat by her bed. The dog skulked underfoot.

The doctor visited three times a day to take the woman's pulse, administer medication and let himself out. He asked several times if the girl wanted to put her mother into care but she shook her head. His wife took the laundry and left a plate of something warm in the kitchen. Sometimes she exchanged a full pot of honey for an empty one.

The girl hardly moved. She watched her mother's features melt and the once fleshy hands sink into a landscape of pale ridges. With all of her exposure to quick, poisoned deaths, the girl disappeared into her mother's staggered journey, her mind darkening. She blurred her eyes. She watched her mother's chest rise and fall with short, insistent breaths until one dim morning just before dawn, her mother shuddered and the life in her face fell like ash.

Holding her mother by the waist, the girl listened to the first spring rain patter against the window and waited for a respectable hour to call the doctor.

§

Listening to the wind press upon the cottage, the girl picked out a slip, a dress and a pair of shoes from her mother's closet. The doctor's wife exchanged them for a cup of tea on a saucer. 'Your mother did this for me, for my beautiful son. When I couldn't look at him and I couldn't take my eyes off him. She put his best suit on him for me. Please. Let me do this for you both.'

In her room, the girl buttoned the same black dress her mother wore when they buried her father. The wind rocked the trees outside and light swam across the floor. The dress hadn't been washed and the girl closed her eyes and put the sleeves to her nose.

Again, she found herself standing in the windy village graveyard behind the church, pulling her hair from her mouth and hiding under her hat. One casket was suspended over open earth; its neighbor hidden beneath a spring-wet mound. Her parents' headstones were exactly the same as all of the others in the graveyard: cut from a granite quarry in the distance.

The priest read from the pages of his missal and the trapper, in his winter coat, held the pages down until the priest closed with a blessing. The doctor, his wife and their son held red roses. She looked at the new church, built from granite this time, beside the graveyard. Her parents once had so many friends and she wondered where they were.

As the gravediggers approached, shovels on shoulders, the priest spoke to the girl, closer now to outmaneuver the wind. 'It's like you've died,' he said, as the trapper went to meet the diggers. 'When you die, people don't recognize you. You might feel alone but you're not. Ask for wisdom and you'll receive it.'

She remembered her journey home, how she asked the way and how answers came. Since she'd been home, she'd forgotten to ask.

The priest put his hand on the girl's shoulder as the shovels hit the soil; she thanked him, handing him an envelope, relieved his service was complete and that the trapper ignored her.

Back at the cottage, the doctor built a fire, his wife put water on to boil and their son turned the soil in the garden.

'The wind was wicked today,' the doctor said.

His wife said, 'I haven't cried in five years,' the accent of her distant island rising through her words, 'and now, I can't stop.'

After they'd gone, when the only sounds were an owl in a tree and the shudder of the fire, there was a knock. The dog barked. Barefoot and still in her mother's dress, the girl got up from her chair, her body crackling, and found the trapper on the step.

'I know this is a terrible time for you,' he said, blanching in the light of her kitchen. 'I came to wish you peace.'

'That's kind...'

'I'm not kind. I'm afraid of you.' He eyed her hair: loose, hanging over her shoulders. 'I know what I saw in the woods. I saw you defy elements and command nature.'

'I didn't command anything.'

'I have never in my life seen wolves behave like that—and you should have been dead in the snow!'

But she remembered his rage behind a rifle. 'You're a killer and you're afraid of me?'

'I make a living. And I wear shoes in the snow like everyone else.'

She remembered the young wolf with a torn foot. 'My father taught me that snares are a cruel and terrible way to hunt.'

'It's better to be the one setting them,' he shifted his weight on the stairs, 'and the world is full of traps. You must know this. The whole village is caught in one and you have everything to do with it. Our farms are fouled. The church burned!'

'It was faulty...'

'People bicker and drink. Hunters think they're the law. Please, the devil causes suffering. It starts and ends with you.'

'I met a devil,' she said, 'and I escaped it.'

He insisted: 'While the rest of the village stays trapped. I'm asking you to come, help us heal this with grace and humility. Don't abandon us. Don't fall into the sin of arrogance. Ask for forgiveness!'

'Sin? Forgiveness? For what?'

'For whatever you did to command those wolves, to survive that cold. It's not my intention to cause you anymore pain but the truth is always painful.' The young man, quite fearful now, descended the steps.

The fire in the stove popped. The owl called. The girl closed the door. Memory stirred as she recalled the little boy from school. She didn't remember him so afraid.

§

The next day, she put the property up for sale. Over a dozen years of neglect made the place a chore for any takers and looking about the cottage, she felt a terrible urgency to leave. Her parents gone, she now saw every corner infected with sorrow; every doorway etched with loss, and she realized that while life had frozen when she returned home, an unexpected thaw softened her.

Serpent's Wake

Again, she heard wolves singing in the night and listened as she sat by the fire. She and the dog looked at one another, mindful, listening. The air sparkled and she felt her mother beside her and sometimes, a curl of tobacco smoke rose from the floor.

Through this thaw, sacred with grief, she wrestled. Sometimes she pretended her parents were in the next room for as long as she could before something broke. Sometimes memories of the serpent fell upon her—striking again and again—until she slid to the floor and stayed there for some time.

She chewed her fingers until they bled and scratched at hives that spread from her neck until her whole torso pulsed. When she was sure the spring festival was over, she walked into town, stalking through the woods for most of the journey, to see the doctor. At his office, his wife greeted her by taking her hat and plucking leaves from her shirt, saying, 'You walked through the woods?'

But the girl was struck by the bare walls. Everything was white. 'Where are your paintings?'

The doctor's wife shook her head, her sadness a flash on an ocean. 'I took them down when my son died. I was embarrassed by them.'

'I liked the birds.'

The woman's eyes welled. 'Here I go again. I've been dry-eyed for years but...' She pulled a handkerchief from her sleeve as the doctor's door opened.

Minutes later, the girl cringed as she sat on the examination table. 'Normal?' Her skin was coarse, scaly, mottled.

'Will this fever pass,' he said, 'or do we just learn to live with fever? That,' he pointed to the red of her rash, 'is the color of the road you're on. It doesn't last forever.'

'What about the floor? I'm always on the floor.'

'You can't fall any further. You'll get up eventually.'

'And what about my hair? Why is it purple?'

'More of an indigo,' he said, peering with his magnified lenses, 'and the tests, oddly enough, were inconclusive.'

'People think I'm a prostitute, even a witch!'

'I say you're an artist.'

She scoffed. 'Will it ever go back to black?'

'I don't know,' he said.

'And what about the ghosts? I think my parents are around.'

'Most people do.'

'You can't give me anything for this?'

'Of course I can, but the truth is you're doing beautifully. Just wait.'

Surprised by his confidence, she buttoned the neck of her blouse. 'What does it look like when I'm not doing well? If it doesn't look like rashes and ghosts?'

'When I look at you, I see your father's will and your mother's wisdom. Yes, this is a horrendous time. But it's not meaningless. As a sea captain once told me, hold fast.'

She sighed.

'Look,' he pointed her gaze to the window where the trio of his wife's bee hives stood in their tiny, walled garden, 'your next jar of honey. It's delightful to watch them.' The surrounding sunflowers and blue hyssop were spinning with bees.

She breathed on the glass.

He continued, 'We'd like to come to the cottage tomorrow if it's all right. That day the three of us drove out to sell the apples, your father asked me to watch over you. I think he knew he was leaving us.'

He then told her to wear loose cotton and make the jewelweed compresses since none of the fancy prescriptions he could write would do any better. 'The skin is an emotional organ. Don't rush it. Eat dark green leafy things and citrus, get a few minutes of filtered sunlight on your shoulders. Take tepid oatmeal baths.'

Back home, she followed his advice and slowly, the rash eased. She stayed on the floor in the dark for hours at a time, waiting for the road to bend.

While she waited for prospective buyers—there were none—she scrubbed. She cleaned every corner of the cottage, chased moths from cupboards, wiped under every piece of furniture, polished every fixture. From room to room she went, tossing buckets of brown water from the kitchen step and starting again. She waxed floors, orange-oiled every cracking trim of wood, got on elbows and knees and scoured every tearstain from the baseboards.

With every stroke of the rag and push of the brush, she saw how, year after year, her mother's power to endure and her father's seeking had imbued the cottage. Every spot of mud or crust of grime or broken

Serpent's Wake

umbrella of a cobweb called the girl to relive each moment of their despair, to bless it, and slowly, to wash it away.

So that she did.

Until she stood back and saw that the cottage was bright again. It smelled like sunlight. It looked like all those days of *before* that were not all times to forget. There were days when fresh biscuits covered the kitchen table and horses whinnied from the barn. Times when her father opened a book to read poems by a man who hailed from across the sea and wrote of a love that joins the pieces of a splintered heart.

Eventually she looked to the rosewood box on the shelf. She wiped away the dust with a rag, revealing red roses and thorny brambles. Inside, she found the sack with the drawstring.

As she worked in the kitchen, she remembered her mother's hands stirring the yeast into warm water. She added sugar to 'charm' the yeast, as her mother called it; the creak of the sifter calling her mother close. As she kneaded the dough, she heard her mother tell her not to overwork it. As she watched the dough rise, her mother reminded her that this yeast was imperious to draughts but still, to cover the dough like a baby with a soft towel. When the loaf was ready—golden and crispy and tall—she ate it warm as a sacrament at the table, eyes closed. And it tasted like goodness; like the light of her mother and all mothers before, passed quietly through the room.

§

The doctor and his wife visited every few days, bringing another jar of honey or a basket of fruit, always commenting about how lovely the cottage looked. One visit, the doctor asked who would harvest the apples from the orchard come autumn. When she looked at him blankly, he said he would find pickers when the time came.

The doctor's wife then asked what she was doing today.

'Closets,' the girl said, a job she had started and stopped many times.

'Let me help.'

So she and the girl sifted through the clothes, bagging most but saving a few things the girl said she would wear herself.

'These are all well and good,' the woman held up a not-too-tatty

Part II: Will This Fever Pass?

red dress with white polka dots, 'but have you heard of mutton dressed up as lamb? Don't rush to be the mutton. It happens soon enough.'

§

The girl was moving furniture in her room to wash the walls when the hunter's knife fell from the slats under the bed. She had forgotten about it over the past year and when she took it in her hand, she felt its rage.

Again, she was barefoot in the snow. The hunter. Boots up. A young, white wolf flashed through the trees.

And she saw how she forgot to tell her father this story.

She found the nick she made when she chopped wire against stone. Blood dappled brown on the horn handle. She touched it to her face, her forehead.

Arise.

Awake.

Words like winged spirits fluttered within her.

She went to the kitchen and plunged the blade into the windowsill over the sink. There, she would see it every day, right beneath the dusty orange her mother had stung with cloves.

That afternoon, the girl found a few apples ready in the orchard and filled the bowl in the kitchen. She cored them and boiled them with nutmeg and cinnamon and ate them over the sink, before the horn-handled blade.

She found paint in the barn and as she uncovered the cans, she remembered the horses that once followed her father and tossed starfields of dust from their manes. As she bent to lift the paint cans, something glistened in the dirt near one of the wheels of her father's truck. She swept a finger and found crushed silver. A whisper wove through her heart: a bell, just like the ones from her dress, from all those years ago, flat and soundless. She turned it in her hand and it crumbled.

She left the paint and returned to the cottage.

The next morning, back in the barn, she sidled around her father's truck. She lifted a paint can and saw a picture tacked to a wooden beam: a postcard, stuck to the wood so long it had curled over itself.

Serpent's Wake

She flattened it carefully as the tack let go, rusted. Cracked and faded, she could still see a handsome ship before a tropical coastline of palm trees and a washed-out sunset. Hadn't the doctor sent this? She recalled the day. Perhaps a year *before*...

Her father had paced in front of the barn beside his wife; the horses pricked their ears at his excitement. He placed the crisp postcard in the girl's hand and spoke about taking them to sea, 'Neither of you have seen the ocean!' Her mother smiled and asked if she should pack a swimsuit. He said, 'You better believe it! Doc says it's the best thing for his boys!'

The girl now turned the postcard to read it but the ink had run years ago. She brought it into the cottage and placed it under a heavy atlas before stirring the paint.

§

Some days, the girl didn't wake with determination. Regardless of what she had planned for the day, if she woke feeling grim, she allowed herself the sanctuary of ten minutes to think of nothing else but her losses and desperate fear of the future. On particularly bad mornings, a boundless terror rose through her body like a beast marking its territory before it swallowed her head.

And there she stayed, blind to everything but despair until she couldn't breathe. When time was up, she pulled herself to her feet and washed her face. She muttered, 'You can do it all over again tomorrow.'

The doctor and his wife dropped by one morning when she was still in a state and she didn't want to answer the door.

The woman tapped. 'It's just us, dear.'

The girl opened the door, eyes burning.

The doctor's wife unwrapped a pie. The curly scent of warm apple, vanilla and allspice bloomed; the crust a dome with heart-shaped vents.

The doctor asked, 'May we?'

The girl led them to the kitchen table. 'Tea?' she said, but the kettle was already going.

'These are your apples,' the doctor's wife said, 'in the pie. The pickers are here.'

'Pickers?'

'Yes,' the doctor said, 'they're busheling and loading them into your father's truck.'

The girl parted a curtain and saw plaid shirts working far off in the trees, surprised she hadn't heard them at all.

He said, 'We'll take them to the same place as last year.'

'Please, yes.'

'When our son died,' the doctor sat at the table, 'there was only one thing I was told that made any sense. The rest of what people said was complete rubbish, though, yes, they all meant well,' he looked at his wife, 'but it was rubbish until someone quoted an old and true religion. Not his religion, but this was a wise man who saw value in all things. He said, "Don't leave the road until the road leaves you." You know who told me that?'

The girl knew. 'My father?'

'A man who grew his heart so big, it had room for everything.' The doctor rubbed his eyes, pushing his glasses to his brows. 'What you're feeling, it won't last. Let it burn itself away. In the meantime, try the pie.'

As that first forkful touched her tongue, she glimpsed the doctor's wife singing in her own kitchen, air alight with spices as her sink filled with blushing peels. The girl ate while the doctor and his wife sipped their tea, a filmy worry in their eyes.

Licking her lips, the girl perked up. 'Brandy?'

The doctor's wife laughed a little. 'Just a splash. You like it?'

The girl took another bite, nodding. 'Brandy and love,' she said, feeling warm and swirly inside. 'I think I have a plan.' She split the crust with her fork. 'I want to see things.' She took a mouthful then lifted the large book on the table to reveal the postcard.

The doctor and his wife exchanged looks.

'My father told me how this ship followed summer around the world. He wanted to take us,' she said. 'You know it.' Her fingers rested on the horizon.

'Of course we do,' the doctor said.

His wife's eyes brimmed. 'Here I go again.' She plucked a handkerchief from her cleavage.

He examined the postcard. 'How old is this? Must be fifteen years?'

His wife blew her nose. 'Your father saved it all this time?'

Serpent's Wake

'We know this ship very well, don't we?' the doctor, a little boyish now, said. 'The old sea captain married us.' He adjusted his glasses. 'I told you about the islands. The captain dropped me off a bachelor and picked me up a year later—desperately in love with an island goddess.'

'Oh dear,' his wife found a second handkerchief in her sleeve.

'It's true,' he said. 'We had a real, maritime ceremony.'

'We had three weddings,' she chuckled. 'One on my island, one on the ship, and one here. I loved being a bride!'

He cleared his throat. 'But that's no fancy liner. It's a polar explorer converted into special transport. That's how the old captain made his money. He only took about a dozen passengers. Medical students mostly, heading to tropical training assignments. He had a soft spot for us medicos—I suspected he'd wanted to be one himself—but he passed away and his son runs the show. I was the ship physician when the boys were small.'

'Twice,' his wife said, 'for a year at a time. I got to take my boys home.'

'Our voyages were colorful,' the doctor shifted in his chair. 'Once when I was ship's doctor, there was a young baroness who took the body of her ancient husband to the family mausoleum on the other side of the world. Then she moved a fleet of antique automobiles by sea. She chartered the whole ship out. Those cars. Beautiful.'

The doctor's wife giggled. 'As soon as that woman discovered you were the ship's doctor, oh the ailments! She kept unzipping her dress.'

He sighed. 'I only remember the cars.'

'I remember lumbago and a heart condition,' she tucked away a handkerchief.

'Now,' the doctor put his fork down, 'this is a ship for people who want to see the world and I say it's wonderful and rather uncanny that you say this now. Just this morning I heard it's due to arrive at the end of the month. I was thinking I'd very much like to pay a visit.'

'You hadn't told me!' his wife said. 'I'd love to go!' She turned to the girl. 'If you go, you'll see my island.' Miles of sand and volcanic rainforest bloomed in her eyes.

'How long has it been,' the girl asked, 'since you saw home?'

Her eyes searched her husband. 'We went with the boys. When was it?

Part II: Will This Fever Pass?

'The year before our eldest went to school.' He cleared his throat. 'We went as far as the island then stayed with relatives for a while.'

'Such fun,' she said, 'but the thought of returning without him, to see everyone and explain...'

'We don't have to explain,' the doctor said as though he'd said it before.

She turned to the girl and spoke, her accent suddenly stronger, 'Some things feel like they will break us to pieces. They don't. You remind me of this.' She collected the dishes.

The doctor said it was time to check on the pickers. He had left his son in charge of them. 'You know, he asked about this place, if you'd want to work something out with him. A lease maybe? We really don't think you should sell it right now. Give it some thought.'

After they left, the girl napped in the sun on her bedroom floor. When she woke to the rumble of the truck, she felt sand between her fingers. She watched the doctor's son back the truck full of apples into her father's barn. He called to her when she opened the window: 'I'll be back first thing in the morning to take them to the coast. Wanna come?'

She shook her head.

In the morning, he came and went without disturbing the girl and when he returned that afternoon, she met him at the door and told him to keep it. 'Please, the apples would have rotted on the ground.'

He climbed the steps, extending an envelope in his hand. 'It's your money.'

She took his hand and looked into his eyes as he took the last step to meet her. He had his mother's eyes: dark and fine and lit from deep within him.

'What?' he asked, casting dimples. The late afternoon sun bathed him.

'Your whole family is so good to me.' She held him on the steps. She shuddered and they embraced as the sun bled orange. Starlings flocked. A chattering murmuration tumbled over the orchard. The flock took one shape after another: a serpent became a crest of a wave; a black sea rushed in on itself.

'Look,' he said, hand resting on her shoulder.

'How do they move like that?' She leaned into him: sweat and apples and sweet cherry wood sawdust.

Serpent's Wake

'Without killing each other?' He shook his head.

She felt his hand travel across her shoulders as the birds rolled in the sky. He kissed her mouth and took a handful of her hair in his hand, the sounds of the starlings fading.

'You haven't cut it once,' he said.

'No.' She lost her edges; everything thinned and the brittleness was gone.

'I like it when you don't wear your hat.'

A twig snapped in the orchard. He rested his forehead on hers, touched his nose to hers and looked into her eyes.

'Hello, soul,' he said with sadness.

She searched his eyes, dizzy.

'My father told me to behave.'

She touched her lips. 'I'm sorry.'

'Don't be sorry,' he backed slowly down the stairs. 'Don't you ever be sorry.'

§

The following afternoon, thunder shook the cottage. Rain hammered the roof, the gutters overflowed, and water poured before every window. She built a fire in the kitchen and set to work. The dog curled up on his rug.

Kneeling on a towel, she scrubbed under the kitchen sink with vinegar. Through the rain, she heard a creak on the steps and leaned back onto her heels. When the door flew open, pinned by the wind, she hit the cupboards with a start. Cool air rushed with a spray; the fire guttered. A broad figure loomed, the sky rolling with the colors of steel. The dog barked, too late.

She winced at the silhouette: thick shoulders, a strong neck and a mane of dark hair seeded with the light of a troubled sky.

The hunter.

A shotgun pointed at the floor, dripping.

The scar tightened.

Right in her kitchen, he leaned on his shotgun. Muddy rainwater fell onto her clean floor as he closed the door with an elbow.

'Hey there, wild thing.' Alcohol drifted on his words and reached her.

Part II: Will This Fever Pass?

The dog growled.

She rose to her feet, though it seemed everything below her waist had turned to rainwater. Her back was to the cupboards, the sink. The table stood between them. Four chairs. A rag dripped vinegar from her hand.

Rain fell from his beard. He looked around the kitchen with a sway. 'Didn't you all just let this place go to hell? Do me a deal? I'll do you one right here on the kitchen table.' His boots scraped a trail of muddy leaves. A leech fell to the floor and searched: fat bottomed, skinny necked, headless.

His scent was ripe with the pong of smoke, sweat, blood. She remembered his appetite. She remembered everything about finding herself alone with him and wondered how it could have happened again.

His shotgun bumped against wood. He wiped his face with his sleeve. His eyes smoked like torches. 'Come on, gimmie a tour.' The open, dirty shirt hung on him like violence.

She didn't move: everything still as stone, except her frantic heart.

'Won't sell to me? Discrimination,' he sprayed the word.

Then he said, 'You look different. A little fat and a spit shine, you're almost respectable. Though we know the truth, don't we?' he leaned toward her. 'There was no goddamn snake. Just lies, that hooker hair, and doing the thing you do best.'

He took a step, clapped his shotgun on the table with too much force and rested both palms against it. 'Tell me the truth. I won't think any less of you.'

She still didn't move.

He raised his voice, 'My hunting dogs were poisoned to death because of you. In the old days, we'd have chased you out of town by now.'

She remembered his hungry dogs. The rag dripped in her hand. She smelled vinegar. The leech searched the floor.

He noticed her dog. 'Maybe I'll shoot yours. In the belly so you can watch him die slowly, the way mine did. How about that?'

Her mind tightened, keeping panic behind her. He was in her house and she had nothing but a bucket and a rag. All the utensils were in their drawers. Pots and pans stowed. A folded tea towel sat in her

Serpent's Wake

periphery. Her father's gun was locked up in the barn. All around her, the tidy kitchen swam like a heat mirage.

He pulled up something sticky from his chest and spat on her floor. The leech waved beside its warmth. 'Nothing?' he said. 'You got nothing to say to me? You were quiet when we met, too. Remember that? I do. And how you hit me in the face with a bottle.' He pointed to his cheeks above his beard, pitted with scars. 'Never got to thank you for a face full of broken glass and frostbite. Woke up to find my fingers frozen solid.' He slipped his hands off the shotgun and held up valleys carved into flesh. He moved around the table, wiping rain and sweat from his face, and straightening his shoulders. 'Know how painful that is? No? You don't, do you? Playing around in the snow all naked.'

Her eyes were fixed on his but she watched the space grow between him and his weapon.

'World's tallest altar boy says you're a witch. Bit much, I know,' he trailed off, 'but he's stirring up that old time religion. Probably pay a visit to you soon, too. Maybe with some pig fat, a stake and some firewood. God. I miss the old days. People worked their shit out!"

The girl was stoic.

'But I know, you got people defending you too. Even that doctor's on your side. I used to respect that man. Even though he married that cannibal from godknowswhere island.' He grunted. 'Yeah, and their son—I'd hang myself too if I didn't know what color I was.' He slid toward one corner of the table, another step closer.

'Say, are you giving it up to him too? If his wife finds out, she'll shrink your head. You know how they do that, right? They peel your face right off your...' he froze. His jaw unhinged. Lightning lit the windows. 'What's this?'

She didn't know what he was talking about, her head reeling.
Then.
On the windowsill beneath her mother's orange.
His knife.
Planted like defiance.

'You goddamned little thief, my father gave that to me. I spent all day digging in the snow looking for it with my fingers black as sin and here it is. You took it, you cow.' With a grunt, he plucked it from the sill. The orange fell, bounced and scattered cloves.

While he eyed the blade, she leapt to another side of the table.

He snarled. 'What did you do? This blade! Sharpened finer than a piece of paper over three generations and look at it,' he pointed it at her. 'You...' He staggered and let out another groan then took an angry step toward her. 'You cut wire!'

Thunder rolled, shaking the roof; lightning flashed. A gust shot wet leaves past the window.

She took another step back until they stood again at opposing corners of the old kitchen table.

'I should have thrown you back into that hole you crawled out of...'

And something woke. A flash, a beacon of light shined down into the depth of her being and she felt the serpent move. Her body remembered first, long before her mind, as her thoughts spun between the hunter and the kitchen and *oh what to do, what to do*. But beyond that, underneath all the spinning fixtures of herself, a coiled stillness glistened in the light with the patience of erosion, of heavy mist, and all the pittering time in eternity. The tickticktick of terror time slowed into the tick...tick...tick...of focused time.

Tick.

Tick.

Tha-dump.

As her body reshaped her mind to sharpen it.

The hunter's speech stalled. His sluggish hand rose to wipe his nose. The blade winked across seconds.

Lightning lit the room, very close now; the whole kitchen white.

Thunder boomed.

The air shimmered.

He said something else.

His face wrinkled into a grimace.

And she knew what he was going to do next.

He lifted his arm to lunge, blade raised.

But she had so much time.

The serpent struck.

She kicked the closest kitchen table leg inward and leapt down on the table with all her weight, snapping the leg and tipping his end upwards; thrusting the corner straight into his ribs. The very point struck him with an audible crack.

The shotgun slid from the tabletop and registered when it hit the floor, spraying buckshot and blowing a hole through the roof. The dog leapt, knocking the hunter against the wall. Plaster fell upon them and the air coursed with rain. An arm wrapped around his torso, knife in his fist, he waved the blade and punched it through the skin of the dog's ear. The dog set his teeth into the hunter's wrist; the blade tore. He cursed and the dog clung, flinging blood everywhere.

The girl sprang for the shotgun and shoved it in the hunter's face. She pumped it as her father showed her and in a terrible keen that rose from every single one of the open gravesites within her, she bellowed: 'Get out of my house!'

The dog let go and flapped his head. Blood shot across the hunter's face.

'You...'

The girl didn't let him speak. 'GET OUT OF MY HOUSE!'

He fumbled at the door and fell down the steps with his father's knife. Rain slanted white.

She stood on her front step, drenched, the weapon leveled, her entire body quaking with ruin and delight. She had never known this sensation, not ever, and bellowed an ancient war woman cry as the rain ran into her mouth.

He cursed, holding his side.

She screamed again—a bottomless sound—until he was gone. The rain soaked her; her dress stuck to her; her hair was plastered to her face. And deep within her, within some cavern of her most hidden self, she felt that calm, black serpent slowly return to a state of repose.

She looked at the weapon in her arms, water beading on oiled metal, astounded by its odor of heat and wrath.

She returned to the cottage and stood the shotgun beside the fire.

Everything was wet and caked with dust, including the leech, which rolled and curled on the floor.

She stepped on it.

She looked at the dog. Milky wet with pink plaster all over, he shook his coat. He scratched at his ear, which hung at a terrible angle.

§

Part II: Will This Fever Pass?

Early in the morning, the doctor arrived with his son. He told her how in the small hours of the night, the hunter was dragged to his practice raving drunk, clutching both a knife and his ribs. Standing before the broken kitchen table under the opened ceiling, the doctor asked, 'Shall we report him to the police?'

She shook her head. 'I just want to go.'

The doctor took in the damage. 'They should see this.'

His son gaped at the hole and went out to the barn to search for a tarpaulin.

When the doctor saw the dog, he unwrapped the girl's bandages, saying, 'It needs to come off.' With a touch of anesthetic, he snipped and stitched the ear. The girl assisted while the doctor's son clambered up on the roof and threw the tarp over the hole.

'You have steady hands,' the doctor observed.

'What choice do I have?' She wiped blood from the dog's cheek with a washcloth.

He packed up his supplies. Then as he zipped his bag, he asked, 'Are you sure you want to sell it? You could just sell off some land instead.'

'I can't stay here.'

'This is your inheritance.'

'I can't live here.'

'How about a compromise?'

Later that day, the doctor watched his son repair the kitchen table before the three of them sat around it. With everything, the girl had forgotten about their kiss but his smile, as he replaced the joint for the table leg, said he hadn't.

At the table, the doctor presented an alternative to a sale. The young man scraped together his savings and made an offer to purchase half the property and lease the other half, allowing her to keep a share, access a rental income, and make big decisions later.

The doctor hugged her. 'I promised your father I'd look after you.' He then said he had an appointment and his son asked to stay to look for timber and shingles in the barn. 'I'll be back in an hour,' he said and the men walked out together.

Serpent's Wake

After a time, the girl wandered down to the barn and found the doctor's son standing there, waiting for her.

She leaned against the dusty wall, 'I'm glad you want this place. You'll make it good again.'

'I wish we could make it good together.' He took her hand.

She said, 'I can't stay.'

'I know.' He kissed her. He ran his fingers through her hair and whispered against her lips. 'Oceans do what mountains can't.'

She touched his face. 'I don't know if I'll even come back.'

'I know that too,' he kissed her again as his father's car rolled up the drive. 'It doesn't change anything for me.'

PART III: AN OCTOPUS HAS THREE HEARTS

Part III: An Octopus Has Three Hearts

In late summer, as the leaves began to turn, the girl packed one suitcase with her mother's clothes and another with the best of her father's books. Between the books, she nested the rosewood box.

She scrubbed the dog and dabbed his wound and bought a ticket to the world. The doctor arranged to take her to the seaport, saying, 'We've watched the captain grow up. I wouldn't send you with anyone else.'

Early that morning, she wore her mother's red with white polka dot dress, believing it more nautical than the others. She pinned her hair under a straw hat and carried a small, leather purse.

When the doctor and his family arrived, he said: 'You look splendid!'

His wife said, 'You look lovely, dear, but promise me you'll go shopping. Think of all those lovely boutiques.' She took in the girl's expression. 'You've never been to a boutique, have you?'

The girl shrugged.

The doctor inspected the dog's ear while his wife assessed the old, square dress hanging on the girl. She slipped the white silk scarf from her neck and tied it around the girl's waist. 'Better.'

'I can't take your scarf.'

'I have dozens. It's too matronly without it, dear. Remember what I said: don't rush growing old.' She handed the girl a woven bag and inside, the girl found a batik dress, deep blue with a fine design of gold, a pair of leather sandals, a clip for her hair, and a velvety, black wrap that melted to the touch. 'It chills at night.' She demonstrated how to wear it around the shoulders. 'Very demure. Please cast those old dresses overboard as soon as you can!'

The doctor lifted her suitcases with a grunt. 'You've brought your father's library!'

'Let me get those.' His son hefted the suitcases into the sedan.

The doctor opened the car door. 'The captain's father gave me this car years ago. A passenger ran out of money and left it as payment, much to his disappointment. When we got to our port, he threw me the keys and it didn't start. It was the beginning of a beautiful relationship.'

Serpent's Wake

'I hope it starts today,' his wife said, pecking her son's cheek and getting into the car.

The girl looked at the doctor's son with a sad and knowing smile that he returned. She thanked him before she and the dog climbed into the backseat. The doctor reversed slowly, so she could say goodbye with her eyes. She removed her hat and looked up at the familiar trees until she slept. Her father's dog stood guard, good ear set on the road.

A couple of hours later, the girl woke to mingling scents of seaweed, pine and sarsaparilla. The air combed her cheeks and before she could see the shore, her heart quickened. She had never smelled such spice.

They rounded a curve and the expanse of the great gray ocean exalted her.

The dog barked. Though she had considered leaving him at the farm, she wanted him with her. She wondered if it was selfish to confine him to a ship, and knew the doctor's son was happy to have him but when the doctor contacted the ship, he was assured that they still transported animals. She paid a fee and trained him to relieve himself in hay. Now, she hugged him to her.

'We're here.' The doctor turned off the ignition. A show of rusty cranes and slanted warehouses surrounded them. When he lifted the suitcases, he said, 'I'd already forgotten how heavy this one is.'

They left the car, rounded the warehouses and entered the shipyard. A rickety mariner's pub stood on the corner. A huge black anchor leaned on the overgrown grass and a few wooden shakes were missing from the façade. They crossed train tracks and approached a tar-streaked pier. Seagulls screamed over a trawler. Moorings knocked; prickly ropes lay coiled like serpents—the girl stared at them. The tide slapped the pilings where dark clots of mussels met the waterline.

Lines of boats were berthed along the pier, but it was the enormous one, the great pale ship at the end, that was hers: the proudest, tallest man-made thing she had ever seen. Six stories high, the ship was tiered with three decks; windows reflected late morning sun with a pearly summit at the top. The girl held her hat.

The doctor's wife breathed, 'Isn't she lovely? Out there, you'll see plenty of cruisers that will make her look small,' she said as they drew closer, 'but she's gorgeous right down to her buttons.'

The doctor, nearly out of breath, said, 'She's about...three hundred feet long. The captain's father...had much of her rebuilt...before I signed on.' He paused then said, 'True devotion keeps her afloat.' He placed the suitcases on a trolley with a grunt. 'There. Good heavens. I'll go find our captain.'

His wife held on to the bag containing the dress, saying, 'We'll carry this one, and we'll be down by the sea.'

While the doctor strode up the gangplank, his navy suit jacket flapping, his wife said, 'Let's get our feet wet!' She led the way back along the pier, past dock workers shifting crates onto train cars and fishermen hauling catch from their icy holds. They came to a beach where sailboats shaped the horizon and the dog could sniff sea grass. The girl let him off the leash and he charged a flock of gulls. With no one on the beach, they easily abandoned their hats and shoes on the pebbled shore and stepped toward the water.

'It's not much,' the doctor's wife said, a little forlorn, 'but it's your first. Wait until you see my island. Soft sand for miles. And it'll be warm.'

The girl shivered. She felt a nudge of memory: sliding toward the river, over pine needles. Her flesh goosed.

The doctor's wife took her hand. 'Are you cold?'

'No.'

The doctor's wife kissed the back of her hand.

Sunlight danced in pieces.

The girl took in the sea, watching how it changed before her, shifting from light to dark to light under passing clouds; every shade from dusky charcoal to snow seared by sunlight. She hiked up her dress and went up to her ankles. The water was cool.

'It should be colder at this time of year. We're lucky.' The doctor's wife removed a comb from her hair. 'Go for a swim.'

The girl didn't know how to swim but she couldn't say it; not to this lady from the islands, who looked more at home at the shore than she ever did in the village with the sea reflecting on her face.

The sound of a child tripped across the beach. A mother chased her small boy as he charged into the water. He squealed.

The girl smiled a little but dared not shine light on those deeper thoughts. With the years spent in the serpent, her body long-soaked in poison, she did not hope for things she could not yet name.

Serpent's Wake

The child laughed.

The doctor's wife said, 'No one tells you that when you become a mother, every child becomes your own. My boy was just like that.' She whispered, 'Just like my people. Water babies who can swim before they can walk.'

She plucked something from the water, dried it on her dress and gave it to the girl. 'Treasure. Once upon a time it was broken, but over the years, the ocean smoothed it into silk.'

The girl turned the sea glass in her palm. The once vivid cobalt was frosted; every point rounded, every edge calmed. From a bottle or some such useful thing, it was now transformed entirely.

They watched the mother carry her dripping, now howling boy, his spine arching, across the beach.

The doctor's wife giggled, rubbing the sea glass clean, 'They never want to go.'

'Ladies!' the doctor called over the sound of shoes crunching on pebbles. Beside him was the captain.

'Oh,' the girl whispered. Despite the couple saying they had known the captain from his boyhood, the girl expected a natty beard, squinting eyes and hook nose; a face blasted by rum and tide; a lumpy body in black boots washed right out from one of her father's books.

He had none of those. He was tall and lean, unlike the stocky hunters of her village, and she put her fingers to her lips.

When the captain saw the women up to their calves in the sea with their dresses pulled taut around their thighs, hair floating loose on the air like smoke and mystical expressions on their faces, he had the look of a man who'd been tricked but was trying not to show it. When he saw this young girl with midnight hair and the radiance of sunlit water and eyes that shone like dark stars, he coughed and tucked in his shirt with a grimace.

And the girl saw in his face the coldest of places; fair and angular with an age that shifted in the light. His hair was cropped short and he was a couple of days unshaven. She had been told that he was from the great north country across the ocean, and for an instant, she saw it: frozen places of birch and great owls and reindeer and singing wolves; where whales had spiral horns and curtains of green danced across heaven. His eyes were the color of the sea and she looked away before she could meet them again. Her heart, and everything under the red of her dress, swam with a surging, unfamiliar current and she heard her mother remembering the night of her birth: 'I dreamt of the sea.'

When the girl looked at the captain again, closer now, she saw the finest of lines around his eyes, like maps of all the worlds he had sailed. His hair caught the sunlight, then deepened to russet, then auburn with a twinkle of gray, shifting like light on water. But his face, his face looked pained. She took hold of her hair and twisted it, wishing for her hat.

She was unsure what to do next. Shake hands? Curtsy? What did her mother teach her of meeting sea captains? What did her father teach her, other than they went down with their ships?

A trio of swallows approached and she felt them—the laughter of the gods—but she did not smile.

The captain wasn't smiling at all. His eyes were set upon her, now ancient icebergs. His mouth was hard, cheekbones vast.

The water slid around her knees sleek as a ribbon and she wondered if he thought her a burden. Her eyes traced the path back to the car. She heard the clinking of glasses and looked to the open windows of the mariner's pub where a curl of smoke escaped. The silk scarf around her waist felt too tight.

'Hello!' The doctor's wife stepped from the water. 'It's been too long! Weren't you just a boy a moment ago?'

'It was more than a moment ago,' he finally smiled. The girl heard his command of their language, but knew it wasn't his first.

On tiptoes to embrace him, the doctor's wife said, 'I'm sorry it's been so long. Your father, he passed just after our boy...' She looked out to sea.

'Yes. Everything happened at once. We've all had our losses,' he glanced at the girl and she wondered what he knew of hers.

Running the length of the beach toward them, the dog leapt upon the captain. The girl apologized and leashed him but the captain scooped the dog's face in his hands. 'I had a dog like him once,' he said. 'He was happy on the ship.'

The dog stole a lick as the captain asked, 'What happened to your ear?'

'Defending his mistress,' the doctor said.

Serpent's Wake

The girl retrieved the shoes and hats and as they stepped onto the pier, she heard the doctor: 'She's very dear to us. If you need anything, please send word.'

'I'm in my father's cabin now. She'll take the one next door. You know it well.'

The doctor turned to the girl. 'We stayed there before the boys. It's perfect.'

The girl nodded but inside, she rolled and whispered like the sea all around her. She knew the captain hadn't taken his eyes from her, and her shoes, though dry, felt soft with sea water; periwinkles tagged along on her heels.

While they climbed the gangplank, the dog kept pace at the captain's knee. The doctor's wife asked, 'How many passengers now?'

'Half a dozen,' he said. 'Transport is up. Travel is down. Plenty of room if you want to come.'

'Don't tempt me!' she squeezed his arm.

The doctor asked, 'Who's with you?'

'Student physicians. The young woman there on the pier,' he pointed from the railing, 'is assisting the ship's doctor before we take her to your archipelago.' He looked at the doctor's wife.

She asked which island and he said a name that sounded like a flower.

On the dock below, a petite woman stood, short sleeves cuffed, a shining black plait trailing her back. Beside her, a tall woman in a flowing cape looked over her collar; she waved to the captain, her hand suspended, before pulling it back under her cape.

'The woman in the cape?' the doctor asked. 'Did she travel with her deceased husband, her automobiles, her horses, or all three?'

The captain did not return the wave. 'Cars.'

'There was a woman, when I was ship's doctor,' he spoke in a hushed voice, 'a baroness who brought her husband's body halfway round the world to the family mausoleum, remember?'

'Yes,' the captain said. 'I was young and unhappy about a body onboard.' He leaned on the railing as a pair of coupés rolled slowly onto a transporter truck. One little car was the color of cream; the other silver as the moon with red seats. The woman's cape was ruffled by the offshore breeze as she snatched glimpses of the captain.

Part III: An Octopus Has Three Hearts

'I don't know where you find them,' the doctor said, 'but quite a number of fabulous women have traveled on your ship.'

His wife lifted her chin, 'It's true.'

The captain turned from the rail. 'There is a certain poet from my village you'll remember, although he's less a passenger and more the resident now.'

'Ah,' the doctor said to the girl, 'I believe I gave one of his books to your father.'

The girl was trying to remember when his wife gently elbowed her. 'Be careful of poets. I was lured away from paradise with poetry.'

'He's on deck.' The captain waved at a grandfatherly man beneath an umbrella in dark spectacles. A cravat adorned his neck and a notebook lay before him. Despite his warm welcome, the girl felt sadness triple-lance her heart.

The doctor's wife whispered, 'Still, be wary. Poets only age on the outside.'

The doctor extended his hand. 'Hello, sir!'

'Are you back aboard?' the poet asked, shaking hands with the doctor. A silver sphere on a chain peeked from beneath the cravat.

The doctor expressed his regret while the girl drew in the poet's sweeping view of the sea. She then looked to the captain who was staring at her, arms folded, mouth an unforgiving line. She felt she was to be scolded but instead, he looked toward the pier.

The doctor's wife drew the girl into the conversation, '...not this time but she'll be joining you.'

'Let's have tea sometime.' His words weren't as steeped in the captain's accent, but a tendril of a northern wildflower uncurled through his words. 'Welcome aboard.'

At that moment, a man, breathless and shirtless, attempted to sneak past the captain into the galley behind him. The captain, without turning, said, 'Shirt?'

The cook, who looked only a little older than the girl, saluted then crossed his arms over his bare chest. 'Well I am truly sorry. I just got back. Started with purchasing a stove and ended with locals taking my shirt.'

'Never admit to that,' the captain said. 'He's new.'

'New? I've been here almost five years!'

'Shirt.'

'Yeah, it's down at the pub. Lost it in a game of darts to a man with no fingertips.'

The girl chilled. She saw the hunter in her kitchen, holding up his hands. She looked to the doctor, but he and his wife were speaking with the poet.

The cook continued, 'Now his gal's wearing my shirt!' The cook ducked into the galley and reappeared in a t-shirt, inside out. He approached the doctor first. 'Hey. Yeah. Nice to meet you.'

The doctor asked where he was from and the cook described a damp seaport where the food was rich, music was currency, and the dark side of the city ate its young. 'I left seven years ago and eventually landed here. Best gig I ever had. You been on this ship?'

The captain introduced him as, 'Ship's doctor twice for my father.'

The doctor nodded, 'Seeing off our dear friend on her maiden voyage,' and introduced the girl who was still shedding the vision of gnawed fingertips.

The cook shook her hand. 'All right, then. Let me know what you like to eat and I'm on it, though I'm pegging you for a vegetarian.'

She held tightly to her hat, despite the lack of breeze. 'Does it show?'

'Only to my expert eye,' he said. 'But the tropical seas will color you up.'

'Please,' the captain motioned for his guests to climb a flight of steel stairs.

The doctor quietly asked the captain about the poet: 'Is he still writing? I'm always afraid to ask...'

'He had retired to the ship just before my father died, but yes.'

'Does he still have that map?'

'It's on the bridge.'

'I'd love to see it again.'

A crewman intercepted the captain at the landing and showed him a folder. The captain said, 'There are some issues I must attend to before we leave in the morning. Can you stay for dinner? The cook's better than he looks.'

The doctor rubbed his chin, 'There's a patient I promised to see tonight...'

'I understand.' The captain led them to a heavy door and opened it to a place of shining brass rails, white wainscoting, and immense black and white consoles of screens and switches. At the front of the room sat a large steel wheel, harkening to an earlier era. Around the wheel, a set of large throttle arms, a series of screens, gauges, phones and radios commanded the space. Nearby, a desk with ball and claw feet was riveted to the floor. The dog poked his head under the chair and wagged his tail.

Over the desk, a strange, tawny skin hung under a sheet of glass. The girl recoiled. It looked like a crushed animal.

'Ah, to see it again,' the doctor clapped his hands. He said to the girl, 'Don't look so horrified. It's nearly two thousand years old.' He turned to the captain, 'I say it's perfect that he gave it to you: the religious have their icons; a captain must have his own.'

It was an artifact; an inked calfskin webbed by cracked landscapes and a chaos of waterways born into a circle. Ink drawings of man-made structures peppered the landmasses. The girl crept closer but despite her hours spent with her father's books, she couldn't place the location. 'I'm sorry,' she squinted, 'I can't make sense of it.'

The doctor pointed, 'East is at the top instead of north. South is to the right. Turn it onto its side in your mind to see one of the cradles of civilization; the setting of many of your father's books.' He pointed to a mermaid holding a mirror, a unicorn with an oversized horn and a sea serpent that sent a wrinkle of cold through the girl. 'In its age, if you controlled this sea,' he pointed to the heart of the calfskin, passionate now, 'you ruled the world!'

She tilted her head.

'This map is an attempt to organize the chaos that is life!' the doctor insisted. 'Let it hatch before you.'

His wife giggled. 'It does hatch, doesn't it? Like a monstrous egg. It's fine, dear, I never liked it, either. My people believe that we sit at the center of the world and we're most certainly not on this map.'

The girl saw towers and churches and letters tiny as insects. Remote lands were cracked by rivers. Dog-headed men posed with frontal eyes and a man used his single, enormous foot as an umbrella. A pair of frightful individuals ate something unseemly from a pot. Along in the

Serpent's Wake

borders, heaven and hell taloned the map while the skeletal dance of the dead and last judgment eclipsed the corners.

The captain recounted the story of how the poet found it along the coastline central to the map. 'Here,' he pointed to a turret. A vintner sold it to him, saying it was discovered under a house in a clay pot, hidden for seventeen hundred years from various zealots who burned memories. The poet bought it on impulse, trusting his eye for authenticity, before he had it assessed.

The doctor cupped his chin, 'It's utterly hypnotic. I have paid many visits to this map.'

The girl's gaze was drawn by a figure in its border: a lone hunter on horseback who cast a backwards glance at the world he was departing. 'What's he doing?' She inspected his expression.

The captain answered: 'Dying.'

'He looks sad.'

'His expression changes with the person.'

She retreated. 'Why a hunter?'

'Why not?' the doctor leaned into the inspection. 'A hunter sees life's trials and beauty; he births foals and kills quarry. To me, he looks worldly. His horse is handsome. His squire and his dog trail behind, well outfitted. His life is rich but he accepts the transition.'

'He looks wary to me,' the captain said. 'Let's show you to your cabin.'

As they left the bridge, the girl determined to map the layout of the ship but found herself distracted by the captain's strides. And the way his face caught the light. When a second crewman stopped him, she knew he'd be leaving them. This crewman's head shined bald and his brow was a furrow; she had never before seen a man like him and stole glances, reading his manner as he spoke to the captain.

The captain turned to the doctor and introduced his first engineer 'and brilliant pilot. Not everyone can maneuver a vessel like this.' The man shook the doctor's hand tightly but ignored the women.

The doctor was perplexed. 'How can you be below in the engine room and on the bridge at the same time?'

The captain answered, 'His voice carries.'

But the engineer was deadpan. 'I never shout.'

The captain continued, 'My father recruited him from a fishing village.' The girl glimpsed scars peeking from the cuffs of the engineer's white shirt: the backs of his forearms crocodiles disappearing into a river.

'What brought you aboard?' the doctor asked.

'No work in my country.'

When the doctor inquired about his country, the engineer named a coastal, equatorial region, '...polluted by imperialists and run by warlords,' his eyes cold as coins.

The doctor, delighted with his new acquaintance, adjusted his glasses. 'I visited your country some thirty years ago. It was beautiful...'

'Before the uprising, it was under martial law.' He turned to the captain and described a tariff on galley equipment. The local harbormaster was also coming aboard.

The captain told the doctor's wife: 'I must attend to this. Next time. Come with us.'

She hugged him. 'Please take care of her.'

'Of course.' He led them to a crewman they remembered, a stocky old salt, who would show them the cabin.

'What a treat to see you both!' The crewman held out a calloused hand and looked more the part of a seaman the girl had expected.

She watched the captain go, unnerved by the engineer's manner. 'He's as friendly as a bullet,' the doctor's wife said quietly, 'but don't worry: there's one on every ship. Best to identify him early and stay out of his way.'

They came to a corridor lined with rivets and doors. The doctor's wife clapped her hands at the door held open with a hook and eye. 'Our old room!'

The girl lingered, admiring the stately door beside it. A blue leadlight transom glowed: the captain's door.

'Your dog's happy,' the crewman said as the dog waggled. 'What happened to his ear?'

The doctor answered: 'Defending his mistress.'

'My kind of bloke, ay?'

The girl found a double bed, a dresser, a closet and little brass lamp screwed to a writing desk under a portal.

'So cozy,' the doctor's wife said. 'We had to be in love to live in here, didn't we?'

Serpent's Wake

The doctor sat. 'I wrote my first paper at this desk.' His wife kissed the top of his head.

There was a sink with a kettle and a cupboard. 'Stow your things, missy. When we hit the swells,' the crewman said, 'loose clutter can kill a body.' He pointed out a little bathroom with the tiniest tub she'd ever seen then backed out of the cabin with, 'Right. Leave you to it then. If you need me, my quarters are just down the end. Sign says DANGER—KEEP OUT in four languages but don't mind that. Bit of a crew joke that stuck.'

The doctor reached into the pocket of his suit jacket and placed a small leather-bound notebook and pen on the desk. 'Your parents would be proud of you.' The mention of her parents stirred the air. 'They always wanted this for you. Make sense of what you see. And remember, everything good starts with risk, and one of these.' He produced another small book and a little twirling sphere. 'An atlas so you'll always know where you are. A compass so you can tell that captain he's going the wrong way.' The doctor hugged her then said unexpectedly, 'If I'd had a daughter...' but didn't finish his sentence.

Lastly, he placed three bars of chocolate on the desk and told her to hold onto them for when she saw his wife's island. He whispered: 'Snake people love chocolate.'

His wife stood at the window, holding her piece of sea glass. Her eyes said that she was remembering something both happy and sad. She placed it on the writing desk then slipped the handle of the bag over the back of the chair.

§

On deck with the dog, his head between the rails, the girl waved.

'Send a message if you need anything,' they had said. 'Tell us when you're returning...' Now the doctor's wife walked with her husband along the pier and she watched them round the pub and disappear.

Looking out to sea, she saw the edge of the world. The ocean looked exhausted, darkening in the shade of flat-bottomed cumulus clouds. She left the railing.

When she found her cabin, she noticed that someone had tilted the transom of the captain's door.

She slid the key into her lock, all set to unpack and stow things. Her suitcases would be on her bed by now. The dog waited, knowing this was their place now.

But the lock stuck. She shimmied the key. She nudged with her shoulder. She pushed harder and flew into the cabin. The dog barked. She shushed him and looked for her suitcases but found only one: the books and the rosewood box. The one with her clothes, however, wasn't there.

She left the dog and returned to the trolley where the doctor had placed her luggage. A crewman said over a pallet of apples and pears that her patience was appreciated; someone would locate it and send word to her cabin. As she turned, a pile of fish half-buried in ice rolled in front of her, nearly knocking her down. Someone shouted.

Back aboard, she landed in the galley. The cook was crouched low, bolting a stove to the floor. She retraced her steps and found herself at the captain's transom, the lead-light dark now.

Her pulse raced as she wrestled again with the key. Her face flushed and she placed a hand on her chest. She heaved the door and was nearly thrown to the floor. The dog greeted her with spit.

Granted, it was just a ratty suitcase filled only with her mother's old clothes, a couple of pairs of warped shoes and a few more of her father's books. That was what she told herself, but it was all she had.

She sat on the edge of the bed in her mother's dress and folded her hands, the doctor's compass in her sweaty palm. Her purse hung over her shoulder—at least she had her documents. A stillness filled her, just as it had in the serpent and a glaze filmed her eyes. She slowed her breathing and didn't move. The dog, familiar with her way in his animal heart, curled up on a rug.

In the corridor, she heard a rattle. A squeak. A trolley approached, bumped past and kept rolling.

She heard footfalls.

Seagulls floated past her window.

The engines of the ship were tested, paused, tested.

Beyond all that, she felt water all around her.

She rifled through her purse and found her father's postcard—this ship, the island dotted with palm trees—all ghosts. She leaned it against the wall at her desk and said: 'Be with me.'

Serpent's Wake

The words, aloud in that lonely room, were like ornaments hung on her heart. She opened the bag the doctor's wife had given her and buried her nose in the dress. Sandalwood. Dye.

She took the pen, dated the first page of the doctor's journal and wrote:

> Port of departure. Man with no fingers seen at pub. Cook lost his shirt. My clothes gone too. Dog in love with captain.

She assessed her impish handwriting and stowed the journal in the desk with the atlas and compass.

She slipped out of her mother's dress into the new one. Made from the softest cotton she'd ever touched, it fell to her ankles. She examined the shell clip and pinned her hair.

At the window, her eyes followed the wharf and the men smoking, past the piled nets and the bobbing fishing boats. She saw a squat lighthouse on a bluff. She had only ever seen them in books and like those, this was brazen white; a curve of stairs was hewn from stone and etched by crusty watermarks. A man in the lantern room wiped the panes and she knew he was the reason the lighthouse looked so solid with its shining, black roof, every tile in place: the great lamp mirrored the afternoon light in the gallery; a crack in its tower had been repaired.

A strong knock startled her. The dog snuffled the door.

She pulled on the door. Nothing. With a sharp tug, the door swept open and she was flung to the floor. The captain lifted her to her feet.

The dog's paws were upon his hip, crowned again by that absurd grin.

'I'm so sorry.' Such teetering heat she felt around this man. As she pulled the dog toward her, she saw that the neckline of the dress exposed her scar and swiftly tucked the fabric to her chest. She also realized her hat was sitting on the bed, her deep blue hair exposed again.

When she looked up, the captain squinted, saying, 'Your suitcase was stolen. We've refunded your account to cover some of your loss. Please tell me if it's sufficient.' He handed her a receipt.

She read the figure; it outweighed any monetary value left in those things.

'Your cabin door is a hazard.' He rattled the handle. 'I'll send someone to fix it.'

'Yes.' Distracted by this dress she couldn't wear, she held one hand over her chest with the receipt, and held the dog with the other, and pushed a loose strand of hair away from her face. When she looked up to thank him, his cabin door was closing.

Back in her cabin, she unpacked her father's books absently until a gentle rap and, 'Only me, missy,' a voice said, 'ship's dogsbody come to fix the lock.' She threw her hair up into a twisted towel before asking him to open the door.

The crewman who had shown her to her cabin opened the door with a lift and a rattle. 'Bit tricky,' he said, holding a heavy toolbox. He smelled like he had just flicked a cigarette over the side.

'Dogsbody?' she asked, adjusting the towel.

'Bitsah?' He hooked open the cabin door. 'You know: bit o' this and bit o' that. Jack of all trades, master of none!' His rolled sleeves revealed an octopus, all eight legs infinity loops. His toolbox opened like an accordion. 'My real trade is a locksmith. I landed here some fifty years ago to do a little work for the captain's father and...well, now I do everything but the cooking. I can boil water but watch me even burn that!' He said it was true but he could make sardines on toast when hard pressed. 'Eat those, live forever.'

He took the lock mechanism apart, oiled the pieces, tested the key and put everything together again. 'Sure there was a trick to openin this door, but what good is it if no one knows it?'

When he finished, they stepped outside and locked the door. 'Go on. Give her a try.'

The key slid into the latch and with a soft click, the door opened.

'Captain also wanted me to install a deadbolt for you.' He pulled a drill from his toolbox. 'Thought after today's theft, you might feel better.' He sighed. 'It's this bleedin port. Who steals a suitcase fulla clothes? Unless someone's got it in for ya—but look at ya—I doubt that very much.'

She imagined the hunter's fingers lingering on her suitcases; his decision to take the lighter one. She returned to her father's books, stacking them on top of a cupboard with her mother's box as a bookend.

'Stackins not stowin, missy.' The locksmith was watching and she looked at the books in her hands. 'Quiet bookish type, eh? An advantage at sea some never learn.' He went on, between drilling holes, 'The sea bores some people to death. Then they start borin everyone else. Books are good. Though you still don't want them sailin off the shelf and knockin your block off. It can happen. I recall one med student gettin a broken nose from his own anatomy book. You can't buy that kinda irony.'

He laughed as he changed a drill bit. 'I say if you're the doc's people, you'll survive us all right. We loved havin him and his family for a couple of turns. They're good value. Damn shame about the son.' He muttered as he worked, 'Whole world ahead of ya. Gonna be a doctor like your pop. Why'd ya go and top yourself?'

Within minutes, the deadbolt was in place and he packed his things. 'See ya round, missy. I'm just on the other side of the captain's quarters if you need. Dinner's at six.'

The girl missed dinner. She stole into an empty galley to take a few carrots and potatoes and scraps for the dog and retire early. At dawn, to the three notes of the ship's horn, they set sail.

With the motion of water around her, she stayed in bed. When she woke, she fed and took the dog below; then with a belly full of leftovers, she returned to bed and was out again.

§

Three days later, they stopped at the girl's first port: a seaside town with rows of shingled inns with black shutters. It took a swell of courage to leave the ship but she needed clothes.

Along the boardwalk, she projected calm but inside she was scrambling. When a man with broad shoulders emerged from a pub and stood shadowed in the doorway, her heart leapt and she hid behind her hat. He shook out a towel; his fingers zipping along the linen, all intact. When he said, 'Good morning,' she didn't answer.

At the corner, she found a women's boutique. It was close to the wharf with a dark blue dress hanging in the window. She tied the dog and pushed through the door; a bell jingled.

While the price tag of the dress reflected the waterfront window, the girl was not deterred. She kept looking over her shoulder: ship was

Part III: An Octopus Has Three Hearts

in sight, flags streaming.

Her mother had worn so much lilac and lavender, but this dress was the color of a midnight sea with a shimmer of tiny polished seashells stitched into the neckline. She removed her hat.

When she finished fixing all the little buttons and looked in the mirror, her dark eyes and hair glowed.

'It works for you,' a saleswoman said from behind the counter, 'and I love your hair.'

Smiling, she touched her hair.

She found a silk chemise to wear under the batik dress and, as the purchases were wrapped, the girl again looked to the ship. The dog stared through the glass door, mouth hanging. The girl replaced her hat and began tucking her hair.

'I wouldn't,' the saleswoman said.

The girl still hid her hair but felt her shoulders relax; she would get better at this.

With her packages and the dog, she returned to the ship.

Nearly.

A sandy beach near the shipyard called her. She released the dog and her shoes and packages and bolted toward the water where she stood up to her knees. She was still for some time, watching little fish gather in her shadow. A jellyfish, a porcelain teacup, rolled past. The tide rose—climbing the shore as the sea marked its own time—before the girl reclaimed her packages and the dog.

The girl crossed the deck and saw the captain disappear from the bridge window. The poet was under his umbrella with his glass of wine. She smiled but walked straight to her cabin. She filled her little tub and sat with bent knees, sponging away all that courage and salt.

§

The ship travelled south along a coastline woven with wind-slanted trees and cluttered dockyards. The girl sat at her window, watching autumn encroach, the sea glass and the doctor's journal before her. The dog scratched then snored. She wrote a couple of banal lines in her scrawl like, 'Bought clothes,' before crossing it out and writing instead:

Serpent's Wake

    Watched the sea tell time against my shins.

    She tapped the compass, tracked her course on the atlas then took to the books. Still wondering how to stow them, she selected her father's favorite: the sea journey of a king flung to the far reaches of the captain's calfskin map. She remembered her father reading with his big voice and how her mother laughed.
    When she looked up from the book, the coast had disappeared. She watched the sea change as the sun sank and darkness collapsed over the vast stretch of water. A deep calm settled upon her as sky and sea conversed and she thought of the doctor's son and how he let her go.
    She missed dinner again.
    Late the next morning, she found them berthed at port. When the girl took the dog below, they were surprised by horses. She'd seen the empty padded stalls before, but now, a line of horses thudded their hooves against the rubber floor. One great red horse extended his nose, crooning, and willed her to rub his cheeks. She complied, memories of her father and his horses rising like fog across water.
    She saw him beside the barn with a new horse, ears pricked. Her father used no rope but the horse followed him. She remembered his voice: 'Be your own nation. Know yours. Know his. Then let your nations converse.'
    The girl climbed the stairs to the galley and returned with a banana. The horse—so red, he glowed gold in ribbons—nickered as she peeled. She slid a palm over his eye and he closed it. Together, they dozed while the dog sniffed and scratched.
    The girl opened her eyes to the locksmith closing a storage container, his shirt black with grease. 'Crew takes this lot for a play every time we make port. Sight for sore eyes if ya wanna watch.'
    He turned and opened a door to a room the girl had never noticed. Past him, she spied a makeshift weight room with a bench and a hanging bag. The locksmith shut the door and continued on his rounds.
    When he left, she peeked into the room. It smelled of sweat and leather. There were homemade weights: buckets filled with dry concrete with a steel pole set between them. She pushed the thick black bag and sent it swinging on its hook.

Part III: An Octopus Has Three Hearts

Midmorning, she followed the horses off the ship with the dog and a book. She ignored the book and stood in the sea as the horses took the beach, gods on sand.

Upon her return to the ship, she glanced up at the bridge window and found the engineer leaning on the lintel; eyes sharp as daggers. Her stomach knotted. She took herself off to her cabin, suddenly fatigued.

Early that evening, the girl found she was bleeding, as her mother said. She curled into her blankets. She covered her eyes and imagined her mother at the edge of her bed, telling her this was a good thing, a woman thing, and that they were strong women; women of blood and fire.

§

Another morning, another port. After the girl stood in the sea and watched the horses run over the border of her father's book, she collected her shoes to follow them back to the ship but changed her mind. She walked away from the ship instead, to lose sight of it, especially when everything about the ship said *Go*.

Like the captain. All she had to do was think of him to feel the rush of bubbles.

Make maps around your eyes.

She walked past the shops that lined the wharf, letting the flags of her ship disappear and found another dress. She bought it, marched straight back to the ship and fell asleep under another of her father's books. She dreamt of the captain, her body twined around his, and woke to the sound of the dog scratching. 'Fleas?' she asked, examining his coat. It was late afternoon; a sun blanched sea lit her window.

At the next port, she walked further from the ship to a windy bluff. She watched white-capped waves and people running for cover as rain began to fall. Slowly and soaking wet, she found a shop that sold rosemary to make her mother's flea treatment before returning to the ship.

Back in her cabin, she whipped off her wet clothes and drew the dog's bath with steeped rosemary. When the scent of split pine filled her cabin, she took the first dip. She sat in the little tub and imagined

Serpent's Wake

her mother saying neither of them would have fleas. The dog took his bath without too much moaning and slept, freshly scented, finally allowed on the bed.

Again, she dreamt of the captain. She saw the steaming waterfall of her mountains, and found herself nude beside him on a slab of slate by the river. She woke slowly; the dark stone warming her thighs; his ear touching hers until she heard the ship's engines cut out at port. She looked at the wall she shared with the captain until she pulled herself from bed and found horses below, returning from the beach. She opened their locker and brushed them as if in a trance.

§

A month at sea and the water changed from gray to blue and palm trees waved from an island. The girl consulted her atlas to trace their route, imagining her father looking over her shoulder, then opened the last of his books and touched the word *sovereignty*.

She closed the book, braided her hair, and left her cabin for the first time without a hat.

She went to the galley to get treats for the horses and found the cook and the engineer, their backs to her, angling and heaving something toward a wide, industrial sink. They were too busy to notice her hair as she watched them push a giant blue fin tuna into the sink. Flinching against the blow of the fish's mass bouncing against steel, the girl saw the face of a creature accustomed to more weightlessness.

'Look what's for dinner!' the cook panted.

The girl saw by the light in the single, black eye, that the fish—blue as the sea and silver as the moon—was alive. She crossed the galley and leaned over the cold lip of the sink and pulled herself toward the creature. Her feet left the floor: a levitation. She forgot the galley and the men. It was only she and the great fish; the sink streaked reflections like moonlight all around her.

The girl touched her forehead to a bleeding gill and closed her eyes. She saw an egg, a sphere of light dancing in warm brine; then a hatchling flitting in a stream of others all the same; she saw a fish grown, fleeing trolling mouths, all teeth and tongue, a pink crack of gill; she saw fish gliding warm and close in chilly waters, crossing borderless seas with tidal knowing; she saw larger fish dodging nets and diving into darkness only to rise toward wrinkling light, to return to the spawning shoals to call forth more life. She and the fish were alone in the world and she whispered, just as she had done to the dying creatures in the serpent, a prayer long lost: 'Go gentle now. Blessings upon your ancestors and upon your children. You are loved. You are loved. You are loved...'

And the great fish died; the shimmer left its eye, its face pale as milk.

And the girl had forgotten she had said such things.

The overhead lights glared.

The silence of the galley hung.

She slipped from the sink back onto her feet. Wiping her face, she found the cook's mouth agape, the engineer disgusted, and leaning in the doorway with his hand on the engineer's shoulder, the poet, his eyes misted.

She fumbled toward her cabin, hearing the cook mutter: 'How the heck am I supposed to eat it now?' and the engineer asking, 'Was that hair blue?'

§

The temperature climbed as the ship headed due south. The cook left meals in the fridge locker for her and the poet looked at her tenderly. The engineer continued to scowl. She wrote in her journal.

> I remember forgotten things with such force. I cannot stand myself.

At port, she left the ship and sought bookshops which she observed, never rented on the waterfront. They sat in tiny alleys away from the sea and had to be earned. As she walked, she felt the mantle of her father's word upon her: *Sovereignty.*

Occasionally, she spied one of the brawnier crewmen along the streets, a man whose extravagant tattoos culminated in a dark firestorm across his face, but he never noticed her, so she continued her explorations undeterred.

She found books by writers who spent time at the edges, homeless, unable to speak, exiled, ill, imprisoned or in an occupied country—and

Serpent's Wake

her collection grew into a community on her dresser, her desk, and within the folds of her sheets.

As she traveled and read, she used the journal. She wrote about the grand things she read on plaques. On foot, she sketched the architecture and statues of men who had won each city. But one day, when she looked up into the eyes of a bronze rider wielding a sabre upon a rearing stallion, she saw the eyes of the hunter: champion, broker of history, thug; and fed those pages of her journal to the sea.

From then, she wrote differently:

> An old lady bookseller with an eye patch handpicked a book for me.

She wrote about the sea.

> The sea is a mirror. If I am shamed, it eats me. If I am calm, it's tranquil. If I am homesick, it's alien. I see myself; lose myself.

She wrote what she was told.

> A woman on a tanker of oil men at port town. Cook says, 'See her?' as she walks the pier. 'They'll swap her for a new one when they get sick of more than just her cooking.'

She wrote about events on the ship.

> This morning, crewmen shout: 'Man overboard!' A form bobbed in the wake of the ship. A lifeboat falls. A mannequin is plucked from the sea. Cheers silence the alarm. I shake at the rail. Cook says, 'It's just a drill, darlin. Just a drill.'

That day, the ship traded coastline for open water, 'to hook a few for the freezer,' the cook told her while she collected fruit from the galley. He nudged her, 'Maybe you can send them gentle to the next life?'

He was sincere but she smiled and shook her head.

'Aw, that's too bad. Made me feel better about killin it. By the way,

I like that you don't wear that hat so much anymore. It was a little weird at breakfast. The blue is cool.' He uncovered a bowl of dough. 'Damn.'

She asked what was wrong.

'Dough won't rise,' and he tossed the lump into the trash.

She considered sharing her mother's yeast but slipped from the galley and watched the ship's wake. Thick fishing poles emerged on the lower deck and it didn't take long for the men to get something and the desperate elegance of a dying marlin drove her back to her cabin. She waited for their catch to be prepared, studying the map, and tapping her compass until the ship turned southeast. She returned topside to watch sunset halo the sea.

'We're out far,' the cook told her, 'but we're headed into the islands,' when a stench cut across the water. The ship's horn sounded through the dusk. The girl and the cook saw a boat. Tattered nets. The ship slowed.

'No lights,' the cook said, handing binoculars to the girl. 'This is bad.'

Shirtless men waved on deck and a third descended upon them with a stick until the men, protecting their heads, disappeared from view.

The ship turned with a shudder and the cook returned to the galley.

That evening, the girl lay on her bed with her notebook over her chest as the ship made port, remembering the smell of decay that came off that ship. While most others were asleep, she left her cabin and her hat on the bed to walk the deck with the dog. The wrap from the doctor's wife draped her shoulders, her hair uncovered and unfurled in the night. The island port was quiet.

In the light of the bridge window, she looked for the captain but saw only his map. She hadn't seen him for weeks.

He did, however, see her.

§

That night, after the girl turned her back to the bridge, the captain, fully bearded now, leaned on the window. After a day of fishing out past the continental shelf, nearly everyone was asleep. He sipped from a ringed mug and scratched his chin, the beard curling into his mouth. Coffee dribbled from stray hairs.

Behind him, the map clung to the wall, the lone hunter perplexed. The poet entered the bridge and the captain asked in their language: 'Can't sleep?'

The poet shook his head and leaned on a cane as he dropped a sealed document on the desk. 'Would you be so kind as to replace the old one?'

'Who'd you cut out this time?' The captain spun the combination of the safe behind his desk and kicked it to open the door.

'Everyone. I've left my immense fortune to a bird sanctuary.'

When the captain lifted the new will. 'Heavy paper.'

'I splurged and hired a calligrapher and a proper lawyer.'

'Too bad I'll never get to read it,' the captain said. 'One day you'll want a bed that doesn't wander. You'll want birches and solid ground.'

'My boy,' the poet tapped his cane, 'I've written enough of birches and there is no solid ground.' He looked to the window. 'She's out there again.'

'Who?' The captain rifled through the safe, looking for the old will.

'Who, indeed.' The poet waved a hand. 'Anyway, this is what I want: an old world cremation like our ancestors. Our real ancestors. Nothing left. Let the sea take the ashes.'

The captain sighed. 'You want a funeral pyre.'

'And don't skimp on firewood.'

'I can't wait,' the captain said. 'Where am I supposed to do this? I'll have to bribe a hundred people. You can't cremate poets anywhere you like.'

'Don't worry. I'll stay lean so I won't burn for days.'

The captain handed over the old will and kicked the safe door closed. The poet sat on the desk. 'I want wine. And music. And lovemaking. There is no better way to stand in the reality of death than to make love.'

The captain looked hard at him, his back to the window. 'Anything else? An albino elephant?'

'A white elephant is a veiled insult.'

'You taught me that.'

'A gift you can't afford to keep and can't discard,' the poet tapped his cane. 'Have I been your white elephant?'

Part III: An Octopus Has Three Hearts

'You're too cheap to feed. Are you planning something? Have you written your eulogy yet?'

'Now that's tacky. You're perfect for the job but I utterly forbid you to say I never complained. Whenever I hear that the deceased never complained, it's as if it was his greatest achievement. Now there's a reason to weep at a funeral.'

'I wouldn't dream of it.'

He yawned and stood to leave.

'Good night,' the captain scratched at his chin.

'You really should shave,' the poet said as he left the bridge. 'That beard is chaotic.'

Since the girl boarded, the captain hadn't shaved once. In the window, the bearded reflection looked too much like his father. Below, the poet waved to the girl on deck; she waved back.

He turned to a pile of papers and cleared his throat. There was the slave ship today: an unregistered fishing boat with all the signs. His ship came upon the craft as they crossed deep sea, their course set for a string of islands where the racehorses were destined. Half-naked, sunburned men waved only to be beaten by an overseer with a truncheon. The captain had coordinates. He could report it, but he wouldn't. His father taught him that terrible forces turn such wheels; forces that would paint his ship red from the inside.

He crumpled the details.

On the map behind him, a serpent devoured its own tail.

Below on deck, the girl still stood at the rail. Over the past weeks, he watched her disembark and noted her return. At the seedier spots, he slipped a few bills to his bo'sun, a trusted friend and largest of his crewmen with an exceptionally terrifying facial tattoo. He had said, 'Keep an eye on her for the old doc,' as the bo'sun unbuckled his tool belt, his rig of marlin spikes and various tools, from his shoulder. 'Don't pick any fights.'

The bo'sun grinned and said, 'Discretion, bro,' as he folded the bills into his pocket. 'Cheers for the beers.'

A decade ago with his father still at the helm, the captain pulled the bo'sun from an illegal cage fighting circuit deep in the southern hemisphere. The old man was furious when his son dragged a hemorrhagic boxer onboard, calling him bo'sun. The old captain howled about racketeering and discretion and the boxer-come-bo'sun heard everything through the thin cabin wall as he recovered from his tremors. The captain weathered the onslaught from his father, unwavering. And his friend, in bed with both eyes swollen shut, said: 'I'm a dead man. No one'll look for me.' And when no one did, the bo'sun admitted he was disappointed.

The captain's father eventually accepted bo'sun for his strength and work ethic, and the slip in his son's obedience was dismissed. He continued to run his relationship with his son the way he ran the ship: with determined practicality. When he caught his son's gaze lingering on a billowing skirt, he growled: 'You might as well run my ship into a reef as get involved with that.' In the language of their homeland—that frozen place where summer flourishes for a few weeks before frost reclaims dominion—his father said the crew would lose respect and it would only ever end with humiliation.

After his father's death, the captain went on what the bo'sun called 'a bender' and had a couple of affairs that ended mildly. The crew ignored them—nothing like his father's predictions—and he got on with the business of managing the ship. His affairs were timed to the ship's schedule and amicably concluded. The last one, the widow whose geriatric husband loved cars more than he loved her, sought comfort closer to her age before returning to the expectations waiting ashore, and the captain had never experienced such feminine gratitude.

Now, he sorted papers at the window. On deck, the girl shook out her hair alongside the ship's endless duties; but entangled in the latest drainage issue, stalled desalination system, broken down cylinder, lost passport or expired relationship with a port authority that could only be mended with a case of expensive rum, was a single strand of her long, indigo hair.

The captain paused to consider the girl, alone on the ship with that one-eared farm dog, and plucked at his beard. His attempt to fortify his charge across the seas of the world as a free man had turned on him. The beard was supposed to say he didn't crave comforts. Or women. But it grew in too thick, and a little too gray.

From the map, a mermaid held up her mirror.

He scratched at his chin. With the ship lights just right, the girl's body shone through the fabric of her dress, the curve of a hip. The black wrap slipped from a shoulder blade. The glow of the waxing moon made her hair iridescent as the skin of a deep-sea fish rising from the gloom.

'See me,' he said in his language to the pane, an incantation.

She yawned; the dog sniffed the breeze.

The engineer pushed on the door as he entered the bridge—duty roster in his hand.

The captain put his back to the window as the engineer asked, 'What are you doing about that fishing boat?' He looked sharply at the captain. 'I know that network. They're dangerous.'

The captain picked a curling hair from his lip, silent.

'Good. I'm having a nightcap. Do you want one?'

The captain shook his head with a yawn.

'You know she is bewitching you.'

'Who?'

'Ha! Who!' the engineer said. 'Your boo hag.'

'My what?'

'Demon woman who comes out of nowhere and steals a man's soul. She weakens him. She makes him grow his beard too long. She makes him sleep on the couch.' He pointed to the pillow and blanket on the bridge. 'You look thinner. I know why.'

'You're crazy.'

'You have a gray beard, no bed, and a boo hag. And the young ones are the hardest to shake.'

'It's not that gray.' The captain looked.

'It is,' the engineer finally chuckled.

'Boo hag. Where do you get this stuff?'

'Your cook and his swamp people. Come on, come down for a drink.'

The captain shook his head and the engineer left.

And this is how it was. The captain grumbled at his papers, his eyes drifting again to the window. The night the girl had boarded the ship, he caught several of the crew standing around in the galley joking about propositioning her. He sent them back to work with: 'Anyone fraternizing with passengers will be paid out at the next port.'

The engineer had said: 'Impressive. You sound just like your father.'

Serpent's Wake

When everyone cleared out of the galley, the cook relayed the fantastic story he had heard from a hunter at the pub who was making sure that girl was gone for good.

Not a whisper of emotion crossed the captain's face as he listened. His father had taught him: 'Never give anything away. Leave that to the crew. They give everything away at every port. Not you.'

When the cook finished his story, the captain answered, 'If you believe all that, you'll believe all the horses below are winners,' and reprimanded him for spreading rumors about their passengers.

Before the girl had boarded, all the doctor had said was that both her parents had died but something in her eyes and carved into her chest said there was, indeed, more to her story. The captain saw that scar when she was flung to the floor by her cabin door—and for him, a sea captain whose life coiled around the molten seas of the world since the day his father first took him from his mother's lap, he'd seen plenty of the strange and the mystical. There was more truth than myth to that old calfskin map hanging behind him; the sea serpent writhing in an inky sea.

He stood at the window. 'See me,' a ghost upon the glass.

And the girl looked. She saw the thick beard and behind him, the map, a fracturing star. She touched her face with a smile.

He looked into his mug. A string of unintelligible words streamed from his lips, then a moment later, a whisper in his language: 'She likes the beard.'

While the girl retreated to her cabin, the captain shaved. The hair crackled under the razor, his face grim.

§

In the morning, a beach on the first of a chain of subtropical islands claimed the girl. She found herself up to her knees in a warm sea, hair swept up under a wide-brimmed hat found in a vintage shop. The brim was so broad that when she tilted it just right, all she saw was water. Her dress, the one from the doctor's wife, was pulled around her hips, a silk camisole fluttering at her chest. Watching the tide come in, she stood rooted as a mangrove. Behind her, the dog rolled in the sand, a knot of driftwood in his teeth.

Inviting as the water was, the girl only went out to her knees. Through the glassy current, she watched dozens of skinny fish, eyes as black as buttons, tube up from holes in the sand several feet ahead of her. Two rivals argued, lashing toward each other in the tide.

Someone entered the water behind her and she turned to see feet sloshing through the surf, pants rolled. The captain. Clean-shaven. Behind him, the dog danced, driftwood sloppy with drool.

The captain asked, 'What's happening?'

'An argument.' Hand on her brim, the fish leaned into the current with menace.

'Garden eels,' he said.

'The water is so clear, I can see everything. Why are they attacking each other?'

'To get girls. Why else?'

She hid behind her brim as his ripples approached her knees.

'I used to swim up to fields of them just to watch them disappear. You should try it.'

She imagined it. 'What was it like, growing up on a ship?'

'It's what I knew.' He told her about the times the doctor's sons were onboard, how they treated him like a big brother. 'The years when the old doc and his family were with us were the best ones. His sons could always get me off the ship for a swim.' He asked about the family.

She remembered the kiss on the cottage steps and felt the flush of her cheeks. She hesitated. Absent when the doctor's son took his life, she was careful as she described their kindness toward her.

The captain cleared his throat and explained that he was on the other side of the world when the doctor's son died. 'My father was in his last weeks,' something in him unfolded, 'so I didn't tell him. He was too sick to handle such news. It would have infuriated him.'

She felt the bones in her legs creak. 'I took care of my mother. I don't know how you managed at sea.'

'My father always said he would die on his ship and in the end, he didn't want to die. Who does?'

Again, they thought of the doctor's eldest son. The captain turned his head sharply.

'I'm sorry,' the girl said.

Serpent's Wake

'Not your fault,' he said. 'It was the world's fault.'

'It's too easy to blame the world.'

'We shouldn't?'

'Only for a little while.'

He dragged his fingertips across the water in an arch. Sunlight danced as rings broke.

She saw mercy in that scattered light. 'My father was fast. He was here, then he was gone. My mother suffered but when it was time, her passing was gentle.'

'My father was not swift or gentle. After a lifetime of fighting, he never stopped.'

She felt a chill and knew he was finished talking about it. She asked, 'Were you ever afraid?'

'Captains are never afraid. That's what my father taught me. Not even as the water rushes in.'

'I suppose not,' she smiled a little at his intensity, 'but what about the man?'

'The man is always afraid.'

The girl watched a pelican soar, regal.

'It's all over now,' he said and she wondered if that was true.

She stole another glance. 'Your beard is gone.'

He touched his chin. The water rolled between them, toes sinking. 'Tide's coming in. How are you finding your voyage?'

'Wonderful,' she breathed, trying to cool the enthusiasm too late.

He apologized. 'These islands are always slow. We stop daily for contracts and the horses. Things will pick up a little bit later but we tend to be a bit slow.'

'I don't care.'

'Is there anything you need?'

She considered his question. 'More books. But I'll find them.'

'I've noticed. Do you have anything I should read?'

'Please, yes, help yourself.' Still too much enthusiasm. She suddenly felt the garden eels watching her now and blushed.

'I used to read all the time. My father insisted.'

'Mine too. He said they were my bridge to the world.'

'My father told me that the world was my bridge to the books.' He laughed. 'Maybe we can meet in the middle?'

Part III: An Octopus Has Three Hearts

She bit her lip.

The eels hovered.

'A draw,' he said. Seawater pin-wheeled between them. 'I was told you're grooming the horses.'

She smiled, wondering if he thought about her down in the hold, her hands running the length of their bodies.

'Travel is hard on them. I appreciate it. Tell me: what is it with women and horses?'

She stayed behind her hat, unsure.

'A secret allegiance?'

'If it's a secret,' she said, 'I can't say.'

'I'll tell no one.' He folded his arms tightly. She watched his reflection. 'Whether it's a medical student or a widow, women are always talking to the horses.'

'I think, maybe, it's because we're similar.'

'Hm.'

'Emotional?' She said it like a question. 'Maybe we both just want to live.'

'Emotional, yes. I've been kicked by both.'

She laughed, a ripple spun.

'I assure you,' he cracked a smile, 'I did nothing to deserve it.' He tried to see past her brim but only saw her chin turn toward him. She watched his reflection: his look, that of a man remembering a dream.

They lingered there, quietly until he checked his watch. 'I must get back.'

'I'll walk with you.'

'Good.'

The dog pranced as they crossed the deck, the poet tipped his hat from his table. They looked up to the bridge to find the engineer, his face lined.

The girl said: 'I'm sorry but he always looks so…angry.'

'If he is, I don't have to be.'

'I don't think he likes me one bit.'

'Beautiful women terrify him.'

Cheeks aflame, the girl turned toward her cabin where she wrote in her journal:

Serpent's Wake

The sea reshapes the world.

§

Warming to a world that opened like a treasure, the very next day sent the girl straight back into the dark.

She rose early, braided her hair, put on her favorite dress and hat and stood on the deck with the dog. This time she let her braid trail from her hat, instead of coiling it out of sight.

The night prior in the galley, the cook asked her if she knew about the island colony where they berthed, renowned for its leadlight glass. Each morning as the sun climbed over the sea, he said, the windows of the eastern-facing esplanade shined like flowers dipped in light and market stalls sold sun catchers he'd never seen anywhere else. 'Take some money with you or you'll wish you had,' he said, lifting the cover of the stove. When the girl asked what was wrong with the stove, he said, 'I think I got fleeced by bandits in your port town.'

So that morning from the deck, she saw a line of tents selling stained glass and jackfruit. Over their heads, windows shone scarlet and emerald, more vivid by the minute. The great window of a seaside chapel bloomed sapphire and she wanted to watch the sun move blue across its tiled floor.

Her dog beside her, she descended the gangplank, light on her feet. Yesterday's conversation with the captain lingered. She smiled easily.

As she touched down onto the pier, the money in her purse jingled and she wrapped a hand to silence it. She smiled at a brawny man who stared as she passed and he fell into step behind her. Too close. She stiffened. Everything within her suddenly rang her back to the ship but she refused such impressions as ghosts and stuck to the pier, her mouth terribly dry.

She measured the distance to the chapel.

On the beach, a whiteout of seagulls attacked something in the sand.

She felt a hand clamp onto her shoulder, heavy as a sack of flour. The dog barked. The man slapped her hat and it whirled to the pier. A round face sweated down at her, eyes targeting.

He pulled her across the pier, tearing the neckline of her dress. Buttons popped. She gasped.

The dog took a mouthful of the man's shirt. When she tried to fight him off, he struck her face twice with his free hand. She touched her nose, surprised by blood.

The crowd along the market tents hushed. Then, a thunder of applause.

A sudden rainstorm, she thought, looking into a cloudless sky. She heard whistling then saw men and women clapping; their faces all a smudge, eyes dark.

She sank to the pier just as a crewman appeared: that tree trunk of a man carved with tattoos. A tool belt was strung over one shoulder. Leather sheaths swung against his hip on a line of silver carabiners. Shouting a string of abuses, face aflame with ink and war cry, the bo'sun yanked the stranger's hand from the girl and pinned it. The man dropped to the pier; the eyes of the bo'sun shined between black rays.

The girl leapt to her feet. She fled, scar exposed.

The applause crunched to a halt, catapulting a woman's shouts over the water.

The girl didn't look back. She and the dog ran all the way back to her cabin.

On deck, the poet called to her, but she heard nothing until the silver deadbolt rasped across her cabin door.

She crept to the corner of the room and sank to the floor. She fell onto her belly and breathed into the floor, searching for the water all around her and feeling the swell of each breath until, within minutes, the captain knocked.

The bo'sun stood beside him, blood on his shirt. 'She was all right. Just a bloody nose. I've had my share of those.'

The captain considered the misshapen nose before him. 'You're a boxer. She's a girl.'

'Yeah, well, sorry. Where I come from, girls drop sandbags like that in one hit.'

She listened, holding the shredded neckline of her dress, and didn't move.

Serpent's Wake

§

At noon when the captain knocked again, she still didn't answer. He slid an envelope under the door and hooked her hat on the corridor rail before returning to the bridge. Inside the envelope, the girl found a needle and thread. And several of the tiny seashells and a single blue button from her torn neckline. She read the note in the light that seeped under the door:

Visit infirmary. Man is detained. I'll be back soon.

She began to sew. Wetting the end of the thread on her lips, she imagined her mother saying the light was poor and she'd ruin her eyes, she ignored it. Then she wondered how the captain knew this button or these tiny shells were hers. She rolled them between her fingers.

As she tied off a thread, the captain rapped again. 'I need to speak with you. Please.'

She tucked the needle into the fabric.

'I have the doctor.'

The dog whined.

The captain said, 'And something for you, too.'

She opened the door and slipped back into her cabin. The captain entered and the ship's doctor followed, half his height, the corridor light blanching her glasses. She said: 'Little dark in here, don't you think? Have a seat. Let's let some light in here so we can see what's what.' She lit the desk lamp. The girl sat before the glow, her cheek embossed with a handprint.

The ship's doctor, her hair short as a man's, walked past the captain, her mouth curled into reprimand. 'When something like this happens, see me immediately.' She handed a bag of ice to the girl.

The captain unwrapped a bone and looked at the girl. She nodded behind the ice and the dog took it to his corner, all business.

The ship's doctor fiddled with the desk lamp and aimed it toward the girl's face. She squinted through bifocals, and the girl looked at the scrawls around her mouth. She was quite hardened but her hands, now on the girl's cheeks, were soft as pollen.

The doctor said, 'Just bruising. You were lucky.'

The captain cleared his throat to speak but the doctor spoke first.

'Yes, you were lucky. You've got all your teeth and both eyes are open.'

'Soften it a little,' the captain grumbled. 'She's not one of the crew.'

The girl replaced the ice while the doctor relaxed her voice with purpose, 'You'll be sore for a few days but you'll be fine.' She smiled stiffly, both at the girl and the captain. 'Keep icing, especially for the first twenty-four hours. Come to the infirmary or the galley to replenish your supply. I have pain relief if you need it.'

'Better,' the captain said. 'Now would you give us a minute?' and the doctor left.

The captain lingered. 'Please let me in when I knock.'

She started to apologize but he stopped her. 'I also need you to do something else for me. I need you to come with us to the magistrate's office.

'When?'

'Now.'

§

When the girl, the captain, his first engineer and the bo'sun met that afternoon with port officials, they sat across from a translator and a rather grave magistrate in a stuffy meeting room. The translator read from a statement that 'The man who frightened the girl is unwell.'

'Frightened?' The engineer corrected him: 'He assaulted our passenger. Look at her face.'

The girl looked hard at the magistrate, grateful the captain was on one side, the bo'sun on the other.

'Who is this man,' the translator gestured to the engineer on behalf of the magistrate, 'and why is he a part of this hearing?' The captain, for the second time, introduced his first engineer and said, again, that he was privy to all aspects of port relations.

'Well,' the translator said, 'yes, we made a note of her face.'

'Not only her face,' the engineer said, 'but the substantial bruises on her face.'

The translator continued to read. The man had a history of mental instability and was perpetually in and out of their hospital. He mistook the girl for his sister who ran off with a merchant seaman last year and

Serpent's Wake

hasn't returned. His mother is distraught and the man vowed to bring his sister back, should he see her. Unfortunately, he saw her once a month at the docks.

The captain frowned. 'How do you explain the applause?'

The translator and the magistrate exchanged words then the translator spoke: 'Police officers have submitted a report.'

'If this happens once a month,' the bo'sun grunted, 'someone won a bet.'

The translator continued: 'There is no evidence of gambling but there was another incident.' He exchanged words with the magistrate, then said, 'One of your crew. A young woman. Dark. Has a black plait. Your medical assistant? She threatened bystanders on the pier with a...' Papers riffled. A pencil sketch of a large sewing needle slid across the desk. Disbelief soaked the translator's expression. 'What is this?'

The bo'sun chuckled. 'A marlinspike.'

The girl looked at the sketch.

The translator repeated the word.

'Only a baby one,' the bo'sun put his hands out about a foot apart.

The engineer said, 'She was assisting crewman on the dock when she ran to aid the victim on the pier. The marlinspike was in her hand prior to the incident.'

'Witnesses say she waved the weapon provocatively.'

'It's not a weapon,' the engineer said. 'It's a common tool aboard ships.'

'Threats were made. Something about offering the bystanders a brand new...hmm.' The translator slid the report toward the men so they could read it themselves.

The bo'sun belly laughed, 'Rectum? She said rectum? Only a medical student would say rectum!'

The engineer and the captain hardly breathed.

The magistrate murmured to his translator, who then said, 'The magistrate doesn't understand why a medical trainee would risk her hands with such activity.'

The engineer answered before the captain could: 'Everyone participates in the daily duties of our ship. All hands contribute to our port routines. She was assisting...'

'Me.' The bo'sun pointed to his chest. 'She was assisting me.'

The translator did not translate any of this. He continued, 'The magistrate understands that it takes only one call to conclude her medical career before it starts.'

Before the meeting was over, the magistrate served the captain a fine and the translator said the bo'sun was charged with the unlawful assault of a man with a mental illness, a charge which would be dropped through payment of the fine.

'Too proper to say rectum,' the bo'sun rumbled, 'but not too proper for extortion?'

The translator closed the folder. The magistrate stood.

The engineer motioned to the bo'sun to control himself but he snarled: 'Tell me I at least broke some bones on your money spinner.'

'No.' The translator twitched.

'What's his bloody address?'

The translator closed the folder.

The captain said, 'The man attacked my passenger. You anticipated this situation but did nothing. My crewman halted a dangerous situation, leaving the perpetrator tender but unharmed. Your magistrate is fining us for self-defense and threatening a member of my crew.'

There was no translation; the magistrate left. The translator paused before he followed him out, saying, 'What a shame we cannot reach an agreement. What a shame for your medical student's future.'

The bo'sun groaned. He turned to the engineer. 'Come on, you know this is bullshit.'

'I know a solitary female tourist is nothing more than a liability. Is anyone honestly surprised?'

The girl looked at him sharply. The captain tore up the fine as they descended the steps of the building. 'We're leaving tonight. I know which fights I can win and this isn't one of them.'

'They need the money,' the engineer said. 'The leadlight and beaches are the draw card here but the bureaucratic corruption leads all the way back to a decaying crown. Same old story.'

'Yeah, thanks for that, mate,' the bo'sun rolled his eyes. 'You know, you're a crap bush lawyer. We needed a real one in there.'

The captain turned to the bo'sun and asked about the medical assistant and her marlinspike: 'You knew about this? Are we talking about the same person here?'

'Er, yeah,' the bo'sun laughed but stopped himself. 'She was helping me on the pier, it's true, but when we saw what was happening, she pulled the spike off my rig,' he pointed to where he wears his utility belt. 'I didn't know what she was gonna do with it. We ran in different directions. After I put the mongrel down, I found her—yeah, that little girl was impressive, shouting and carrying on like that. I had to drag her back to the ship.'

'Why didn't you tell me?'

'Didn't want to upset you, bro. Trust me. Some things go more smoothly if everyone looks genuinely surprised.'

The engineer snapped: 'You should have told us. I was unprepared for that. How the hell did she pull a marlinspike off of your rig?'

'She's quick. Another rescue case,' the bo'sun laughed and elbowed the girl. 'Ship's fulla them.'

The captain said, 'We don't know how serious they are about reporting her.'

The engineer shrugged. 'It doesn't take much effort to crush a medical student.'

§

Years ago, the bo'sun had a grandmother who told him: 'A man amounts to all the little things he does, so do a little right.' Within the hour, he shattered his savings to get to the magistrate's office and pay the fine before they weighed anchor.

When the bo'sun had looked up from his grapple hold on the pier and saw that petite young girl waving a marlinspike with her black braid swinging like a cobra; when he heard the applause falter and the crowd turn to her outrage, the once-boxer was moved.

'Moments like this,' his nana had told him, her voice majestic as rocky beaches of his youth, 'make your heart grow big.'

So, while the crew notified the passengers and prepared for departure, the bo'sun strode back to the magistrate's office and slammed a pile of bills on the translator's folder. When the magistrate emerged from his office, the bo'sun stared long with his face of iron, until the man began to sweat. Then in the language of his island home, the bo'sun slapped his own chest and sang the chant he had always used before his fights: *Listen to us! We are fearless in the storm! We climb to heaven while you blow in circles like dust! Blow away, while we ride this storm to glory!*

No one moved.

The bo'sun pushed through the doors, shouting: *We die; we die! We live; we live!*

Neither the magistrate, nor his translator, understood a word and back aboard, he pounded his fists into the heavy hanging bag below and never told anyone what he did.

§

That evening as they left port, there was another rap at the door. The girl answered, hoping for the captain but found the ship's doctor, the medical student holding a tray, the cook beside her. The medical student clipped into the room on kitten heels. The doctor introduced her as her assistant, 'Though for how much longer, who knows?'

Balancing the tray, the young woman offered a warm hello. 'It is good to meet you finally, despite the circumstances,' she said, her words threaded together like song. Her eyes were large and penciled, though smudged from the day's events. 'It could have been any one of us.'

The student removed cutlery, a bowl and a plate from the tray and placed them on the desk. 'We thought you'd like some soup. I have more medical skills than this, I promise you, but I'm glad you don't need them.'

The doctor pushed her glasses onto her head. 'You can have all the medical skills in the world, but people still say it's the soup.' She looked at the cook: 'No offense.'

But the cook's eyes were soulful with regret. 'I feel so bad, darlin,' he said. 'I told you to go see those damn windows.' He pointed to the bowl. 'Soup's got dumplings. Galley's got loads of ice if you want to see a friendly face, no offense,' he turned to the doctor.

The girl felt pained at the crowd in her room. 'I hate being such a bother. I'm so sorr...'

Serpent's Wake

The doctor snapped, 'Don't you dare apologize. Since when is going to a chapel at nine o'clock in the morning asking for it?'

The medical student hugged the tray. 'You barely made it off the ship! And that clapping? I had to put a stop to it.'

The doctor glowered. The student read her face and blurted: 'I wasn't going to use the spike! I harm no one, right! But I see harm? In front of me? I stop it!'

'Oh you're going to change the world,' the doctor put her glasses back on. 'Don't you know it's the world that ends up changing you? You're in the galley until further notice. I hope you're enjoying that tray.'

The student considered it.

The doctor continued, 'The magistrate threatened to end your medical career right here, before it even starts.'

'He has no case,' the young woman answered.

'Don't get sassy. He does.'

§

Over the next set of weeks, the ship dotted along a curvaceous archipelago of islands and the girl submerged. She did not speak for days, not even to the dog. Smiling hurt, so she stopped. She watched the sea from her window for hours and never left her cabin in daylight, slinking out to retrieve the cook's meals and care for the dog in the dark. Hiding her black-blue then yellow-green face became routine. Ports came and went and as the blow to her face faded, the rest took longer. She wrote in her journal:

I lose myself. I dissolve like bread in water.

She found herself below with the chestnut horse and as if he knew, he crooned a deep purr. She rested mute against his shoulder, awash with the pulse of the ship's engines.

The door to the weight room opened: the light simple, the smell sweaty, the bo'sun slick and slinging his rig over his shoulder. He hadn't noticed her. She slipped between the horse and his stall wall as the bo'sun stowed his bench press and he was halfway up the stairs before she breathed again.

Part III: An Octopus Has Three Hearts

Another morning and she went below to find the horses gone, delivered to an island estate. She stood, hands hanging at her sides, eyes burning, before returning to her cabin.

Wretched moments scratched into her solitude; moments that ambushed her at dawn when most others were asleep. The ghost of the serpent had followed her, tracking the churned ocean wake then sidling along the prow of the ship, waiting to slide aboard while the crew dreamed. And sometimes just before sunrise, she found herself at the steel door of her cabin, sheets about her knees, heart pounding, groping frantically for a way out that she never found. She woke; the serpent closed its mouth.

The dog studied her face. When he realized that, once again, they weren't going anywhere, he reclined, sullen.

The girl returned to bed.

Another morning, another fright at the cabin door. Groping for the handle, she shook away the bright white panic and slid back into the dark.

I don't know where I am.

Sunlight cracked her window into shards and she felt the menace of another day. Some mornings, when the landscape was only sea, she fumbled for the compass but the needle just spun. The endless rolling sea, dense with the sunrise, stung her eyes.

She scratched at her neck and the shrieking in her head quelled a moment, then rose again. She scratched. Blood ran.

'I'm all right.' She groped with red nails, trying to believe.

Nothing is all right.

'I'm all right.' She rested her forehead on the cabin floor. And like a disciple aimed in the direction of some holy place, some glittering, solid place that many hands touched far in the distance beyond the curve of the globe, she hunched over her knees and clung to the thought that somehow, all was well; there was meaning somewhere in all of this. The crows still shouted in the trees and wolves still crooned their freedom; that one white wolf crossed forests wiser to snares; that a stand of pines still led to a river where falls churned with good sunlight; that the doctor's son replaced the rotten cottage steps and a team of horses again stood in their stalls, sucking mouthfuls of wet chaff from a bucket; that there was more goodness and grace in the world than

Serpent's Wake

darkness; and that life, by its very nature, craved, pursued and loved new life, and that was the force that guided her. She refused the sense of finality she felt—that she was finished before she ever began; that there was nothing for her anywhere; that she was too broken to mend and too twisted to rise and meet the dawn with an open face and clean hands.

All of these thoughts turned into water until they soaked the floor.

And she pretended that someone was beside her: a good angel, a wise old woman who had seen all these little sadnesses before and so much more.

She imagined a hand on her shoulder and shuddered until she felt the hives rising along her neck and recognized the blood under her nails.

Stop searching.
With your fingernails.

So she breathed. In and out. Staring at the floor that pressed her nose.

The worst is behind you.
Trust.
Life.
Trust.
Yourself.

When she was ready, she washed her face and the water stung her neck like tiny needles; a pain which sang her alive and allowed her to focus again. She patted the rash dry and rested her hands on it. Then she crawled into bed.

Lying there, she considered her strange new prayers. No more little girl utterances for safety or forgiveness or this thing or that. She uncurled the old memorizations from *before* and released them to the sea. She saw them drift one by one from her cabin and into the water like soft, white petals, leaving a swirling trail in the wake of the ship for the hungry ghost of the serpent to eat.

§

A knock.

The light from the window said it was midday. The girl rose, her mouth sticky; the dog scratched at the door. She threw on a dress and wound a light scarf around her neck.

The medical student had a bag over her shoulder and asked if she could come in. The cabin was a mess and the girl apologized. 'I'm not here to see the cabin,' she said. 'I'm here to see you, even though—strictly speaking—I'm on galley duties. May I come in?'

The girl sat on the edge of the bed, grateful for the scarf. The student took her pulse and blood pressure and looked at the skin along her arms and legs. 'No wonder you're sleeping so much. You have malnutrition. Your heart is racing and you have low blood pressure. You're dehydrated.' She pointed to the girl's shins. 'Do you see these bruises? The captain would lose his mind if he knew this was happening on his ship. If you're going to be such a radical eater, you must educate yourself.'

She pulled her bag onto her shoulder.

'Are you,' the girl said, 'in trouble?'

'No, not really. As for what I did, I still cannot imagine any alternatives.' She stood. 'Before I go, can I ask, how on earth do you get your hair this color?'

The girl blushed, touching a hand to her hair. 'I don't know. It used to be black.'

'You don't know!' The student leaned in for a look. 'I am sure I will come to your cabin and catch you crushing sea snails into your hair.'

The girl started to smile.

For the next several days, the student left notes to find her concoctions in the galley, inviting her to try new foods: lentils and black beans and pine nuts and roasted mushrooms as big as her hand on piles of spinach. Alone in her cabin, she ate goat's cheese and turmeric and ginger and chickpeas and lots of black pepper, and slowly the bruises faded and she slept a little less.

§

One morning, she woke easily. She slept so well that she missed the inching of dawn and the ship was already at port. When she pulled

Serpent's Wake

herself from bed, she felt good for the first time in the long, steady slide that was a strange few weeks.

The dog yawned with a fart and leapt to his feet.

When she laughed, the dog bounded to her.

Outside, the color of the water and the heat from the pane surprised her. How the world had changed. The water was a lighter blue than the sky.

She pressed her face against the portal and saw flowers: small, street-side marigold gardens and geranium-stuffed window boxes. Garlands spiraled flagpoles. Boats rippled with flags. Saints stood on petal-covered platforms and angels sang over the street she could see.

Peaked windows, archways and haughty bell towers crafted the skyline of a former colony, of old missionaries still traceable in the city's profile; but the girl sensed deeper roots that led into the volcanic hills. She saw old tribes in the faces on the pier, in the bright clothing, and the braids of the women selling corn fritters.

Along the docks, banners flew bright white against the currents. They looked like airborne snakes wriggling from their poles and for a moment, the girl's heart skipped. She scratched into her journal:

> We looped back west from the islands and we're close to the equator. What is this place that shines after such a dark night? Angels everywhere.

She heard a knock. Before she answered, she tied a scarf around her neck to hide the fading rash.

The crewman who fixed her door on the first day stood there, holding his cap. Dogsbody. Locksmith. 'Mornin, missy. Captain requests your presence at breakfast.' Formal was awkward but he did his best. Half his hair was plastered to his head, the other half stood up like matchsticks.

'He does?'

'Yep, time for breakfast. You can't miss this one, missy.'

The girl flushed. 'I don't mean to be such a...' she stopped herself.

'Aigh, what happened to you would scare anybody, especially bein a girl. Did ya hear that there was indeed bets that day? Somebody won a bucket of money.'

She looked at the floor, embarrassed.

'Aw, it wasn't nothin personal.'

She shook her head.

'Oh, you look like you're gonna cry.'

'I'm all right.'

'There is good news,' he said, trying hard now to improve the mood. He told her that the medical student was in the clear. 'Not a mark on her record but I am sorry, missy. I've never been particularly good at consoling women, though I'm pretty good at givin em reason to cry. Anyway, you can rest easy that the bloke was flogged pretty good. Won't be so keen next time.'

'That's terrible.'

'Eh, for some, it's the only way they learn.' He scratched at his scabby head.

'The crewman who stopped him,' she said, 'I've seen him around the ship and sometimes, I swear he's following me at a port. Has...?'

'Aigh, naw, naw,' the locksmith tittered. 'The bo'sun? Followin you? Not him, he's too busy with ship business.' He was a twitchy liar. 'He likes to stretch his legs and get new tattoos, unlike me. Only ever needed the one,' and he turned the octopus toward her. 'No need to stretch my legs. I get landsick. Over fifty years on this ship alone! I prefer the predictable chaos of the seaman's life.'

She wouldn't let him change the subject. 'He's hard to miss. I think he loves a fight...'

'Course he loves a fight! He was a boxer! Good one too til the ring nearly killed him. Built like an icebox with a face like a fist. And that ink job! But he's a good man down to his boots. For all his strength, he's got *discretion*.' He said it like a magic word. 'He and the cap have known each other for yonks, too. Anyway, I feel better with him around. I'm useless in a fight. You know, I'm nearly seventy? Don't look it though, do I? Secret's in the sardines.'

'Really? No...' She thought he looked eighty and knew he wasn't the only one lying now.

The locksmith bent with a crackle to scratch the dog. 'Hey there, geezer. Good to have a dog aboard again.' The dog licked the crewman's face. 'Do you wanna come to breakfast, too? Of course, you can.'

Breakfast would be the first meal she'd share with anyone, aside from the dog, in months.

She imagined her mother: *People get strange when they eat alone.*

She looked to the window. 'What's the holiday?'

'Real old one. Saints' day for the church but for the locals, it's for the ancestors. Rub ochre on gravestones, eat honey cakes, drink wine, spill some on the ground for your dearly departed. Cap gets us here every year, just like his father did. You have to be street-smart but there's no trouble here, missy.'

When he left, she fiddled with her scarf and pinned her hair. She sat on the bed and mopped her face with a damp cloth.

She considered the man on the pier and his circular hunt for a sister who ran away. She thought of the bo'sun, his fervor in thrashing the man, the medical student waving an enormous sewing needle at the jeering locals. All of this somehow belonged to her; it was inside her and she carried it wherever she went. She rested her eyes against the damp cloth; ashamed and tired of feeling ashamed.

Her thoughts turned to the crew. Surely everyone knew everything. She groaned into the washcloth.

An invitation.

To breakfast.

The agony of breakfast.

She'd been at sea for well over two months and hadn't gotten to know anyone aside from the cook, and that was out of necessity. The medical student was trying. She waved to the poet but never spoke to him. Solitude might drive some mad, but for her, it was a vice.

She thought about the locksmith and his refusal to leave the ship. He was doing the same as she: creating his ship-world and abandoning the rest. Fifty years. In 'predictable chaos.'

She imagined her mother saying: *You need people.*

What if they see my scar?

Her face still pressed into the cloth.

She listened. *Everyone has scars. At breakfast, people are more concerned with what's on the plate.*

She pretended her mother was standing there. 'OK, Mama.'

But her mother wasn't finished. *For heaven's sake, not everyone's looking at you. Wash your face and get on with it.*

The girl could almost smell orange and cloves. Bread in the oven. She saw that certain sideways glance her mother had when she thought she was right.

Now gimmie kiss.

The girl slid the cloth from her face; the dog wagged his tail, hopeful.

She stood, rinsed out the cloth and hung it over the sink. She washed a plate and some cutlery—a knife, a fork and a spoon—she used for her meals and placed them to dry on a towel.

She brushed the dog and washed his face. After a couple of weeks of neglect, he pedaled his foot as she worked his coat. 'I'm sorry,' she told him. 'You're not meant to be locked up like this.'

When she arrived topside, she was surprised by the formality of white tablecloths. The poet sat under his umbrella beside the engineer who slid papers into a folder and left. A warm breeze carried the scent of tropical fruit and flowers. Melon and papaya. Fat, fleshy hibiscus. Syrupy lilies.

The poet waved her to him; his steel-frame sunglasses reflected a sea of white and he wore an ascot to match. She remembered the warning from the doctor's wife and couldn't help but smile.

'My dear,' he called, 'this is a special occasion. Would you have breakfast with me? I'm afraid our captain has been detained.'

She slipped into the chair beside him; the dog panted in the shade of the umbrella.

'The sun is strong here, isn't it?' He removed his glasses. 'Our journey is heating up.'

'I've never felt sun like this.' She fiddled with her scarf.

'Too hot for scarves,' he said as he touched his ascot, 'so we're both hiding something.'

The girl shuddered.

He continued, 'You know, it's a whole year without winter for you.' He told her that the closer they sailed to the equator, the warmer it would get. When they passed the equator, the seasons would flip and it would be summer again.

'Do you miss winter?' She searched for small talk.

'I don't miss anything.'

Her hands shivered as they ran over the table. 'Tablecloths. This is an occasion.'

'Quite. Did you see the dolphins? Look. Even they're here today.'

Serpent's Wake

She straightened to see the water and saw nothing. Then a pewter dorsal fin broke. And another. 'Oh!' She stood. 'There!' Then in a quieter voice she said, 'I've only seen them in books.'

'The natives say they carry the dead on their backs. Have a look before they disappear.'

She peered over the railing. A set of flukes rose and sank. A dark whorl of an eye met hers, even from that distance. She dreamt a moment, the water around the creature, its smile tilting. The dog stuck his head through the rails.

'One saw you, didn't it?' he asked. 'That knowing look will leave you guessing for the rest of your life. Tea?' He lifted a kettle from a trivet to pour steaming water into a transparent teapot where a tight tangle of tealeaves sat dry at the bottom. Steam from the spout plateaued, lazy in the humidity.

She returned to her seat. 'Please.'

Hot water hissed over the leaves and they uncurled like ferns on fire. 'A local leaf. A round flavor. Do you know what it's called when the water hits the leaves?'

She shook her head.

'The agony of leaves.' Tealeaves expanded and collapsed. 'High drama. In a teapot.'

She knew there'd be agony at breakfast but this surprised her, her hand pulling the dog close.

'The dog is fine. Let him seek. Apparently, dogs need to seek or they go mad.' He looked at the dog and said, 'Don't you?'

She looked at the breakfast tables, the passengers, the crew. 'No, he's all right.'

'When the dog says one thing and the owner another, believe the dog. Let him go. He'll be fine.'

She looked into his eyes, unhooked the leash and said to his muzzle, 'Be good.' He assumed seeking in daylight, a novelty, and politely visited every table.

'Look,' the poet said, 'the leaves are copper now. A good brew.' He ceremoniously poured tea into their cups.

When the vapors rose to her nostrils, she caught scents of toast, flowers and apples.

'If you close your eyes,' he said, 'it shows itself.'

She knew how to see that way, and imagined white star jasmine and a trail of honey.

'Complex, isn't it? Many years ago, when I was introduced to the silk trade teas, my palate awoke. Those first teas, kissed with honey straight from a beehive, called me alive to the whole world.'

She remembered the honey from the doctor's wife, closing her eyes to sip. First she tasted the jasmine; then a citrus tang blossomed; then a smooth, biscuity tone reminded her of her mother's perfect bread.

'Can you taste the layers?'

'Does it start with flowers and end with flour?'

'Yes! It takes you straight home to the kitchen, doesn't it? I'm so glad to share this with you!' The teacup rested in his hands. 'This is your first party with the dead, isn't it?'

Confused, she looked toward the pier and saw the paper skeletons dangling from the iron street lamps, all jagged teeth, ribs and joints. One had red roses for eyes. Children ran along a pier in masks shaped into skulls.

'People are perverse, aren't they?' he said. 'Celebrating death in order to kiss the ground of their lives. This festival always makes me feel a little less accusatory. Ekes out the poison and washes it into the sea.'

The girl looked at the flowers everywhere, tea unfolding on her tongue. Some were bright and picked this morning, others limp from the day before.

'You've been sequestered in your cabin with all those books. Reading is wonderful but I hope you'll join us more.' His eyes sparkled. 'I say you're good luck for this ship. Our very own mermaid come up from her kingdom.'

She blushed and felt the skin of her scar tighten across her chest. 'Far more interesting than the truth,' she heard the sharpness in her tone.

Too much solitude, she heard her mother, *can make you hawkish.*

The poet swished a fly. 'This ship holds so many stories. I'd like to know yours.'

The girl liked this poet. She determined to relax, even though her dress was sticking to her. The dog returned panting, and lay at her feet with a thump.

Serpent's Wake

The poet dipped a hand into the suit jacket that hung on his chair and produced a small, black flask. He dribbled liquor into his tea and the flask disappeared again. 'Medicinal purposes,' he said. 'Now where were we? Oh yes. Our stories. Many years ago, when I was still very much a young man, I left the priesthood to become a poet.'

'You were a priest?' The girl didn't know one could leave the priesthood.

'My mother always wanted one and I did my best to oblige. I had a good parish but I left to study with a master poet whose work I utterly relished, quite secretly I might add, while studying in the seminary. Such tiny, simple poems. Perfect as diamonds that led me to a cave in the East carved by dragons, and there I spent years drinking good tea, minding someone else's bees, and writing bad poetry—it takes a long time to make diamonds.'

'What happened to your master poet?' she asked, her mind glittering with peaks and shadows.

'Sailed into the mist. Although, one could say on this particular morning, he's right here at our table. Frowning at me. He had a spectacular frown.'

The girl felt his affection. 'You loved him.'

'And you're forthright. Yes, tremendously.' He reached under his ascot and pulled out a chain and a little silver globe. 'There's a little bit of him in here: a smidge of stolen ashes.'

The girl had heard of cremation but no one in her village would have dared such a thing. Everyone was buried in the same cemetery, lined up in rows, all with the same granite headstones, cut from the same quarry; many erected their stones even before they were dead.

The poet dropped the chain back into his shirt. 'He would have loved this feast. Especially the parade. For such an old crank, he loved a parade. It passes by, right down there.'

She winced at the thought of a throng of strangers.

'Not one for parades?' he topped up their tea. 'At least try the honey cake and light a candle at the cathedral.' He pointed to the set of stone spires spiking over the village, a bell tower in the center held dominion. 'It sits on a temple that's thousands of years old. Solid rock descending into ancient catacombs and even deeper caves. Infinite coils. I'm too old now. I can get down but not up and I'm not ready to

Part III: An Octopus Has Three Hearts

be left there...but I tell you this: if you speak to your dead there, they shall hear every word.'

She examined the spires, the exclamation of a bell tower.

'It's been a pilgrimage site for thousands of years, even before the birth of the church that holds the lease now and I suppose it will continue to be when the next church builds another, most likely higher, spire.'

She liked this poet more now as he looked out to the cathedral, muttering now. 'Doesn't a religion become another of mankind's monuments to himself, just before another knocks it down?'

She considered her last encounters with church: the hunter's threats, the trapper's judgement, the funerals, the blue windows of a chapel she never got to see, and asked: 'Do you really believe that?'

'Maybe. But there is a truth to each of them that not a single one of them can own.' He swirled the tea in his cup and finished it. 'You must see all the ribbons as well. Petitions. Loving cries from the heart, each one. Can a doorway be a state of grace? Then I suppose every state of grace is a doorway.'

Someone stepped under the umbrella. 'Good morning.'

That voice.

The soles of her feet ran with tidal foam.

'Good morning,' she said. 'Oh would you get down?' she scolded the dog.

'Trying to get on my good side,' he told the dog. 'You should know I don't have one.'

The poet scoffed, 'First the beard, now no good side?'

The captain looked toward the skyline. 'I'm happy to see you in good company. I hope you'll enjoy it here.'

'In light of her recent experience on a pier, my boy, don't you think an escort would be prudent?'

'I'll get one of my...'

The poet clanked the lid on the teapot. 'And you know I'm too old. I cannot climb off and on this ship like I once could. Someone needs to take this girl to see what lies beneath that magnificent church. Why don't you take her? Especially now that the scary beard is gone.'

She smiled a little and the captain looked into the dangerous seas of her eyes. 'Right. I'll fetch you after breakfast.' And he left, visibly ruffled as he climbed the stairs.

'Fetch you!' the poet scoffed. 'Heavens. He's talking about a beautiful young woman here not a newspaper. That man needs to get off this ship as much as you do.'

'Was the beard scary?'

'Terribly. He grew that preposterous mass after you boarded. Didn't you notice? I've known him since he was a child and he's never done that. I hope it's gone for good. I'm too old to be on a bloody pirate ship and I haven't the fashion.'

The girl couldn't help herself; she laughed.

'Our captain. He acts older than I do. Heavens what I would give to have my body, my youth back.' The flask appeared and disappeared again. 'The vigor! Anyway, let's get right down to it,' the poet leaned in closely and almost whispered, 'are you in love with the captain?'

Surprised, the girl dropped her eyes to the tablecloth.

'Coy thing,' he said. 'If I were a young woman on this voyage, I should be in love with the captain. He's handsome, intelligent. A tremendous good side, no matter what he says. And those otherworldly eyes. He's insular, I know, but we're working on that. I've told him his whole life, if you do not rise to meet the sea, the sea will rise to meet you—and it will be hungry!'

The girl sighed and looked to the pier below, the gathering crowds, the skeletons.

'The truth is,' he pointed to his notebook, 'I always write the best poetry when there's a love affair brewing. I was here when your friend, your doctor-uncle, courted his island bride. That chapbook won a prize! On another voyage, a rather mature woman had run away from her heartless husband and lunged into a stormy spring-autumn tryst with a young crewman. She was a woman alight. You know the captain turned a blind eye? This was our captain's father, of course. He knew exactly what was going on but he didn't fire the boy as he might have. Poets have a way with words. And then there were mine. Lovers who spoke in poetry but who never wrote a word.' He paused, a little dreamy, then said, 'And these days? An empty notebook. Only the agony of leaves.'

The girl sipped her tea, 'I'm sorry. I'm doing my best. I didn't mind the beard.'

'Oh, you're charming. I don't mean to be selfish. Would you like a little sparkle in your tea?' He gestured toward his jacket.

'Oh no, no thank you,' she said. 'I'll keep my wits about me if I'm going to be alone with a sea captain.'

He smiled, 'Smart girl. Anything can happen in the underworld.'

Breakfast was served. While this might be standard on other ships, it was unusual here, where breakfast was collected, not delivered. The bo'sun slid plates across the tablecloth, his singlet revealing tattoos that matched the work on his face. He said, 'I hope you enjoy the service along with your breakfast. Had me a bath and a shave.'

The poet thanked him, placed his napkin on his lap with fanfare and said, 'Ambrosia of the gods!'

'No blinkin idea what you're talking about but yeah, you're king for a day. Don't steal the napkins. We're trading them before we leave port.'

The girl seized the moment, buoyed by the poet's vibrancy. 'Sir,' she said, 'I didn't get a chance...'

The bo'sun snorted. 'She called me sir.'

'...I didn't get a chance to thank you for what you did on the pier.'

'Hey, my pleasure.' He shot her a warrior's grimace before turning back to the kitchen.

The girl turned to the poet. 'I don't mean to be rude, but he scares me.'

'He scares everyone, but he's a pussycat. You should have seen him when the captain dragged him on board. A wounded lion.'

'Dare I ask?'

'Dare you,' the poet looked sly. 'He and the captain played as boys along the shipping route. Their lives diverged: one boy groomed for the helm of a ship, the other for boxing. The money was steeper in illegal fighting, as were his debts and his injuries. One boy took the other from the pit that held him and brought him here. An old captain raged about his son's indiscretion but was powerless to impress that fear upon his son. It was a love story of another kind. God, I wrote reams...'

'It's a beautiful story,' the girl said. 'Here I am, traveling the world with people I don't even know.'

'If you really look at him, you'll know him,' the poet chuckled. 'The heart eventually shapes the face.'

Serpent's Wake

The girl looked back to the kitchen, where the bo'sun held another plate and saw that the tattoo on his arm was not just spears and circles. It was the sun. He winked at her.

Before them, pomegranate seeds streaked papaya and golden pineapple on a bed of marigolds. In the center, nasturtium flowers coveted a triangle of honey cake. On another plate, zucchini flowers were battered, a nest of golden trumpets.

'A feast!' the poet cried. 'Have you ever started your day eating flowers?'

'Flowers for ghosts?'

'Maybe we're all ghosts,' he answered with honey on his chin.

When the captain returned a half-hour later, the girl had removed her hat and wore nasturtiums behind her ears. Most of the passengers and crew were on deck, finishing breakfast and aiming for the street. The cook rested his boots on the railing, beer bottle in his hand and nasturtiums in his hair as well. The medical student sat beside him. The cook pulled the pencil from her hair and threw it overboard.

The poet asked the captain: 'Come to fetch her?'

'I must be back in an hour,' he said.

The girl thought he spoke too loudly and the flowers suddenly felt limp. 'If you have too much to do, please, I can go on my own.' She reached to remove the flowers from behind her ears.

'Leave the flowers,' the poet touched her hand. 'And leave the hat. You won't need it.'

'Allow me,' he said, quietly now.

The girl turned to the poet, 'Breakfast was lovely. What will you do now?'

'Watch the parade from here. See the kisses of the dead sparkle on the living.'

The girl looked at him, wondering how he could speak of the most intimate gestures of her mother.

He continued, 'Spill a little wine. It's noon, isn't it?'

The bo'sun leaned over the table and poured his red, saying, 'Uncle.'

'Do you want anything?' she asked.

'Light a candle for me, too.'

§

When the girl and the captain stepped from the pier, the parade was upon them. In a crackle of drums, he pulled her close. He guided her through a sea of bodies and skeletal masks. Firecrackers snapped over cobblestone as a rainbow of feathered dancers hurled past. Jostled and flinching, she knew she would never have come into this melee alone. Smoke poured from open grills and candlewax from the night before had melted into puddles underfoot. As the captain and the girl walked, their soles ran yellow and red.

She started at the screech of penny whistles; her cheek brushed his shirt. His scent, like soap and crisp paper, touched her lips. Mounting the steps of the church, she looked up to a gargoyle poking its tongue. The captain pushed against an enormous wooden door. She stepped past him into the dark.

When the heavy door closed, she was blind in a crumple of darkness.

Stone blotted the din of the street; her eyes adjusted. Feathered wisps brightened around them. She touched them. Ribbons. White, orange, red, blue, green, yellow, purple. Thousands, maybe tens of thousands of ribbons were knotted through a wire mesh that covered the walls. Each was stamped with inky crosses, wheels, stars and moons. She looked up. The ceiling looked like the belly of a tropical bird.

The captain said, 'Prayers.'

Some were fraying into dust. Some were crisp, as though knotted moments ago.

'So many.' She ran a hand over them.

'Mine, too,' the captain said, then clarified, 'when I was younger.' He looked to the ceiling, 'That one. There.'

She followed his gaze, trying to discern which of the thousand ribbons might be his but when she looked back at him, his nose twitched. She said: 'I didn't know you were funny.'

He broke the faintest smile. 'Follow me.'

He opened a door to the nave and the church compounded with light and space. Sunlight poured in shafts through stained glass windows, mirroring the rhythm of arch and beam. A tiny, solitary woman in black was bent in a pew, a handful of beads dangling. They walked along the aisle and the girl stole glances: the old woman wore a headscarf tied under her chin, eyes closed to this world but wide to another.

Flowers climbed the steps to the altar: white lily trumpets, red dahlias with faces like lions. Saints, all shiny and serene, peered from alcoves. Beneath vast, colorful windows suspended in rock, an unexpected happiness bounced within the girl like songbirds chasing seeds over stone.

The captain dropped coins into a box and descended a set of stairs: rectangles of limestone at first, then hewn directly from the stony earth itself and sloped in the middle from wear. She followed. Candles lit the stairwell; the walls were kissed emerald with algae.

The captain stepped onto a landing. A blackened arch held tiers of hundreds of tiny, flickering candles. A dozen wooden pews sat empty under a dozen red lanterns. The walls were damp with memory.

The captain picked candles from an open box. 'For poetry.' He lit one from another and placed it into an empty holder. He lit two more without a word and dropped coins into a copper box.

She lit two and watched the flames cloak their wicks.

The captain motioned they were going down, further still. A wooden handrail had been pounded into stone. Iron nails wept rust. She touched the rail, worn smooth. Her head felt light; her strides jerky.

The intrusive sensation of descent was unwelcome.

The captain's footfalls mimicked her heart.

Then her heartbeat punched ahead.

Her stomach churned.

A line of torches.

Curls of smoke.

Sooty walls.

Oil.

Another landing. Sweat against cool. She exhaled, better now on solid ground.

'Catacombs,' he said. Open rectangular cavities surrounded them, hewn into walls from the floor to ceiling where bodies once fit, all empty now. Carvings had been etched into the walls. Boats. Skulls. Wings. Fish.

Part III: An Octopus Has Three Hearts

She touched the stone and felt the march of souls.

'Older than the map. By a thousand years or so,' he led them through a dusty channel of stone.

The captain walked quickly. Images slipped past her. The bones gone. Were they this dust or buried? Stacked somewhere? She'd read of churches that turned bones into walls. She looked at her own knucklebones, pale in torchlight.

She caught her breath. Another set of stairs.

Another cavernous descent.

She was ready to stop.

Return to the ship.

Too far down.

Troubled air.

But the captain was ahead of her.

She followed, one hand on the railing, one tangled in her scarf over a swelling sensation. Each breath shorter, higher, until it was darting in her throat, rocking back and forth like a tiny skiff in a storm.

Each step grew more wretched.

World turning on itself.

The air fled.

And she knew, she knew, she knew that this is where she couldn't tell the real from the blunt edge of remembering as it scraped the crimson of her mind. She knew she was faltering, but she couldn't stop it. The more she tried to stop it, the more her heart bailed buckets of blood in a little boat going down, down, down.

The captain's form grew waxen. She slipped on something wet; she caught the railing. The tunnel rolled. Dampness slid down the walls. The torches dimmed.

She gasped and didn't know where the noise came from.

Her eyes clouded. The walls grew ribs. And flexed. And tightened, sticky. One hand clung to the railing; the other clutched her scarf and when she looked, she saw a filthy hand balled under her chin. Hot and cold, her chest heaved.

Not enough air.

Not enough.

Not.

She closed her eyes and remembered everything. The dark. All that dark that tried to use her up. So long, alone, in the dark. Whole world gone. Hanging in the void.

Then she heard it. She didn't hear it exactly, but she *heard* it.

The slow...

Tha-dump.

...lurid...

Tha-dump.

...heartbeat.

Tha-dump.

She slipped. She landed on her bottom. She hung by a hand.

Wet seeped from the corners of her eyes.

She listened. Like she used to. Sound was a way out, a way through. She heard water.

Opening her eyes, she saw her hand on the railing above her head. Water trickled. She saw the stairs, torches. And slowly, a whisper at a time, the air began to return, breath by breath. And the walls exhaled around her. She saw the captain hammering up the steps toward her.

'What's happened?'

Her voice was trapped in her throat.

'Are you all right?'

She put her forehead to her knees.

He sat.

She felt for the solidity of the step. When she could, she said, 'I felt ill...'

But then, as if he hadn't heard her, the captain asked, 'What's happened?'

She didn't answer.

'Do you want to go back?'

'No.'

'We'll go back.'

'No.'

'Take your time.'

'Yes.'

And they did, alone in the navel of the world. She breathed. He worried. The sound of water trickled somewhere.

He said again, 'We'll go back.'

Part III: An Octopus Has Three Hearts

'I hear water.'

'You do.'

She aimed to stand. 'I felt ill. It surprised me. That's all.'

He got to his feet and put out his hand. 'This place does things to people. And you've been at sea awhile.'

She remembered the locksmith and his fifty years. 'Maybe I'm landsick.'

He took her arm and they walked to the landing where a soft skin of smooth stone absorbed the sounds of their feet.

She breathed.

An enormous golden cave, like the chambers of a giant heart, bloomed. The girl removed her sandals. Red candlewax from the street stained her fingers. Cool stone touched her feet. Firelight played on walls. Tiny rays of sunlight beamed from somewhere far above them.

The girl slipped from the captain.

He cleared his throat, a rumble through silk.

She blotted sweat from her face. Those stairs had grabbed her. Unexpected. Uninvited. She hiccupped. It echoed.

She followed the contours of the cave with her senses. It smelled like wet petals. Every breath reverberated. Stalactites hung like icicles: some thick as the swords of dead kings. Stone curtains wove serpentine across the floor. Shimmering pillars joined ceiling to floor into the molten profiles of men and women. All sparkled, a galaxy. The girl blinked at orbs of moisture in her lashes.

'Eccentrics.' His whisper echoed. The captain pointed to a rabble of what appeared to be sleeping stone butterflies, mid-flutter, angled every direction. 'They grow their own way.'

'What shapes them? Currents in the air?'

'No one knows.'

'They're not bound by gravity.' She pointed to a cluster of ivory wings but did not touch. 'So fragile and no one's broken them.'

'Not here.'

The girl looked past the captain. 'Where's the water?'

He moved along the rippled floor.

She took a few steps. A flash lit between pillars. She turned. A troop of people appeared. Red fabric wafted; she thought they must be in the parade. But they were silent where every hint of a sound carried.

Serpent's Wake

And they were gone.

Her skin prickled and the floor slanted.

Ancestors, her heart said.

'What?'

'Did you see...oh, I don't know what I just saw.'

'It happens,' he whispered, 'here.'

'I've never...'

'We're in the underworld.' He sat upon a stone beside a pool, water trickling from the wall behind him, and she saw the boy who strung ribbons for people he loved. Upon the water, specks of blood red saffron drifted. Honey cakes were piled on the ledge and red wine had been spilled, again and again, over stony ground. Carvings etched the ceiling overhead, patterns taking shape. Women emptying water vessels, weaving, holding babies, their hair twisted up into a grinning serpent on each of their heads.

'This was a temple.' He stretched his legs before him.

'Snakes.' Her stomach turned.

He told her what the poet had told him years ago: 'Yes, snakes shed their skin. Their venom makes medicine.'

She shied from the strange women, staving off the urge to tell the captain what she knew of snakes, of ambush and death; there was no healing elixir there. She rattled a slow breath and found the red saffron floating on the water's surface, leaving golden streaks behind.

When she found the captain's eyes, tenderness ached in his face. She knew she caught him wondering about her, wondering what he said or didn't say, wondering at the shadows in her eyes. She knew the divinity of this place was all around them, spun up from the ground and thrown down like spears from heaven and she knew she would never have persevered to this heart of the world without his help. She would have gone as far as the chapel, returned to the ship, smiled at the poet and said: 'Of course I lit a candle for you.'

She would not have seen the ancestors.

Or cave's long teeth of time.

Or the snake women.

She touched his cheek; he looked up at her. She stepped between his knees and peered into his eyes. The cavern darkened and she saw the very shimmer of his self and her heart opened to its light. Gratitude,

Part III: An Octopus Has Three Hearts

in that moment, felt like sadness swirled with joy, and she smiled.

He blinked at her with surprise. He took her hand, lips pressed tightly together into that sharp line of his mouth; eyes bright with fire and water. He placed her hand over his mouth. His lips moved under her fingers, whispering in his own language: *From the moment I saw you, my love, you joined the pieces of my life and sang me alive.*

Though she didn't know his words, she understood. Her hip slid against him and for an instant, she wished their bodies would fuse into stone, just another among the pillars that surrounded them.

She let him pull her off her feet, into his lap; he turned his face in her hand, covered his eyes with her long fingers. Her body encircled him and she uncovered his eyes to look into them. She remembered a passage from one of her father's books and said, 'Heroes can turn villain for this, in such a sacred place.'

'And villain to hero?'

'Are you a villain?'

He loosed her hair from its pin. Nasturtiums fell to the floor. 'Why do you keep something so beautiful tied up?'

'Why do you?'

A shift in the air, coming from the stairs. 'People.'

'Mortal?'

'Terribly.'

'I cannot...'

And she remembered another book of her father's: the sea captain who forfeited his wife's most precious years for war and adventure.

By the time the others arrived at the base of the stairs, she was dipping her fingers in the water. The cook and the medical student waved. The captain was on his feet with his arms folded. The girl touched her face and ran wet fingers across her forehead.

The cook whistled an echoing birdsong. 'Beautiful, isn't it?'

The girl looked into the nasturtiums she had brought with her, and saw the face of her snake in the center of each bloom. She sent each one floating in the pool. She stood, casting a final glance back to the women who wove them into their hair.

§

Serpent's Wake

That afternoon, the girl lay nude across her bed, examining candlewax on her fingers. Perhaps, if she willed it, she could leave her serpent in the heart of the earth: abandon it to those wise women. Perhaps, she already felt lighter.

Then there was the affection she heard in his language, she heard him say it again and again. She thought of a wooden woman mounted to a ship hull, her breasts open to the sea air, carved hair flowing. He could have her always and lose nothing. And she could have him and he would never know where she'd been.

When the medical student and cook had arrived in the cavern, the captain and the girl took to the stairs. She followed him slowly, holding his hand through the catacombs, the chapel, the church. They passed through the crowd, where the cafés were packed, and the dancing had started, and their shoes absorbed another layer of wax.

He didn't look at her all the way back to the ship and returned her to an abandoned deck. Before he left for the bridge, he finally turned to her: 'Here you are; safely returned.'

In her cabin, she dropped her clothes. The dog rolled onto his back, a subdued greeting in the heat. She let her hair fall over the side of the bed to the floor, longer now and brilliant to the roots.

As the hour grew late, singing rose from the streets. Fireworks painted her window. She knew the captain was on the bridge. Alone. She got dressed, took the dog and left her cabin. From the deck, she saw the bridge lights and started to climb.

Careful, her mother said.

The girl stopped. She turned and headed toward town.

She found the poet at a table in front of a café, the globe with his master's ashes peeking from his shirt, beneath his ascot. Beside him, a beautiful young man sat with a skull mask atop his head like a hat. The poet waved his cane, relief washed over his face at the sight of her: 'Join us!'

She sat beside them and pulled the dog to her legs.

The man emptied his carafe of spiced wine into a glass before her and left to refill it. She smelled cinnamon and gunpowder.

The poet leaned into the girl's ear. 'I'm tired. I can't stay much longer. And if I do, there may be unkind rumors. Would you help me back to the ship?'

She nodded. 'Who is he?'

'Another hopeful poet.' In the light of the sparklers waving in the street, the poet looked older than he did at breakfast. They sat quietly until the young man returned with his carafe.

The girl sipped the wine, sweet as apples and crushed berries spiked with woody spice. She watched the crowd while the poet spoke and the young man scratched into a notebook. The cook and the medical student laughed at a nearby table; he pulled off her sandals and held her feet in one hand. The bo'sun passed by with a woman on each arm. The girl looked toward the ship, to the captain's light. The dog stood to leave.

The poet took up his cane, asking, 'May we?'

When they finally stepped onto the pier, he groaned. The planks were lamp-lit and spotted with crepe paper. 'Is it quieter on the ship?'

'Much.' She felt the alcohol like a mist behind her eyes.

'Good.'

The dog sniffed at the ocean scent rising between the planks.

Then the old man touched the girl's hand. 'Tell me.'

She said, 'He lit a candle for you.'

'And a thousand candles for you?'

She looked out at a dark sea and said nothing.

'He's a fool. I have half a mind to climb up to the bridge and flog him.' He tapped his cane along the pier and yawned, 'Maybe tomorrow.'

'Tomorrow then.'

The poet coughed. 'I've had too much wine.'

She licked her lips. 'It was good wine.'

'I can't manage it like I used to. And I'm afraid I won't make it...'

'What?'

A little further along the pier and out of sight from the street, he slipped between two berthed fishing boats. 'I beg your forgiveness, with deepest humility...but old age has got me. Would you please turn your back?'

She obliged and heard him take a few tired steps until water hit water.

He sighed. 'Brings a tear to the eye. Thank you.'

'It's all right.' Her dog sat, his back to the poet as well. There was a pause and she thought he was finished, but a drizzle followed along with a long groan.

Serpent's Wake

He finally zipped his trousers and muttered, 'Small mercies for the old. Oh, I'll have earned a headache in the morning.'

She turned to walk with him again.

He frowned, thoughtful. 'Oh that captain of ours! His father was a dear friend but he ruined the boy. What's he worried about now? How can he look at you and keep up this performance?'

They looked at the sparkling lights of the pier reflecting on a black sea.

'You know he fancies you. You exude something of the mystical. You might as well have wings dragging on the ground behind you, dear. You don't need a bloody poet to see he's utterly enchanted!'

She shook her head, 'It doesn't matter.'

'Don't be so quick to let go.' He shook his cane. 'Hold fast to worthy things.' He took an angry step but the planks were uneven. His shoe caught. He stumbled and cried out.

The girl threw out a hand to steady him but he swung his arms and the handle of his cane snagged his necklace.

A pop.

The silver globe struck the pier and their eyes chased it. It bounced and rolled toward a wide crack between the planks. It disappeared with a watery plink.

'Oh no!' The poet melted to his knees over the crack in the pier.

The dog circled him.

The girl found the broken chain and picked up his cane.

'I've lost him.' The poet stared into the darkness. 'After so many years.'

She held the broken chain. 'Maybe someone can dive for it in the morning? It went straight down.'

'Oh, my dear, no. I wouldn't dare wrench it from these forces. Not these.' Bent to the pier, he whispered, 'You broke your pearls; I found each one...'

She wondered how much he'd had to drink and realized she had no handkerchief for him just as he, nodding slowly with wet cheeks, produced one. She asked, 'Are you all right?'

'No,' he said. 'I'm praying. It keeps me from howling,' he sniffled. 'If I must weep at all, let me weep with the voice of thousands.'

She looked at the stars.

Part III: An Octopus Has Three Hearts

The sea waited on ceremony.

'You know,' he said, 'people think I just make it all up. But I don't. What is this?' He pointed between the planks. 'That the last little piece of my old master, the man who rescued me from doom, the last little piece that I held so dear should depart into this sea on this night when the veil between worlds is so thin? What is it but poetry? Life is poetry, not the other way round.'

He muttered, laughing now, 'He would write a poem about it. Piss freely upon my resting place, for I am not there.'

The poet took hold of the girl's hand and with some grunting, they were back on the path to the ship. At the gangway, he said, 'Wicked man. He never wanted me to have it in the first place. I stole it and he stole it back. His final poem.'

The poet laughed until he coughed. 'I'm overtired and overexcited. My head will be sore tomorrow. And my heart. I need a sleeping pill tonight.'

After taking him to his cabin, the girl wrote into her journal:

> A spell is broken. I am unafraid as we approach the canal where one sea drinks the other, away from winter's home straight into the sun.

§

The following morning, as the horns blew, the girl finished sewing her favorite dress, one button and one tiny shell at a time. It wasn't perfect—she'd missed years of learning with her mother—but it was good enough.

As she snipped the final thread, there was a tap at the door.

The poet asked, 'Am I intruding?'

She shook her head. 'How are you feeling?'

'Tender in head and heart but I earned it,' he leaned on his cane. 'Would you like to sit with me on deck as we pass through the canal? The locks are quite a show. Besides, I have a good tea I've been saving. The dry leaves look like little golden snails.'

She took her wrap as the dog, off leash, led the way.

On deck, they sat before the agony of leaves and watched the mules, boxy little automobiles guide the ship along the concrete sleeve of a lock until they paused before a colossal gate. As the lock filled with water, the ship rose to a towering height, 'Nearly a hundred feet above the sea,' the poet said, to meet the lake. Around them, immense cargo ships and sleek passenger ships awaited passage.

The girl imagined her father with his dog at the rail. She asked, 'How long before we reach the ocean?'

He poured the tea: the golden snails disappearing into an opaque brew. 'The rest of the day, so we might as well enjoy it. We're changing worlds, you know. Forgiving past debts and releasing sadness.'

She thought on forgiveness—still an empty word.

'You're not wearing your hat,' he said.

She ran a hand through her hair, loose on the breeze, vivid. 'No.' She looked up and caught the captain watching from the bridge. When the engineer appeared beside him, she looked away.

He asked, 'What do you taste?'

She closed her eyes. 'Earth. Molasses? And cocoa?'

'Precisely. So how can something so gold steep into something so black? I say it's perfect for crossing a jungle. You know, the whole world passes through here.' He looked into his teacup. 'All the glorious colors of our humanity.'

'You were right,' she said.

'About what?'

'The festival. The poison washed into the sea.'

He smiled like a cat.

'I felt it. It happened underground. Thank you for sending me there.'

He sank into his chair, cradling his teacup.

'Tell me,' she said, 'why should we celebrate a short cut? Why not trace the coastline; go around?'

'So you're in no rush, are you? Neither was I the first time. Be careful: this ship has a habit of collecting people,' the old poet tapped his cup. 'But this short cut—thousands of people died to deliver this passage. Imagine that. This grueling effort in drawing us all closer together. I tend to believe that every true embrace unfolds on the edge of some kind of tragedy.'

She looked up at an empty bridge window and said, 'I don't know anything.'

Part III: An Octopus Has Three Hearts

'Oh dear,' he said, 'you're in love.'
'I don't want to be. I've made my peace.'
'That's terrible.'
'No, I am good at acceptance. Besides, I don't trust my perceptions.'
'You don't?'
'No. I don't know how to describe it. I...'
'Swoon.'
She said nothing, her thoughts muddied.
'It's in your eyes.' He shifted in his chair. 'You lose control. What an enviable thing that is. I say if you see his goodness, you see him better than he sees himself. And he, you.'

The poet thought for a time then said, 'Say yes to things. Keep saying yes.'

As the lock opened and the ship coursed into the lake, the locksmith emerged from the galley wiping breakfast from his chin. 'Day off!' he said. 'Goin to my quarters for a kip! If you need me...eh, don't need me!'

The lake expanded. The temperature was perfect and the girl's wrap slid from her shoulders. The poet tipped his flask into his tea and the girl pretended not to notice. The dog snored.

After a time, she asked, 'Why an octopus?'

'On his arm? Well, I know a man with a rooster on one foot and a pig on the other, each a talisman against drowning: those animals hate water.' The poet topped their cups. 'So why an octopus? There is meaning everywhere at sea, right down to the knots; perhaps why so many come here when the rest of the world grows meaningless. I don't know if he knows it or not, but an octopus has three hearts. Beautiful and intelligent creatures. An octopus is clever. He's resourceful and skilled at tearing himself from a trap. I've seen a formidably sized octopus squeeze through a hole smaller than that,' he pointed to a narrow scupper, designed to drain water from the deck. 'They're capable of doing things most animals cannot: they can change the color and texture of their skin, even regrow lost limbs.'

The girl remembered the young white wolf, loping through the woods. 'What did he lose?'

'Not even I know that. Sometimes when one has finally got free, he never speaks of it again. Tattoos can tell stories the sailor cannot. Or maybe it's not the story that matters so much as the victory.'

Serpent's Wake

'I understand. I think I am forgetting things at sea.'

'Yes,' the poet said, 'and it's easy to forget what you're capable of. I've seen you standing on the shore. Go swim. I'm sure you've done things much harder than that.'

The girl looked at him.

'Say yes.' He drained his cup. 'Make some waves.'

She finished her tea. 'Make some waves? The engineer?' Brazen now, she asked, 'Why does he hate me?'

'Why do you care? He can't see far enough past himself to hate you, dear. He's a serious, devoted and ingenious man, but he is terribly hurt.'

'He looks at me as if I'm the devil.'

'It was his deep capacity for compassion that nearly broke him.'

'It sounds like quite a story.'

'Definitely not mine to tell.'

'It also sounds like more love poetry.'

'It is all love poetry.'

§

When the ship emerged from the canal that evening, it headed north for two weeks, stopping periodically along the coast for contracts. Just as the hull touched wintry waters, the ship completed a delivery for an art dealer and swung southward again.

Back at the warm, bustling coastline north of the canal, the ship made port to conduct repairs and fill the stores. The captain had avoided the rowdier seaports along this trade route, ensuring a quiet ship to await parts, a partial crew change and a couple new medical students bound for tropical posts. The girl and the poet met daily for tea while the captain watched and worked.

The night before the ship was set to start its trek across the vast southern ocean, the captain was barefoot and stretched across the couch on the bridge. The poet had told him, 'Surrender,' but he only answered, 'I fear costly surrenders.'

Since the cavern, he hadn't gone near his quarters. He dozed.

The engineer stepped onto the bridge with a bottle. 'Hey, you awake? I got this from the market today. Triple-distilled.'

Part III: An Octopus Has Three Hearts

The captain sat up.

The engineer held out a mug.

They drank in silence until the engineer said, 'The man who sold this to me? He said it had a hint of fragrance, like the scent of a woman who has left the room. He was a good salesman.'

'Do you smell a woman in this?'

'No, but it's been a while since I've smelled a woman.'

'Well, they smell a lot better than this,' the captain said.

After the alcohol warmed the men, the captain asked the engineer why he let the girl annoy him so much; a girl whose parents were dead, who knew the good doctor, and who didn't do much more than read and drink tea with the poet.

The engineer, caught between his drink and annoyance, said, 'She has blue hair and I saw her make love to a tuna.'

'You did not. She pitied the fish. Judging by its size, it was even older than you.'

'You don't need any more crazy women on your ship.' He capped the bottle. 'Look at your ship's doctor. And the medical student you cannot trust.'

'They're not crazy.' The captain drained his mug and rested it on his belly. 'They've just had to deal with men like you.'

The engineer turned the bottle in his hand. He asked the captain if he'd heard all of the cook's story about the girl: especially the part about the snakeskin the hunter pulled from a sack under the dartboard. 'Did he tell you about that?'

The captain yawned and shook his head.

The engineer told him.

The captain listened carefully, then concluded with: 'Do you, an educated man, believe in country fables?'

The engineer tightened the cap on his bottle. 'There is always truth behind the country fable.'

§

The ship was out to sea when the girl slipped into her favorite dress for the first time since she'd repaired it. She paused at her window, before the new ocean. There was no land in sight.

When she went below with the dog, an onslaught of crewmen jogged up the stairs in wigs, grass skirts and coconut shells that slid around on chest hair. Strings of sand dollars hung from their necks.

'G'day!' the bo'sun was first. Long, blonde locks contrasted with his dark, bushy brows and tattoos. A fishnet studded with cowry shells was slung around his waist.

The girl pulled the dog back to let them pass.

The locksmith popped his head out from behind the bo'sun. 'Crossin the equator, missy,' he said from under a waist-long black wig woven with seaweed—the only thing different from his usual attire. 'No need to be alarmed. Situation normal.'

'Get yer coconuts out for the line crossin!' The cook was semi-dressed as a sea nymph, a tatty red wig sticking to his stubble. Vintage fishtails hung over his shoulder, the scales sun-bleached pastels.

The locksmith pushed seaweed from his eyes. 'Out-runnin a storm so we gotta hurry. I'll go get the sea god.'

'Quick!' the cook rattled his necklace of bottle caps. 'Before the cap changes his mind!'

'Got the bubbly?' another crewman asked.

'Aye!' a chorus.

'Go! Go! Go!'

The girl hugged the wall then took the dog below where she found the engineer scratching away at a clipboard, the top of his head shining under the narrow tubes of lighting. In short sleeves, his old scars rippled well past his elbows.

'Are you heading up?' she asked over the hum of the ship's engine's, buoyed by the crew's cheer.

He looked only at his clipboard, pretending, she could see, that the engines drowned her out.

She persisted, 'Don't tell me they do this every time we cross the equator…'

Again, he ignored her.

She frowned, saying, 'You might look nicer in a wig,' and unclipped the dog's leash. He sniffed the sawdust and hay in wide circles.

Both the engineer and the dog turned their backs to her. When the dog was finished, she cleaned up and slammed the waste container, hard.

Part III: An Octopus Has Three Hearts

'You want to talk to me?' The engineer sliced the air with his clipboard, approaching. 'We will talk.'

She pursed her lips, surprised by his sudden arousal.

He moved in. 'Leave the captain alone. The man has got enough to do without you making nonsense for him.'

She didn't move. 'He barely knows I'm here.'

'I don't believe that and neither do you.' His eyes narrowed. 'It is my job to make things go smoothly for him and I will tell you something—you would not even be here if it were up to me. There is no money in passengers. Passengers! Always people running, hiding, bringing problems with them. You are a liability. You proved it on the pier.'

She took a step back. 'That was my fault?'

'Yes.' He never blinked; she felt his breath skip across her nose. The air felt close and hot, the thrum of the engines pounded.

He continued, closer still: 'You are a bold child who knows nothing. Women, like children, should never travel alone. If you do, you deserve what happens to you.'

'I was told by your crewman that the port was safe.'

He scoffed. 'Nowhere is safe!'

In that jaundiced light below deck, his scars flashed against the severity of his face and she knew that instant he didn't do that thing to himself. It was done to him.

She leashed her dog. 'You can't speak for the world.'

'What do you know, girl?' He left her there with sawdust sticking to her ankles.

She climbed the stairs, heart pounding. By the time she got to the crowded deck, she was shaking.

The doctor's wife was right about him. 'Friendly as a bullet. Stay out of his way.'

As the girl looked about the deck, she found the captain in uniform, standing with his arms folded against the railing. She'd never seen him in his dress whites. All around him, his crewmen were wigged, buxom and draped. A few sat, flapping mermaid tails over their feet.

The poet was dead center, presiding. Someone had smeared blue paint all over his face, chest and hands, but he still wore that trademark ascot, gold for the special occasion and a long necklace strung with red coral and silver ring pulls plucked from beer cans. A flowing white beard, apparently torn from the stuffing of a pillow, flapped in the breeze, lopsided. A towering foil crown topped his pillow stuffing eyebrows at an angle. When he saw the girl, he waved his cane, now a foil-wrapped trident, and said, 'Behold, another virgin!'

Beside him, his stubbly mermaid queen—the cook—sat with a humbler crown, a fishtail and bikini top of sea stars slung under two ill-shaped papaya. The medical student, flanked by a couple of new students, couldn't stop tittering and even the ship's doctor held her glasses over her lips. Champagne flowed into mugs.

The captain mouthed, 'Where did you get that?' to the bo'sun, but he just swished his wig.

The locksmith held a weathered scroll that looked as if it had done the equator crossing a hundred times already. He was mid-stanza but stopped to say: 'And so, oh, hello, missy,' and continued. 'We ask the seas to bless us, for the winds to be kind to these sailors, as they cross into new territory...'

The captain stared at the girl. In uniform amidst all these wigs, bottle caps, coconut shells and sand dollars, he looked embedded in a carnival.

'...should any of these journeymen...'

'Or journeywomen!' the medical student called.

'...or journeywomen—pardon—fall overboard, we ask that the sharks be too fat to bite, the jellies too slow to sting and that your dolphins push them in the direction of sweet tempered island women...'

'Or men!' she called again.

'...right.' The locksmith took the champagne bottle and poured a few glugs over the side. 'And that the currents caress them to safe harbor...'

With the sky forlorn, the ceremony unfolded rapidly. Someone pressed a mug into the girl's hand. The dog waggled at her knee.

'...and so yer land-lubbers no more!'

A cheer hoisted over rising wind. Champagne sprayed.

The captain spoke closely to the locksmith, who had tucked his wig under his arm.

The girl slipped back from the crowd and swept bubbles from her eyebrows; she watched the captain, as covertly as she could, over the lip of her mug. Lunch was announced; another cork popped. She shielded her eyes from the spray and the captain was gone.

In a shrill, queen mermaid voice that made the dog bark, the cook announced: 'Ahem! Before lunch! Everyone! I say, everyone!' He adjusted his sea stars, nearly losing a papaya.

The bo'sun returned the captain to the deck, the blonde wig flapping over muscle. The captain's chin was down, his eyes in shadow.

The locksmith replaced his wig and cleared his throat. 'Since the crew are, technically so-to-speaking, in charge a mere minute more, we declare that as the king of the sea here has his queen,' he rolled his hand to the blue poet and his queen, both waving imperially, 'so the captain, too, must have his bride.'

The poet raised his trident to the heavens then slowly lowered it, pointing to the girl. When she saw this, she looked for the engineer, afraid, but he wasn't there.

The bo'sun pushed in beside the girl, a wild sneer on his face. He clapped his hands around her arms and pulled her directly toward the captain.

She stiffened but when the path cleared to the captain's face and she saw the pale nudity of his regard as the clouds rolled overhead—she let herself be led. She looked at the bo'sun as he tossed a necklace of bottle caps over her head and released the dog.

The captain bowed slightly, but the bo'sun grabbed his hand and wrapped it around the girl's waist.

And she was pulled close to him.

And she felt faint.

And like fire and ice all over.

And she again searched for the engineer who wasn't there.

The scar hidden beneath her blouse sang as if exposed to the sun.

The stiffness of his uniform swept over her bare arm, her cheek, her neck.

Her heart cantered so loudly, she thought surely, he must hear it.

His scent—soap and crisp paper—unrolled about her.

Her mouth went dry and she pried her lips apart with a sweep of her tongue.

The poet smiled so brightly that without another thought, the girl succumbed.

Serpent's Wake

She rested her head against the captain's shoulder and surrendered, just as she had beside the saffron peppered pool in the belly of the world.

The trident waved. The cook swung his wig like a lasso and tossed it at the medical student.

'Right, all hands,' the captain said, 'give the passengers the rest of the booze.'

'Kiss your bride!' the poet shouted, his exuberance officiating a wedding he knew he'd never see.

The captain put his hand up. 'Congratulations for crossing the line.' He turned to his crew, 'Posts.'

The sun emerged from the clouds, brightened the deck and disappeared again.

The locksmith told the crew, 'All right, pull up your socks or you'll be wringin em out.'

The bo'sun plucked a bottle from a seated crewman. 'What are those legs painted on? Get goin.'

The cook chucked his sea stars overboard and the passengers followed him to the galley.

Still, the captain's arm, his hand, remained where it was. The girl barely breathed. Her body curled against his, she felt the length of his torso, his hip, his thigh, all throwing heat. Something in him had changed. She felt it and was powerless beside it. Despite the engineer's warning, she wanted to whisper: *You're a ship captain. Marry me. Have me. Carry me to bed.*

But she said nothing.

He cleared his throat, not looking too closely at her, and said, squeezing her with the greatest of tenderness, 'We're outrunning a storm. It's come up fast so we have to move.' Then he said, 'I hope they didn't embarrass you.'

'Not much.' Her voice was strained but not from embarrassment.

His arm relaxed. 'These ceremonies are always…' He searched for the right word.

'Fun?' She tangled her fingers in the bottle cap necklace.

'Thank you for being so gracious.' He let her go and looked down at her dress. 'You fixed it.'

'Yes.' She touched the tiny seashells in the neckline.

'Good.'

She found the leash hanging on the railing and caught her dog. In her cabin, she hung the necklace from the lamp beside her father's post card. She flung herself onto her bed and watched the sea glass shimmer in the bubbling light. The scent of the captain lingered on her skin, in her hair.

She felt the ship change course and pick up speed.

§

Later, under a sky smudged with impending rain, the girl returned to the deck to watch white caps. Waves charged the hull and the ship rocked. She could hear the sound of lunch, a few passengers still enjoying the party, despite the proximity of the storm.

The captain appeared at her side as she rested her hands on the railing. She turned to him.

'It's getting rough,' he said over the wind, 'so if you feel ill, there's ginger tea in the galley,' but he recognized her delight with the boiling sea. 'You don't get seasick, do you? Of course not, but for your safety, I ask that you stay in the galley or your cabin.' Lightning scalded the horizon and the dog stood at the length of his leash, pointing toward cover.

The captain's voice changed. He said, just above the wind, 'I can tell you. I've heard the stories.'

She swayed in his direction.

'I don't care about any of it. You can stay with us as long as you want. You're welcome on our ship.'

A shadow inside her moved.

The captain waited for her to respond but she just looked at him with darkening eyes.

'Well then,' he said, 'please, take shelter.' He retreated toward the stairs, hands still deep in his pockets, legs striding over the tilting deck.

She felt salt filling the air. Her skin grew taut. The waves crashed; a gray wash charged like the shoulders of gigantic buffalo. Rain fell in fat, slow drops, spotting the deck.

Lightning flashed. The dog moaned.

Though her hands were clamped on the railing, she felt like she was falling. A writhing sense of betrayal jumbled her thoughts.

No sanctuary.

This ship, a trap.

Who told?

The doctor?

No.

Would he?

Maybe.

The blackness of the serpent was all around her, stealing breath from her lips. Poison dripped from her fingertips as they curled around the wet rail. The sea exploded into a mist of salt spray, stinging her eyes.

She looked at her dog, cowering, pulling on his leash and suddenly, as if something else entirely had pushed into her being and crushed her with its weight, she felt an urge to take that dog in her arms and feed him to the sea.

Throw him in.

Throw him.

Then horror.

At the theft of these thoughts.

At whatever was left of herself.

Just as she began to feel she belonged somewhere, the sensation crumbled. She saw, once again, that she was still the mess from the mountain village, spat up from a story that would never die.

With the pounding of the ocean churn, her whole body remembered the belt of the serpent's strike. She caught her hand mid-scratch under her scarf, fingernails sliding over flesh.

Don't.

Scratch.

But she did. And her scarf fell away, loose, and blew away high into the wind and over the sea like a panicked bird until it disappeared, until the wind devoured her senses. Lightning split the sky, releasing pounding, white rain; the world went deaf. The deck heaved; her knees buckled.

Anger shot across her ears: 'Get into your cabin!'

The engineer, bracing the stairs, his palm motioned to sweep her toward her cabin.

Part III: An Octopus Has Three Hearts

She reached for her dog. His claws skidded and she dug her hands into his black coat as if searching for something, but all she found was fright. With the next thunderclap, the dog urinated on her feet.

She stumbled across the deck with the dog, threw open her cabin door and sealed it with the silver bolt.

The wind screamed and the ship yawed. Her books fell from their perches and slid across the floor. Her desk chair toppled and the lamp flickered.

Don't.

Scratch.

But she did and as she did, so did the scalding disperse for a flash; the wild sea of her thoughts threw her up for a breath. She caught it and went down again, dragging her along her own powdery, black-bottomed sea.

The dog huddled halfway under the bed. He panted and drooled.

The necklace of bottle caps swung from the lamp.

The sea glass slid across her desk.

The ship creaked.

Sink, she thought.

Can't do this anymore.

Can't leave it anywhere. Follows me.

The serpent, now a sea serpent, black as the coldest deep, rose from the stormy sea and showed itself as if all the despair and cruelty that ever mounted the world swelled to its true form and opened a gargantuan mouth.

In the hideous roar of the wind, she heard: *Nowhere safe.*

And with that, her mind locked.

And the world got very, very small.

She saw herself searching the cabin for a way out. She pulled her arms from the sleeves of her dress and ran her hands over her scar. The ship threw her to the floor and she stood with violent purpose. She leapt at the portal but it wouldn't budge.

Her hands groped through piles of books for cutlery from solitary meals, for a knife. She would slash herself to bits: tear this stubborn life away, this sticky ribbon of a life that refused to end and had only ever lived in some halfway in between place ever since.

Serpent's Wake

She found a spoon. Threw it, striking the dog's flank but he was stone.

Books slid across the floor. The chair rolled.

The girl, a thousand miles deep within herself couldn't stop this.

Pounding at her door.

'Miss!'

She gritted her teeth.

More pounding.

'Miss! Emergency!'

She was kneeling on the floor, bare-chested, ready to saw through flesh with a dinner knife.

The pounding unlocked her mind, called her to see herself in this slanting room. The lenses in her eyes twinged as they focused on the blade touching her wrist in the rocking light. She sucked in a breath.

The knife fell.

'Emergency!'

She knew the voice. The locksmith.

She scrambled to her feet. Hunching against the pitching waves, she pulled her arms through the loops of her dress and threw a wrap over bleeding rash. She flung open the door.

The locksmith jumped at the look on her face. He clung to a rail as the ship rolled and shouted, 'Holy! Are you all right, missy?'

'Terrified,' she braced herself in the door jamb.

'You and me both!' He swayed. 'Captain's keeping us out of the worst of it.' Then he told her that the poet fell. 'There's blood. Are you all right with blood?'

'I'm fine with blood. Let me change.'

§

In the poet's quarters, the girl sat on his bed, braced against the wall. He was lying across his blankets, the gold ascot brown with blood, one hand attempting to fix it. 'Oh stuff it,' he mouthed under the racket of the storm.

Pillows braced his head and a broken arm. The blue from the ceremony was gone and he wore a fine silk shirt. A bandage about his head bloomed red. 'Still bleeding, isn't it? I can smell it...'

Part III: An Octopus Has Three Hearts

The girl's hands were sweaty inside the gloves given to her. She smelled acetone wafted from the poet's breath. The ship pitched as she braced his head with another pillow.

She said, 'What did you do?'

'Dramatic irony. I can't write anymore. I tried to kill myself.'

He had lost his balance with the roll of a wave, slamming his head upon a marble-top table and breaking his arm. Blood sprinkled his cabin door where he'd collapsed in the hallway; his cane, still a foil-wrapped trident, lay on the floor.

'Am I so fragile? I've lived too long already.'

The girl unwrapped gauze the ship's doctor had given her.

'Had to have the marble.' He glanced toward the offending table. 'They didn't tell me it was cursed.'

The medical student leaned into the doorway, returning from chaos in the infirmary, a cannula kit in her hand. Approaching the bed, she braced herself, sliding in kitten heels. She turned to the girl in a fresh pair of gloves, 'I'm glad you're fit enough to help. The doctor is overwhelmed with the fire in the galley. The others are helping her in there.'

'Fire?' the poet asked. 'What happened?'

'One of the new passengers tried to fix a stove in the middle of all this. It came loose. There was gas. People got hurt and nearly everyone is seasick. I tell you—stupid people can kill us!'

Through the wail of the storm, retching occasionally echoed, a sound that could almost be missed—but not quite. The girl wiped blood from the poet's eyebrows.

Despite the crisis, the student's hair was pinned in a perfect twist lanced by a pencil and her tidy white jacket was neatly pressed. She swabbed the back of the poet's hand, explained that she was inserting a needle into a vein so they could administer pain relief very soon and taped it down.

When he asked about the storm, she said: 'We are still ahead of it,' she said, 'would you believe it?'

She touched the sleeve of the poet's shirt. 'Uncle, I need to see your arm.'

'It's heinous,' he told her. 'Tell the captain my will is final.'

Serpent's Wake

'People don't die from a bump on the head and a broken arm,' she said. 'I thought you disliked melodrama.'

He chuckled weakly and said, 'I always liked you.'

'Stop talking in the past tense,' she scolded. Pinching the fabric of his shirt between her fingers, she said, 'Oh, I am sorry.'

'What?' both the girl and the poet asked.

'This shirt is exquisite. There's no way I can tear it.'

'You're right,' the poet said. 'A king's tailor made it for me.'

'I can't roll it. Your break is too high. I'm sorry.' A scalpel sliced the fabric.

The poet cried, 'Ugh, without anesthetic? One of a kind!'

The unforgiving angle of the poet's upper arm was revealed.

'We need morphine,' the student said, 'and a splint.'

'God! Yes!'

She slipped a sleeve over his wrist and pulled it up over his arm. He yelled. She apologized then began to inflate the splint. He whimpered.

'The pressure will control the pain,' she said. 'We're going to get you to the infirmary as soon as we can, but first,' she opened his bedside table and shook a bottle of pills, 'have you taken any of your sleeping pills today?'

Dazed, he shook his head through a fog of pain.

'Are you absolutely sure?'

He nodded.

'I'll go get the doctor.' She staggered to the door.

The poet called after her: 'Lose those shoes!'

The student waved for the girl to speak with her at the door and leaned in closely to project into her ear: 'He's lost a lot of blood. He's had too much to drink. Keep him talking, all right? The infirmary is full but he's priority. We're trying to find a place to put the passengers who were hurt in the galley. We'll get back as quickly as we can.'

The girl returned to the poet's bedside.

He said, 'I hope she said nice things about me.'

'Raved about your poetry.'

He smiled. 'Flattery. Take a book with you tonight. That one.' He gestured.

The shelf was packed so tightly, she didn't want to leave a gap during the storm. 'I will,' she said. 'She asked what you're writing next.'

'People always do. But this knock made me see, I'm too content to write. Life had its way with me. It left me jilted and even more in love.' He watched her. 'If you're not careful, contentment will sneak up, even upon you.'

'So how did it happen?'

'I told you I couldn't write because there were no love affairs on this ship but look at our cook and this lovely girl here with an eye for silk.'

She nodded.

'And there's you. And our captain. Roiling in a love affair and you don't even know it. Some say this is the best part!'

'I say it's awful.'

'Oh you are in love.'

'I'd rather hear about contentment. I can't imagine such a thing sneaking up on me.'

He looked to the door. 'She told you to keep me talking. A bad sign.'

'The way she tore the king's silk makes me think we should do what she says.'

'All right. Well, our captain, he's like my son. And did you hear her call me uncle? The sweetness of it. You know her splint is working. I can breathe.'

He sighed. 'Granted, I'm far more chaste than I'd predicted, though I don't miss the turmoil. Once I finally held my lovers, I never knew what to do with them. My curse. That, and the drink. Alcohol and self-pity are so cliché.'

The girl tore open a packet of gauze.

'My master told me if I build a world that I behold in my old age with despair, I have failed. That is, if I was lucky enough to reach old age as he had. He was big on luck.'

She placed another layer of linen but the blood was seeping. 'Does drinking mean you failed?'

He looked at her directly. 'Some say yes.'

'Maybe we're all bound to fail,' she said. Her own sensitivities felt close and she hoped, distracted for once, he wouldn't notice.

'So if I failed, is contentment a form of penance?' He laughed uncomfortably. 'There is nothing worse than a contented poet. I despise happy poems.'

Through the wall, the sound of retching resonated along steel beams.

'Perhaps he's reading "Festival of the Larks" by some such happy poet?'

The girl placed a strip of fresh bandage on his head and he touched it. 'All of my lovers are dead. I had three and they're all gone now. Sailed away.'

'I'm sorry.'

'I was blessed to have them.' He tried to move, to readjust his arm but abandoned the effort. 'God! What have I done? Did that young doctor say she was going to cut it off? She's a lovely little lady but she looks strong enough to do it.'

'Oh no. They're just going to set it.'

'The splint helps but a lion still gnaws on it.' He drew a jerky breath. 'A great, biblical lion...'

'They won't be long.'

'You don't know that, but I appreciate your effort.'

The girl snipped a piece of tape.

He thought a moment then said, 'Everything dries out...my hips, knees, fingernails...the writing. The thing I treasure most, the thing I thought made me who I am, that I sacrificed everything for...that thing, releases me. Oh the sensation...the fearlessness. Just like this...'

He raised his good arm and splayed his fingers into an open palm under flickering light. 'I didn't know I could do that. Do you know? Maybe you do. Treat the world as if you are farewelling it and bless it with every breath. I said that for years but I didn't know what I was saying.'

He placed his hand on her arm and gritted his teeth through a yawn. 'Oh pardon. I'm sleepy, which I suppose, is unfortunate.'

She returned his yawn and a single tear fell from her eyes and the veil parted. The grim realization dawned—of what she was about to do when the locksmith pounded on her door minutes ago. Her shame burned, unquenchable.

He squeezed her arm. 'What were you doing before they called you in here?'

Tears blurred the lines. She couldn't lie; she couldn't tell the truth.

'Look at me,' his voice tender against the storm.

Part III: An Octopus Has Three Hearts

'No,' a little girl's voice.

'Look at me.'

Her eyes rose to his.

He studied her. 'I know that look.'

He placed his hand on her as she sniffled.

She barely whispered, 'I'm sorry. Here you are…and I'm…'

He stroked her arm. 'I know this place.'

'I'm so ashamed.'

'Don't forget how it feels. Now you know this place too.'

'You know…'

'I did. I do.'

She choked on her words: 'I lost my family, my home, my faith. I have no anchor…'

He touched her cheek. 'Your home is everywhere. Your family, everyone. Your faith did not rise from something handed to you by a man. It's not written in a book and it certainly isn't something that can be torn by predators. It's within you, already opening like an infinite puzzle box. All yours. But you already know this. You wear the marks of one who knows, of one who earned her wisdom all alone in the dark and saw by a light that didn't go out. This faith is beyond the grasp of both men and serpents.'

Serpents.

The girl put her head down and wept as the sea rocked them. She wept her losses and her futile secrecy. She wept the road she traveled and the frightful, open space ahead. She wept her parents and her village. She wept the abandoned tenderness of the doctor's son and her guilt at wanting to heave her closest friend, her father's dog, overboard. She wept the prospect of belonging to everyone and everywhere and how that felt like dying too. She wept her way around the poet's words. And she wept that she had wanted to die, and that she had to die again and again, but not by her own hand. She had to die by love, to die and rise from the torture of fear into the blessings of life. And when she looked within, she saw her faith burning gold, and it looked like nothing else she'd seen *before*.

And these tears that took so long to come would not cease.

He touched her hair. 'I know.'

'How do you know?'

'When I left the priesthood, I got lost. First I lost mother church. Then all of my friends, even my family, though later, we made a kind of awkward amends. I was in exile until I could grow my life again and I stood on that precipice.' He pointed to the tissues. 'Don't be shy, dear. Blow your nose.'

'I'm a mess.'

'You're holy.'

She blew her nose, a wet trumpet over the roar of the sea. 'I imagine you were a good priest.'

'The best. Humble too. But I was a better poet.' He lifted his good arm to hold her. 'You'll be all right. Come out of the dark. It's beautiful.'

She let herself be held. The ship rolled and the light tossed shadows. She looked at the title of the book he wanted her to have. 'All is Gift,' she said. 'What does that mean when things are stolen from you?'

'Even theft is gift.'

'That doesn't make sense.'

'The more you lose, the more you gain. Lost, stolen, given away. You grow rich. You'll see.'

She shuddered.

'Hope,' he said, 'is easier than regret. Conjure it into being if you must. Release it into yourself like tiny sparrows, one at a time. And see what happens next.'

Moments later, the ship's doctor and the medical student entered the cabin. They changed their gloves. They both wore thick yellow boots that squeaked and the girl wondered at the state of the galley. She sat up, wiping her eyes.

'We're in love,' the poet said. 'It's very difficult for her to see me in pain.'

'I can see that. We're going to give you morphine and move you to the infirmary,' the doctor examined his eyes. 'Have you had morphine before?'

He turned to the girl, 'To think you would have missed this.'

She stood to make room for the team, holding onto the wall.

'Come back here,' he said, 'and hold my hand.'

The doctor repeated: 'Have you had morphine before?' as she snapped the top from a glass ampoule.

'Yes? No? I don't know,' the poet said. 'I smoked opium...oh wait, no, hashish with mountain gods in the East. Does that count?'

'Opium counts; hash does not.' The doctor tapped the needle, consulted with the student then said, 'I know you had quite a bit to drink today but did you take any other medications today? Did you take any of those sleeping pills today?'

'No.' He shook his head.

'Are you sure?'

'Of course I'm sure.'

'Allergies?'

'Happy poetry.'

The doctor aimed the syringe into the cannula and the morphine drifted. He blinked at the ceiling, his grip on the girl's hand softened.

'The morphine is easy. There it is, blossoming like a cherry tree.'

The doctor said they should give him a few minutes. She would ask two of the crewmen to move him.

He closed his eyes. 'I see flowers...soft, pink blossoms soft as the skin of a baby bird. I see exploding golden chrysanthemums, faces like dragons.' He began to slur. 'Yes. And oh look,' he opened his eyes and ran his hand over the blanket. 'All over the bed. Velvet. I can smell them. Am I on a bed of crushed violets?'

'You're delirious,' the girl said.

'Did no one tell you? All is well,' the poet drifted.

The doctor took his pulse and monitored his breathing. She turned to the student. 'He's good to go. I'll be right back.' She left, bracing the wall as she went.

The student told the girl, 'Just keep holding his hand.'

He looked asleep but suddenly, his breathing shortened. His chest fell sharply. And didn't rise.

The girl touched his face.

The student shouted his name. No response. 'Get the doctor!' She pounded his chest.

§

The girl lay in a sea of books, her head on the dog's flanks; the poet's book in her hand. The approaching dawn reshaped the room.

Serpent's Wake

The wind had fallen from a roar to a whimper and the waves sank back into the sea. The course steadied. The echoes of vomiting silenced and the crew tripped off to bed one at a time. The doctor and the medical student drank cold coffee in a broken galley while the cook wept. The girl sat with them until she couldn't bear it anymore. The poet's body waited in the infirmary.

Footfalls.

A pause.

Three gentle raps.

She knew who it was. She slipped over her books and opened the door.

The captain's eyes asked if he could come in, his face ashen.

She nodded.

He stepped into her cabin and watched as she cleared a path with her feet. She sat on her bed, still holding the poet's book, the ravaged skin of her neck exposed.

'What's happened?' the captain touched her shoulder.

'Nerves.' She adjusted her blouse.

He righted the desk chair and found the discarded knife on the floor. 'It gets more interesting.'

'This,' he lifted her mother's rosewood box from the floor, 'should be somewhere safe.' He placed it on the desk and sat. He examined the bottle cap necklace, telling her that the doctor was writing a report. 'Please speak with her again to ensure everything is correct.'

She nodded.

'He always came with us to write.' He lifted the sea glass. 'Then, when my father got sick, he never left.' The air quivered. A puff of land slid into the portal's view. The captain rested his head in his arms.

'It happened fast,' she said.

He snarled: 'I know. Morphine. And it looks like he lied about the sleeping pills.'

'He lied?'

He told her the doctor was running tests but yes, they were almost certain he had taken a few before his injury. 'He probably didn't think it mattered. What's a couple of pills? Until you throw morphine at it. And booze. And the rest. And this storm. I did everything I was supposed to do. It followed us.' His anger crackled. 'But he shouldn't have been hurt in the first place!'

Part III: An Octopus Has Three Hearts

She watched seagulls outside the window, knowing it was easier to be angry, to savor the anger because, soon enough, it caved to something bottomless. She looked at the island with a dull sense of relief. 'It's like he knew.'

'What did he say?'

'He was content. He was home.'

'And how should that lead to his death?'

'I'm not saying it right, I'm sorry. He spoke so honestly, so beautifully—not like me. I don't know. He just seemed ready.'

'Ready. What is ready? I'm never ready. My father ailed for years on this ship and his final year was a nightmare. It should have been a relief when he died, but...' His throat seized. He whispered, 'When death comes, we feel everything at once.'

The girl thought how death took freely from her and she had learned to yield. For the captain, however, it appeared it was an insult that death should come at all. 'We do feel everything at once. At times like this, everything is close.' She said, 'What does the hunter on your map say?'

He told her that the poet, the day he had the map mounted on the bridge, pointed to that lone hunter and said, 'Our story is this map. Let nothing you touch own you but love everything you touch,' and how utterly impossible that was. Then the captain said, 'The hunter has resignation. I have outrage. How can a man love and lose all at once?' He sat up suddenly, 'I apologize. I'm gruff and generally awful at the moment. I am not myself.'

'So be gruff. Be awful. Lose yourself. It's safe in here.'

'Is it?'

'Yes.'

'With your knives and books all over the place?'

'Utterly safe.'

'All right then,' the captain rubbed his eyes. 'Let me say how he talked about you. Always. He asked me: "Have you put her at the helm yet? Let her wear your hat?" He teased me daily: "Have you kissed her? Held her in your arms and seen your best self? This is how it is: you are the ship; she is the sea." God! He told me the ancestors were watching, waiting with anticipation, holding their collective breath. The man was relentless.'

She remembered the agony of leaves, 'He thought I should be in love with you.'

'He told me to tear a hole through this wall,' he stood and palmed it, 'like "a titan claiming his bride." I argued with him. I told him I could never touch you and he called me a liar. He said we touched every time I saw you and he was right. I insisted I was too old for you.'

'Are you?'

'More than a decade and those are a sailor's years. I can't imagine...'

'I can.'

He looked down at the desk.

She continued, 'But I don't believe I'm anything more than a favor for an old friend.' There was more, but she couldn't frame it with words. Poison. Ruin. She squeezed the poet's book in her hands.

'I have reinforced that impression.' The captain's eyes glistened and he noticed the postcard. 'My ship. When my father was alive.'

'Sent to my father. He wanted to take this journey but never could because of what happ–' she stopped herself.

'What happened?' his question struck like a dart.

She knew she didn't have to say anything but his eyes said, *Tell me everything.*

She asked, 'What were you told?'

He repeated what the crewman had said about her past. '...twelve years, inside the throat of a giant serpent. You escaped. Walked home, barefoot in the snow for miles, commanding a pack of wolves. Is it true?'

'No one commands wolves. I don't know why people keep saying that.'

'Maybe they wish you did.' He asked if the doctor knew everything.

'Didn't he tell you?'

He shook his head. 'He told me your parents died and you leased your farm to his son so you could travel.'

'Well,' the girl said. 'Now you know.'

'I already knew.'

She looked to the portal.

He leaned back in the chair. 'On deck, I was trying to apologize for how I spoke in the cavern, but I've offended you further.'

'What did you say?' She wondered what, precisely, he regretted.

'About snakes. The idiotic things I said about snakes,' he scowled. 'I can't imagine how that made you feel.'

'But your story had hope. Mine is just ugly. I thought I was free from it and now everyone on board knows.'

'They've known for a while. It's a remarkable story and I meant what I said on deck. Stay with me, as long as you like.'

On deck, he spoke like a professional: 'stay with us…'

There in her cabin, she watched the light rouse the sea.

Eventually, he said, 'Perhaps it's only fair then…' He unbuttoned the top buttons of his shirt. After the third, he stopped. Old stitches swept his breastbone.

The girl wanted to ask what happened, but her mouth was full of sand. *Little sparkling grains of humility,* the poet might have said.

'My mother was a sad woman; the marriage reluctant. My father was always at sea but when she grew more unstable during his absences, his "wretched expeditions" she called them, he took me away from her.' Then he described a time on the edge of his boyhood when he thought his parents were mending things and he spoke carefully, as if these memories were rarely touched. He recalled how his mother met them unexpectedly, bringing a trunk full of toys and smart clothes; and how he watched his father's face tighten.

'Then she announced that the marriage was over and she was taking me home. We were at a port closer to our country then. A lawyer was waiting on the pier with train tickets and I saw him: a thin man with glasses but no eyes. A man who was paid to engineer my final departure from this ship. Well, I wouldn't go. And everything fell apart.'

He told her how the three of them battled at the top of the gangway with the lawyer below amplifying the sense of ambush. His mother yanked the boy's wrist but he clung to the rail, causing exactly the kind of scene his father abhorred. His mother screamed at his father in their native tongue, assailing him somewhat privately until the poet arrived. Her words were smoking: 'Raising a boy like this! Surrounded by rum-soaked, dirty buggers! I'll have the boy examined for syphilis!'

The boy, stronger than his mother realized from his life at sea, wrenched himself from her. 'And I fell. I saw the pier racing toward me. I struck a cleat,' he pointed to his chest, 'and then, water.'

He told her that a crewman—the locksmith—went in after him. 'I remember the air on my face and coughing up fire. Covered in blood, I cursed my mother until she went away. My father never said a word.' He told her how their mutual friend, the doctor, was onboard and had nursed him back from that place, but his wounds ran deeper than the points of that cleat.

'I hated my mother,' he said, buttoning his shirt. 'A decade went by and mariners know curses stick. I was told she had every illness imaginable and then she was dying. She sent for me but I ignored her.'

The girl listened, her arms tight around her knees.

'But I saw her once after that. After her death. Just for an instant, just after I had tied a dozen white ribbons.'

The girl leaned toward him. 'Maybe that's all she wanted.'

He reached for the girl, to where she had inched toward him on her bed. The skin of her neck glowed like scales and she felt his urge to take her in his arms. But he withdrew, 'I don't know how to do this. I have no compass. No map.'

'In the desk.'

'What?'

'The drawer.'

He opened the drawer. 'I know who gave you this. He probably told you to keep me on course. So keep me on course.'

'I will.'

'I must get some sleep.' The chair creaked as he got to his feet. The sea rolled with first light. A soft, green island ringed with white sand grew larger in the window. 'You see this place?' He told her that the doctor met his wife there, then he mentioned the poet. 'Thank you. For all that you did for him.'

She stood. 'But I know he gave me so much more.'

She reached for him. She watched his eyes drift from her fingertips to her face. She knew he had been set on the door until she touched him. She unbuttoned her blouse. The skin of her scathed neck exposed only the roof of what was her sad church. Her fingers progressed until the lash of her scar was revealed, her breasts raked by the plumage of poison. This would repel him and she could be done with all this.

'Now that,' he said, 'is a scar.'

She was burning; her mouth sealed shut.

'You'd put more than a few crewmen to shame with their jellyfish scars.'

She looked at him, incredulous.

'Stay with me. How many more times will I have to say it?'

'Many,' she whispered, 'many more times.'

He touched her, warm on the cool of scarred flesh, his fingers drawing her heart to life. 'I look at you, every time I look at you, I want this dawn. I want you to lead me. Stay with me.'

Fireflies. His scent combed across her face: paper, soap, worry, grief, relief. She inhaled the ache of his being and slid her fingers through the gaps between his buttons. With no compass. No map. Just the dawn ablaze.

He touched a thumb to the point of her chin and kissed her. 'Stay with me.'

Her blouse slid from her shoulders as she rose into his kiss.

'Stay with me.' His teeth brushed against her lips. His hands slid through her hair, and over her breasts, hips, the small of her back. His body rocked with hers like the sea itself, through all the books beneath them, and he remembered: 'If you do not rise to meet the sea, the sea will rise to meet you.'

He lifted her tightly against him, her bare toes skipping across her books as she kissed him. When he reached the door, leaned his back against it as he grasped her hips.

Their faces touched in homecoming; how could all turn so finely, so sadly, so completely over the course of hours and through this hallowed moment of grief? Their hands traced the other's cheeks, above the bubbling wake of their bodies.

Into the softness of her mouth, he said, 'Stay with me,' and lowered her to the floor.

She placed her hands on his shoulders. His fingers rested on her scar, lingering. He unbuttoned the last of the buttons past her navel, pushed the blouse to the floor, and turned her toward the light of the window. She looked down to see her body reflecting the sea in that morning light. She shimmered.

'Do you see? I've been around and around this world and I have never been called to the steps of anyone like you.'

She was no longer trembling.

He opened the door, a little. 'Stay with me.' He slipped into the deserted hall.

'Many more times.'

She closed the door.

She stood in the reflected light of the sea. 'Who are you, that you can love this?'

Her fingers rested on the window: the one she tried to break just hours ago; and she looked at her hands, the hands that had held the poet, just as his body released its last poem.

PART IV: BLOOD & FIRE

Part IV: Blood and Fire

When both the captain and the girl woke hours later, the ship was at port. They found something of themselves wound together through the steel that divided them and drifted there, recalling the taste of the other. Then they found grief again; that sharp, waking grief that snags and startles the heart.

When the captain arrived on the bridge without shoes, the bo'sun handed him coffee.

The captain said, 'Hot here.'

'Stinkin hot,' the bo'sun wiped his face, 'for ten in the mornin.'

The captain asked for an update and was told the island had escaped the brunt of the storm so they were welcomed by old friends and there was plenty of assistance if they needed it. During the storm, the captain had pushed hard, blew two engines, and made it smoking to safe harbor. Repairs would crawl along on island time, taking three months or so, but everything had to stop and this was the place to do it.

The captain emptied his mug, his face sour. 'Coffee's terrible.'

The bo'sun said, 'Galley's a wreck. Got an electrical mess below too. Got a diver down on water intake and they're opening up the bypass valves. Gonna blackout the power soon for an overhaul. Gonna be a hot one so we have generators for the galley and the infirmary. Oh yeah, and half the steering's gone.'

'And this.' The bo'sun handed him a torn paper and sweated at the window. 'A reply from the old doc.'

'Morphine sensitivity devastating. Concussion, alcohol, age, blood loss, hypnotic use…respiratory failure…we grieve with you…' There was also a photo and the local name of a plant.

He handed the image to the bo'sun. 'I need this plant.'

'I know just the man who can get it.'

'Round everyone up to meet on deck in an hour.' When the captain asked him to knock on the girl's door, his crewman raised an eyebrow, but the captain looked at a console. 'She was with him when he died.'

When the bo'sun left, the captain radioed nearby contacts and presented the remaining passengers with their connections. The passenger who had tried to fix a stove during the storm would be first to meet his new ship, in handcuffs.

Serpent's Wake

The captain kicked open the safe on the floor behind his desk and found the poet's will under banded piles of notes. It was stamped with a red wax seal: a crane danced before the sun. He broke the crane in two and the paper opened. A familiar white ribbon slipped onto the desk.

'I can't read this,' the captain said to the calligraphy. 'If you did anything, you did it with lions and laurels.'

He scanned and saw details for a cremation and a box of ribbons to be found in the poet's cabin. Then he saw his first engineer's name cited as the lawyer, full credentials at his thumb. The captain's eyes twitched.

He folded the will and kicked the safe door closed.

Minutes later, he was on deck with the crew and several of the islanders. An old man with black teeth and a head of tight gray curls traced a knobby finger along the shoreline.

The girl sat among the crew in a scarf and a modest shift in the heat. Beside the girl, the bo'sun sat arms folded, shirt ringed with sweat, rig over his shoulder. The engineer had his hands clasped over his head. The locksmith and cook sat side by side with a few more able crewmen. The ship's doctor and her medical student looked unkempt.

The captain reviewed the night's events. The doctor answered pointed questions and confirmed the presence of sleeping medication in the poet's system. 'It doesn't mean his death was intentional,' she said, 'so don't say that.'

The bo'sun pushed back from the table. 'So you stuffed up.'

'Don't say that either,' she sprang back at him. 'As I said, he, for whatever reason, was not completely honest with me.'

The captain stepped between them, reading out the confirmation from the old doc.

She retreated.

Strained, sweaty looks were cast out to sea as the poet's wishes were discussed. The captain gave the ribbon to the cook and asked him to find a box in the poet's quarters. The locksmith blew his nose into a filthy handkerchief.

The old islander pointed again toward the sandbar, saying it was underwater now but would be dry by the afternoon. 'We will have twelve hours. Water will sweep the ashes clean by sunrise.'

The ship's doctor nodded.

The islander said, 'We all knew him. Good man. No permit. Just get rid of the tourists.'

The captain said, 'Five o'clock tomorrow afternoon.' He turned to the engineer and said, 'Bush lawyer, come with me to the bridge.'

On the bridge, the captain placed the poet's will on his desk. 'I've noticed that you're not insulted when we call you our bush lawyer?'

The engineer shook his head slowly.

'When you're a real lawyer.'

The engineer nodded.

'You finished law school—got a degree?'

The engineer nodded.

'Tell me, how did you find the time to study law and engineering?'

He looked past the captain at the great map where a headless man held a spear and a basket. 'How does a man begin...'

'Try.'

The engineer described a quiet conversation with the poet, a year into his appointment. 'He spoke to me about the way I assumed everyone was guilty. He said: "The highly suspicious always have something to hide," then he asked me what my something was.'

'So what the hell is this?' The captain tossed a copy of an engineering degree on his desk.

'A forgery made for your father.'

The captain crumpled it. 'You played apprentice on my ship? You could have killed people.'

'When I met your father,' the engineer clasped his hands, 'I was living out of a boat taking whatever job I could get. He saw me haggle parts for a liner bigger than this and he said he liked my style. Your first engineer had run off with a woman and your ship was stuck with overheated engines in the tropics. Do you remember?'

'I remember everything. My father trusted you,' the captain opened a window, the midday heat roasting the ship now. 'Look at the galley to see what happens when a man calls himself an electrician.'

The engineer drew a deep breath. 'I put myself through law school fixing all kinds of machinery at a shipyard. For over a decade, all through my studies, I fixed everything until a man drove me from my country.' He touched his arms, the ripples lit with sweat. 'People think this is some kind of ritual scarification. It was a warning.'

'What are you talking about?'

The engineer stalled, exhuming a story long buried, then started slowly. 'Back in my country, when I was studying law, I knew for years about a man who was trafficking. It was very bad.' His eyes were leaden. 'I was nearly finished with school and I learned that nearly everyone knew what the man was doing but no one stopped him because they were poor. So I took pictures. A professor showed me how to bypass my country's justice system—run on bribes—and report this to an international commission. The man found out about my pictures.'

'What kind of trafficking? Drugs?'

'Young boys and girls. The only thing in plentiful supply in a world growing scarce in everything else.'

On the map behind the captain, the hunter looked betrayed; the man using his foot as an umbrella, appropriate.

'The shipping world is small.' The engineer clutched his forearms. 'If the wrong ear hears about a lawyer of my color managing ship engines—an uncommon combination—they will come with acid. Yes, I lied and I kept the lie until it became truth. But,' he looked at the will on the desk, unfolding in the humidity, 'he saw right through me. He paid me to qualify as an estate lawyer through a correspondence course based in his country. I did whatever he asked. He was a good man. You know,' he said quietly, 'they kill men like him where I come from.'

The captain poured water into his mug.

'I assure you...' the engineer began.

'Assure me. That's what lawyers do best,' the captain interrupted. 'Do you know what my father would do to you?'

'No.'

'Shoot you in the arse as you left the ship.'

'This is when I find out how much you are like your father.'

The captain picked up the will.

The engineer, his voice cautious, said, 'You have read it, so you know.'

'Know what?'

'He left everything in your care.'

'I read enough to see cremation and your name.'

The engineer leaned on the window. 'You must return to your country to finalize the will.'

The captain sat on his desk. 'You kept a dangerous secret.'

'Secrets do not keep.' He dropped his gaze. 'I am sorry. I will pack my bags and join the passengers leaving today. Please do not shoot me in the arse.'

'You know the situation below,' the captain said, 'and how we always lose crew on this island, even when we're not dead in the water. Still, I ask, what kind of man are you?'

Sweat rolled down the engineer's temples. 'I have been devoted to your ship for a decade.'

'And devoted to your lie.'

'Yes.'

'Don't bullshit me ever again or you're off.'

'Yes.'

'I mean it.'

'Yes. No bullshit.'

Then the captain asked, 'What about the snake story?'

'I only repeated what I heard.'

'Stop gossiping,' the captain said and the engineer looked stung by the word. 'No one's going to broadcast your background. Now fix the mess below.'

§

In the galley, the girl found the cook at a table. His mop and broom leaned against the wall; an open wine bottle before him. A generator purred somewhere nearby as he announced, 'Don't come in here without good shoes.' His boots sat beside his chair, his bare feet propped up the table. On the instep of one foot: a tattoo of a pig; the other, a rooster; both making a fuss as they rode the surface of a wave.

She showed him her boat shoes and sat across from him. The galley was a mess; burned, wet, stinking of bodily smells.

The cook poured red wine into a mug and slid it toward her. 'He called this oaky. Smoky oaky. What do you think?'

As she sipped the poet's wine, it sucked the moisture from her mouth. 'It's OK.'

'No. It's oaky. Better with food. If you're hungry, there's stuff in the fridge. Hot food's on hold with my stove broke. You know it's from your port town. Buncha thugs. No offense. My town's a buncha thugs, too.'

'I'm sorry,' she said. 'I'm more from the mountains.'

He heard her attempt at a joke and smiled a little.

She said, 'Can I help?'

'Everything needs a bleach. Nothing like glass and blood in the kitchen. And puke. Can't forget the puke.' The cook's voice cracked. 'Whole goddamned world's upended.' He poured more wine.

The girl took up his broom and pushed broken glass into a pile. She found the dustpan.

'Gloves.' He tossed her a pair and followed as she swept, his boots clunking against the floor unlaced without socks. He yanked a bracket from the wall and threw it into a pile. 'Sometimes shit happens too fast for me. Pardon my language but I am so off duty right about now.'

The girl found the bleach.

'When he...' the cook unscrewed the cap for her. 'When he...'

She looked at him.

'Was he scared?'

'No,' she said, 'he was talking about flowers. Violets.'

He wiped his face with his shoulder. 'So it was as fast as they said?'

'Yes.'

The cook took up his mop. 'We were having such a good time. First time he let us paint him blue. Never let us do that before.'

'I'm sorry. It wasn't fair that I was with him.'

'Aw, don't look for fair in this. Who wouldn't want a beautiful girl at his bedside when he goes? Look at you with that midnight hair and all. I say he was in the very best of company.'

She looked into the bucket of glass.

The cook mopped until the engineer entered the galley, a drill in his hand, saying, 'I warned you not to buy that stove.'

'Don't do it, man,' the cook aimed the mop.

The engineer's drill weighed in like a pistol.

The cook raised his voice, 'I wasn't even here when it happened!'

'Where were you then?'

'The infirmary! Carrying a passenger who dropped his guts,' he pointed, 'right where you're standing.'

The girl slipped off the gloves and examined the galley's herb collection.

The engineer turned to her, 'What the hell are you doing in here?'

'I'll come back in a minute,' she told the cook, leaving the gloves and taking a sprig of rosemary.

The engineer blocked her path.

She looked into his eyes. 'What.'

He said, 'It disgusts me that you were there with him, doing nothing but watching him die.'

'So what would you have done?' She leaned toward him. 'Tell me. Since you know so much. All I hear is how brilliant you are. The engineer. The pilot. The bush lawyer who rescues stupid girls from magistrates. Well? Maybe you can tell me how to save a man from himself.'

He didn't answer; his drill, limp.

She pushed past him.

In her cabin, her heart pounded; the dog thumped his tail on the floor. She sat on the bed her head in her hands until she heard a knock. The captain held the poet's notebook and a bundle in newspaper.

The girl assumed it was a bone for the dog until he handed it to her; it was light. She smelled a familiar, waxy scent, a hint of hops, before she saw the star shaped flowers, orange instead of yellow. Jewelweed. She looked at the captain with surprise.

'When I wired the doc, I asked how I could help.' He touched her neck. 'He said the flowers are a different color but the effect is the same.'

She hugged the bundle and thanked him.

As he sat at her desk, the sound of wood-chopping began to worm through the ship. Onshore, a ring of lanterns lit shirtless men swinging axes.

'I need a favor.' He opened the poet's notebook. 'It's the only one in here and it's appropriate. None of the crew can do this. Would you read it tomorrow?'

She reached for him and tasted his grief before he left.

§

The captain didn't immediately join his men on the beach. The girl heard the unusual sound of him entering his own cabin. He unlatched a cabinet to find his father's axe hanging by leather straps and took it by the handle.

He and the girl both looked from their portals to the fading sunlight, to lanterns casting golden spheres on the beach, to the bo'sun and the engineer dragging pallets across the sand, leaving deep scores behind them. Flying foxes, hundreds of them, made a sunset pilgrimage across the island's volcanic skyline toward the mango trees and fruiting palms at the other end of the island. At the shoreline, a cluster of children swam before dashing from the water toward their waiting mothers and aunties. A small fishing boat was dragged ashore by three men; they jumped out, pulled an enormous manta ray onto the sand and cut it into chunks.

And the captain wept in a way he had never done before. Not the way he did for his mother, a woman ever remote to him; not for his father, a man carved from salt and anchor points. He wept with silent but extravagant boyish loss; and the girl, on the other side of the wall, held the silence.

When he was finished, he straightened, took up his axe, and went down to the beach.

§

At dawn, the girl patted her neck with the jewelweed compress and took the dog below. She found the door to the weight room wide open and the bo'sun, covered in sweat, sitting on his weight bench with his back to her. She didn't make a sound.

In the galley, she found the cook and the medical student sitting on the spotless floor, knotting white ribbons to a bamboo stretcher. The cook looked up, eyes cloudy, and resumed his work.

The student kissed his cheek. 'I have to get back.'

Her dog curled up to watch as the girl took a handful from the box and sat cross-legged. The ribbons were the same that feathered the cathedral atrium—stamped with little inky crosses, wheels, stars and moons. Only white; all white. The girl knotted, working silently, fingers warm and thoughts traversing delicate places as the air shifted. With each ribbon, she wound a prayer around the bamboo:

I hope your crossing is gentle.

Part IV: Blood and Fire

I hope the poems are like diamonds.
I hope your master sails to meet you and his spectacular frown has turned.
I hope your lovers who spoke in poetry have much to say.
You shared your light and it grew me.

The girl looked to the cook as she tugged a knot. She had been whispering and he, ribbons in his lap, hands empty, was moved.

She blushed: 'I'm sorry...'

'God, would you stop apologizing? I just don't know how I'm gonna get through this.'

When the box was empty and the simple bamboo frame was transformed into a downy, sleeping dragon, the cook made coffee and peeled a boiled egg for the dog, who had learned, 'Ya want breakfast?' from him. When the engineer and the bo'sun appeared with their mugs, the girl left the dog with the cook and went to the infirmary.

The ship's doctor stepped out from behind a curtain in a surgical smock, looking over her glasses. 'Do you want to see him?'

The girl nodded.

The curtain parted, revealing the poet in his best suit: tailored, creamy ivory.

'That suit,' the medical student followed them behind the curtain, 'is the color of an orchid in my mother's garden. Not white. Not cream.'

The doctor tugged on her gloves, 'He told me what he wanted when the captain's father died. This suit; no shoes.'

'I gave him a pedicure,' the student said; his toes white as porcelain, nails a row of waning moons.

The doctor held up silk handkerchiefs, one red; one gold. 'Which one?'

'Gold,' the girl held out her hand. At the touch of the silk, the girl remembered her father, a memory that started in her throat. She had buttoned her father's shirt over the broad chest and heart that broke. For him, she folded a white cotton handkerchief and placed it just so in his pocket, as her mother wept into her fist. She tried not to look at what was left of her father too closely, since the best of him had flown away.

The girl moved toward the breast pocket, handkerchief light as a draft. His ascot was missing and the wingtip collar was open, unbuttoned. She spied an old wound on the side of his throat until the doctor reached and buttoned the collar right to the top.

The student said, 'I was taught that today, a temple will burn so his soul can fly home.' She touched the poet's hand, 'Uncle, we will meet again.'

The doctor removed her smock. 'I was taught we had one shot, then heaven or hell. After everything I've seen, I think this is it. It's noble to live a good life, for goodness sake alone.'

The student tilted her head with a sweet smile. 'I always knew you were noble.' She gave the doctor a fierce hug. 'I'm going to miss you so much.'

The doctor stiffened. 'You always argue with me. Always insisting the world gets better with every person you heal.'

'It does. Besides, it's the soup anyway, remember?'

The doctor sighed. 'I had your hope once, but I saw too much as a relief worker. I'm talking about innocent people with their lives ripped out from under them, and for what?'

The student interrupted, 'And if you saw what I saw, you would argue with you, too.' Reflected in her hazel eyes were veiled mothers who shouted at armed men in the street. 'My mother said she put chili in my milk.'

The doctor accepted that and the girl gathered the gold handkerchief like a tapered candle and folded it. She asked the student, 'Are you leaving?'

'Soon. My next appointment is a few islands away.'

The doctor asked the student to finish up and left.

The girl slid the handkerchief into the poet's pocket and gave it a light tug. 'My mother taught me this.'

'Strange how our mothers teach us things we'll never do for ourselves.'

The girl touched a wingtip on his collar, 'What happened to his throat?'

'Help me?' the student opened the curtain and unlatched a silver hatch in the wall. Cold air swept across their faces as they slid the poet's body back into cold storage.

Securing the hatch, she turned to the girl. 'He told me that many years ago, he tried to end his life. To tell the truth, I had arrived on this ship very broken hearted. This man sensed it. We talked a lot. I told him there was a doctor back home who was supposed to be training me, but he misused his power and events left me very hurt and deeply ashamed. He showed me his scar and said: "When you're at the bottom, look up and see the glory.'"

§

The day melted away while the captain seemed everywhere and nowhere at once. The girl thought he might visit her but he didn't. She returned to her cabin to dab her neck and watch the sun's path from her window. The dog panted. She opened her journal to write but closed it again.

Slipping into the dress from the doctor's wife, she left the chemise on the bed. It was too hot for layers, and the scar only peeked if she bent forward. The rash had mellowed with the homespun medicine.

As she braided her hair, she considered the captain and thought perhaps he regretted his actions. Before heading down to the pier, she released him. She chose to accept his kindness and forgave his affections. As she tied off her hair, she let him go.

As the tide retreated, the girl stepped with her dog along the sand barefoot and saw the men stepping back from the bare pyre on the sandbar.

Nearby, a group of women called their children from the lolling surf.

'Water babies,' the girl remembered the doctor's wife and her ache for her people. These were her relatives with their seashell combs and skin shining in the late afternoon glow. The girl from the mountains watched the children leaping about in the surf. She marveled at the miracle of their confidence, and all that grows such a thing in a child. She saw the love that rained down on them from the women who caught them and dried them and wrapped them and led them home.

A breeze rose off the water and touched the girl. Sea grass whispered. It was finally warmer onboard the ship than it was on the beach.

A crewman planted torches along the sand ahead of her, lighting the walk from the ship to the sandbar. The breeze sent them guttering.

Serpent's Wake

The crew and some islanders gathered, all in t-shirts and shorts. Another small group of people descended a dune, the old man who had showed them the sandbar in the lead.

A single voice rose above the breeze and a woman with a large, red hibiscus tucked into her hair walked across the sand, singing to the ship. She wore a t-shirt over a long skirt. Without understanding a word, the girl knew she sang a lullaby and turned to face the top of the gangway.

Six of the crew stood on deck. All in white shirts, the captain unshaven, the ship's doctor, the locksmith, the bo'sun, the cook and the engineer carried the poet, his body wrapped in muslin; a thousand white ribbons rippling in the breeze. They descended the gangway slowly and touched the pier barefoot as the woman sang. Behind them, the medical student in her green dress, held a collage of white orchids.

When the pallbearers reached the sand, the crowd escorted them, passing one torch at a time, the woman's voice trailing. The girl glanced at the locksmith, huffing through his mouth as he walked.

To see the ribbons now was a different matter from the galley, and the girl's throat tightened: they rippled like all the prayer and hope and love of one man's life. To her, they read: *This was me. What you saw and what you didn't. I still say all is gift.*

The beach was silent as the pallbearers lifted the poet's body above the pyre, tall as the captain, bamboo creaking. The poet's feet faced the sea. The crew stepped back beside the captain, who put his hand out for the girl.

She opened the poet's notebook. Trembling, she felt a touch to her elbow: the medical student. The girl took a slow, deep breath and read:

> I am
> Rich, for I have known you;
> You of the many faces and the one.
> I am
> Relieved, to have suffered;
> Whole, to be cleaved;
> Found, to know exile;
> And free, to be caught.
> My eyes light from within;
> It is you.

A circle of breath and silence;
It is you.
Days dim; I fear nothing.
That which became me
Knows the way home;
And a feast of our days awaits:

A place set for each one.

The girl looked up; the torches sputtered.

The captain breathed a moment. A wave etched white along the sand.

'I dislike speeches,' he said, 'even more so after that...but the man insisted.' The captain paused, sharing his words with the murmur of the sea. 'As you know, he was from my country but he left it to say he was from everywhere...' He relayed an account of the man's life as a son, a priest, a poet, an uncle, and now as he had discovered from the will, a mentor to young poets.

'And he complained. He complained ceaselessly and with such self-discipline, it was lyrical. He observed the ways humanity refused its own treasure and wove it into his vision of goodness. If you knew him, you know that he saw precisely who you were, despite your best efforts,' he looked at the engineer, 'and who you could be,' he looked at the cook, 'and he pushed you toward the lover of life that is your deepest yearning,' and he looked intently at the girl.

'When my father was dying, he and I had many long talks. I asked him then why he left the priesthood: a decision that came at a great cost. He told me that he longed for a world where none were lost, one with room for all at the table. The only place he truly found that, he said, was in poetry.'

The captain looked out to sea, gratitude waning to sorrow. 'May all the kindness that was the sum of his life return to him now, and carry him home.'

With help from the captain, the medical student, on tiptoes that sank in the sand, laid her orchids upon the poet's body. The old islander came forward and whispered over the body. He patted the muslin over the poet's feet.

The pallbearers each drew a torch from the sand. Six flames leaned into the base of the pyre and spoke in smoke. Reeds soaked in rainwater from the very storm that saw him out were placed over the body, and a whoosh of burning drowned out the roll of the sea.

They backed away.

The fire rose.

The sun touched the sea and threw pink gold into the sky.

The ribbons curled against the damp reeds and the girl turned with the captain, who was looking away. Torches lit the way back toward the ship, where blankets had been thrown on the sand.

The girl and her dog followed the crowd; she let him off the leash and he walked beside the captain. The cook and the bo'sun began to dig, unearthing steaming plantains and potatoes and reef fish wrapped in banana leaves. Bright red coals glowed from sandpits and were covered again.

The captain poured wine in mugs, glasses and cups. The crew and the islanders sat as food was shared. The medical student approached the girl and told her that the ship's doctor was quite melancholy and that the poet would not appreciate her brooding.

As the girl watched the student sit with the doctor, the singer with the red hibiscus approached. She leaned in and touched the top of the scar on the girl's chest; the girl startled. Beside her, the old islander leaned on her arm, his smile dark from betel nuts. He said, 'You're the doctor's people. His missus is my niece. Tell her to come home.'

A hand to her chest, the girl was surprised to be connected with someone, with home at that moment.

The singer introduced herself as the man's niece as well; the doctor's wife was her cousin. She parted the side of her skirt, revealing a large scar on her thigh.

The girl dropped her hand from her chest just as the captain touched her waist. He said, 'Come with me?'

She nodded and reached for the woman. Their hands touched.

The girl and the captain walked with the dog trotting ahead, past the ship, away from the blankets and the food and far from the colors of the pyre in the distance. A full moon hung, dreamy and bright. Stars brightened.

He asked, 'Do you want anything to eat?'

'No.'

'I don't either. I'm going to let them go on without me. I've been too long without a proper sleep.'

'Will the crew mind things?' She looked back to see the engineer staring at them, large banana leaf plate in his hands.

'They'll keep it in focus,' the captain said. 'We're good here.' He told her that the old islander knew every plant there and that he found the jewelweed.

'You've known him a long time?'

'Yes. Did the doc ever tell you about the snake people?'

She nodded.

The doctor's wife was one of them.

Overwhelmed, she looked to the horizon. If the captain was going to disappear again, she didn't want to talk about snakes. 'Such a full moon. We can see in the dark.'

'Yes.' He turned back to the distant pyre. 'Gruesome. I won't go near it until the tide takes it away.' He scratched at a growing beard.

'Do you want to go back to the ship?' she asked. In the moonlight, he looked ghostly.

In answer, he sat. He stretched his legs and fell back into soft sand. 'The sand is warm.'

She sat and the dog curled up on the other side. He invited her, raising his arm. She hesitated.

'Stay with me,' he said.

'Many more times,' she answered.

'Stay with me.'

Eventually, she reclined. There was so much of him and here she was again, free to touch him. A shower of stars filled her. Resting her head on his chest, she listened to the captain's breath. His heart beat under her ear. She asked him, 'What's changed?'

The captain pulled her tightly to him, fingers in her hair. 'Everything.' His voice passed both through his lips and his chest, 'Death changes everything. Stay with me.'

'I will,' she said to his ribs. 'Tonight.'

'No.' A crewman's singing broke out at the bonfire. 'Stay with me.'

She didn't answer, letting his words hover over the dunes.

'I can be clumsy,' he said, 'and insular.'

Serpent's Wake

'Sometimes I don't speak for days,' she said, 'and yet I speak when I don't even realize...'

'How will it be with us then?' he asked.

She nuzzled his chest. The dog snorted.

The mood down the beach turned to laughter.

When the captain spoke again, his voice was raspy. 'They'll carry me off the ship the same way. I don't want a house or a farm or any of that.'

Remembering the hole blown through the roof above her parents' kitchen table, she said, 'Neither do I.'

'What do you want?'

'Sovereignty. I want my life to be my own.'

'Like horses just want to live...'

'You remember.'

'Life at sea is that.'

She thought on that. She said, 'You are both free and not free. Life at sea is a paradox, like everywhere else.'

'I am free, right here, with you.'

She slipped a leg over his and dug her toes into the sand.

'Stay with me,' he whispered, pulling her tightly to him, as sleep enveloped him.

She listened to his breathing widen and his heartbeat slow. She kept watch.

There she spent the night, curled against him, drifting beneath the heavens and embracing the length of him. She watched the tide pull from the shore and the moon's train shimmer over black water.

She heard the beach sing love songs, then drinking songs, and in the small hours, she heard mischief. Feet thumped up and down the gangway; the giggling and snorting of grown men ruffled the air. She heard machinery wailing on the ship; the scrape of metal on metal.

The captain stirred but didn't wake. And she held her place, watching the tourniquet of stars. She saw planets arch and the sky turn, brightening with an expectant sunrise over the ocean. When the sun brimmed and spilled its colors, seabirds called. The dog rolled over in the sand.

The captain said, 'You stayed.'

'I did.'

'Another sunrise with you,' he rolled onto his hip. 'I'll get greedy for these. Did you sleep?'

The girl touched his face with sandy hands.

Then she looked past him. Against the scarlet dawn, no more smoke poured from the pyre. The tide encroached upon crumbling ash, a collapsing sandcastle. They stood.

As they approached the pier, the locksmith called from the gangway: 'It's all done. No need to go out there now. It's all done.'

§

In the galley, the captain poured the coffee.

'Have you, uh,' the cook flipped some bacon to the dog, 'been to your cabin yet, cap?'

'No.'

'Oh.'

'Why?'

'I had nothing to do with it.'

The captain looked at the girl.

At their cabins, the girl saw it when the dog bounded through her door and disappeared. The captain asked, 'What?' but she entered her cabin and closed her door. When the captain entered his quarters, the dog leapt upon him. A doorway had been cut through the steel wall by drunken sailors with an angle grinder.

He rubbed his beard and looked at the girl who sat on her bed.

The dog danced between rooms.

The captain knelt. 'Marry me.'

'I already did.'

And he swept her into his arms and carried her over the jagged threshold.

§

The captain was about to leave her sleeping in his bed, when he kissed her eyes. She yawned and embraced him again, sand in her hair.

He went to the bridge and asked the bo'sun to round up the crew. The captain sent a message to the doctor and his wife: 'Marrying her on your island. May I ask for your blessing?'

When the crew assembled on the bridge, voices were phlegmy. The captain stood with his back to them. Silence fell like a fog.

The bo'sun broke first, 'We can hang a door, real easy...' and the rest of the crew chimed in.

'We've got just the one in storage...'

'Aw, we're real sorr...'

'It was your idea!' the cook pointed to the ship's doctor.

She threw her hands in the air. 'Can't you idiots tell when I'm joking?'

'Not really,' the medical student said.

'There are a million ways to grieve,' the captain said, 'but drunk with an angle grinder? Don't cut any more holes in my ship. Hang a door before dinner.' On his way out, he stopped the engineer. 'Where were you?'

'Below, working on the steering in the crawl space.'

The captain returned to his quarters to find her hanging from the edge of the rumpled bed, her hair cascading to the floor. She splayed her fingers and toes.

He sat on the edge of the bed. 'You're not wearing a stitch.'

She pulled him into his sheets, whispering, 'I never will again.' She pulled off his shirt and hooked her toes around his ankles. Their bodies flushed with the light.

Eventually, he managed to tell her, 'They're still coming to fix the door. You need...sovereignty.'

'Yes.'

He breathed, 'What have you done to me?'

'What have I done?' She combed her fingertips over his temples.

'You've opened all the windows.'

'Yes.' She held his head.

'And all the doors.'

'Yes.'

'There's light everywhere.'

'Yes.'

'There are all these other rooms.'

'This is how I'll love you.'

Part IV: Blood and Fire

§

As the crewmen prepared to hang the door, the bo'sun winced at the angle grinder, saying, 'It's gonna be right noisy.'

'I'm going,' she said.

Before they'd arrived, she made the bed in the captain's quarters, even though he'd told her not to, and she read the spots on the sheets. *We are blood and fire.*

She had found her edges, good ones this time, and looked at the sheets in disbelief. A surprising new ache lit her thighs and the joy was so novel, she felt frightened of it as much as she wanted more. She wanted to wrap herself around him until she passed out.

She limped as she entered the corridor and knew she should visit the infirmary. She looked back toward the writing desk and was blinded by midday sunlight shining off the sea. She shielded her eyes and saw the sea glass perched there, glowing from its heart.

When she arrived at the infirmary, the medical student told her that the doctor was ashore visiting friends.

She was relieved. 'I'd like to talk with you.'

The student pulled out a chair and they spoke into the evening. When the ship's doctor returned, the student was saying, 'It would be wise to assume that you can have children.'

'What's happening?' the doctor asked.

'A honeymoon,' the student said.

'Was there a wedding?'

'Right under our noses.' Then the student asked, 'Can we show her?'

'Good lord!' the ship's doctor said, as the scar was revealed. 'Have you seen a doctor about this?'

Later that night, she watched the captain open the new door. She was nude on her bed with the poet's book open: 'I don't deserve anything: not the hammer and tongs and not a single grace, but shower me in all...'

The captain tested the hinges absently, in his hand a message from the doctor and his wife: 'Welcome to the family. Blessings. Blessings. Blessings.'

§

The next morning, the cook handed her a white ribbon in the galley. 'I saved one. Maybe you can work it into your flowers or something?'

She hugged him and asked if he'd seen the captain. 'He's everywhere,' he said, 'like parsley in the soup.'

When she met the captain on the stairs, he surprised her by taking her in his arms. He said, 'Word has got out.' Some of the women on the island wanted to help with a wedding dress. He asked if she knew that they were all the old doc's in-laws.

'Yes, but I was just going to wear...' she began, remembering the agony of leaves. She looked at the captain, his face close and open as the morning breeze that dazzled the ship, his eyes holding her as they did in his bed. She said, 'Yes.'

When she asked him who was marrying them, he said the old islander who had found her plant. 'He has a ream of credentials,' he said, 'every church with a mail order.'

As he left for the bridge, the medical student approached her with a cleaved custard apple; its skin the texture and shade of crocodile hide. 'I've still got another few days before I'm off. Is there anything you need?'

'Yes, you,' she said, and they shared the silky fleshed fruit that tasted of vanilla and pear and spat dark, oblong seeds from the deck.

Later, the captain fastened a silver chain around her neck. Her blue sea glass was suspended in sterling wire and glinted between her collarbones. 'I took a chance,' he said, 'taking it from your desk. I can undo it.'

'No. This is how it is with us.' She kissed him and soon it was all she wore as they wrecked his bed again.

§

That evening, the bo'sun and the captain rowed to a nearby reef in a skiff. A tug on the line and they brought up a fat, red snapper.

As the captain rowed back to shore, the bo'sun killed the fish quickly and sent its entrails back to the sea. He thanked the fish the way his grandmother taught him. When he'd heard about the girl whispering to a dying tuna, he told the captain on the skiff, he had been reminded of his nana and how she did that too.

Back on the beach, the men grilled the snapper over orange coals. Bats bickered in a palm tree, their wings so large, they sounded like someone shaking a tablecloth. The captain opened a bottle of whiskey.

The bo'sun rolled tobacco grown on the island in thin white paper, saying, 'She's wounded. You sure about this?'

'You don't smoke. What is this?'

'Buck's night. Got smoko. Whiskey. And as your best man, I gotta ask if you're crazy. You just buried someone as close to you as your dad and now you're gettin hitched.'

'I know what I'm doing.'

The bo'sun laughed. 'People don't know shit before they get married.' He turned the fish on the coals. The flesh spit. 'My nana raised me while my parents tried to kill each other. And just look at yours.'

The captain sank his feet to his ankles into the cooler sand below, the whiskey warming. He passed the bottle. The bo'sun divided the fish onto banana leaves.

'Listen to me.' The bo'sun reclined on the sand, burping into his fist. 'You just got a big shock. My nana told me, "Never make big decisions when the house is on fire."'

'The fire's out. Besides, I made this one a while ago.'

'Oh yeah, you've known her, what? Five months?'

'Almost six. It happens.'

'And you're not crazy?'

'No.'

'Remember I asked. Cheers, mate.' The bo'sun raised the bottle.

Later that night, the captain returned to his cabin and touched the shared door. It was closed. She was in her own bed the night before their wedding.

His feet were sandy, his belly warm with snapper and whiskey. He couldn't resist. One kiss. Then back to his cabin.

Soundless, the latch turned in his hand and he stepped into her dark cabin. The dog bumped against his knees. He crept to her bedside and leaned to kiss her cheek.

There was a creak.

Serpent's Wake

A flash in the darkness; a squall of bedclothes. The dog barked. A blow to the face sent the captain into the wall. Words sprayed from his mouth as he clutched both his eye and his head.

The desk light awoke.

Naked and splayed as a spider over her desk, she clung to the wall all fingers and elbows and toes. A loop of bed sheet hung from her.

He yelped: 'It's me!'

The dog leapt about.

The captain snarled before another string of words escaped. He looked at her, white, frozen. 'I came to kiss you! To kiss you!'

She found her breath and dropped her shoulders and brought her feet to the floor. She held the captain. 'I smelled whiskey and smoke.'

He squeezed her. 'Celebration!'

In the infirmary, the ship's doctor was in a set of striped pajamas with her glasses on her head. She said, 'You're not even married yet.'

The captain pressed a bag of ice to his eye.

The doctor turned her. 'You got moxie, kid.'

'And a helluva right hook!' The bo'sun leaned on the door to punch the air. 'She's right for you, bro! She's right!' His laughter echoed up and down the corridor.

§

The following morning, three days after the poet's ashes were sent adrift into that warm sea, the captain stood on the beach. In his dress whites, he squinted at his ship with a swollen eye, the dog grinning at his knee.

The medical student crossed the sand a second time with a bouquet of orchids—this time yellow and pink. She balked, with the most respectful apologies, when she saw the traditional dress that the local women had proposed and wore her best dress instead, a turquoise A-line for special occasions.

The bride descended the gangway on the cook's arm. The poet's ribbon and ginger flowers crowned her hair, which the captain had asked she wear down. Garlands of orchids and two strands of shells covered her breasts; the serpent's mark at the center, canvas under sea glass. A long grass skirt met her ankles. In her hand, she held her father's favorite book, the one that traced the shores of the captain's map: her bouquet.

That morning, a pair of island women had come to her cabin—the old islander's niece and her sister. They laughed as they adjusted the grass skirt; they hugged the girl and whispered motherly things against her hair. As she stood stripped to the waist, they strung flowers over her chest and showed her how to wear the necklaces they'd made: layers of cowrie shells and spokes of mother of pearl. They asked that she give one of the necklaces to their cousin—the doctor's wife—when they saw her again, even though she wasn't sure when that would be. The women went through her clothes; the red and white polka dotted dress a favorite. They found the chocolate and she asked them to take it. They told dirty jokes, she observed, at the door that joined the cabins.

Now on the gangway, the skirt swished. Her hands quivered. The cook placed a hand over hers. 'Not too late to turn back...'

Over her shoulder, the engineer leaned on the deck rail but she looked instead toward the old man's niece below on the sand. She wore the polka dotted dress with a blazing red hibiscus. When she started to sing, the bride started to walk.

She closed her eyes and saw her parents and the poet beside them. When she opened them, she saw the old man and her captain; beside him, the bo'sun. The captain's eyes were brimming and bruised; his clean-shaven straight mouth was stern until, as if he couldn't find the strength to be anyone but the man who had kissed her in the underworld, his smile at last met the maps around his eyes.

§

At dawn, the captain woke her with a kiss. 'Come swim with me.'

She stretched and hooked her legs around his.

'Let me recover before I'm crawling down the stairs. Swim with me.'

'I don't know how.'

'Then it's a good day to learn.'

In the quiet of the early light, the captain took her down to the mirror of water along the beach. They dropped their clothes on the sand and stepped into the sea, warm as their bodies.

'It's easy,' he held her. 'Relax and remember what it's like to fly.'

PART V: PRAYER LABYRINTH

Part V: Prayer Labyrinth

As the captain left the girl to her breakfast on deck, her hair wet from their swim, he slid his fingers across the nape of her neck. Kissed with seawater, she collected toast from the galley and after a moment of hesitating, she sat at the poet's table, beside his empty chair.

She chewed absently, marveling at the sensation that rose from her hips to her shoulders, until she realized the toast tasted of the freezer, even under a puddle of mango jam.

'Ya want breakfast?' the cook called to the dog, who scampered after him for an egg and some mackerel.

The medical student sat with a sigh. 'I'm off.' Her dress was all business—amber, collared and nipped at the waist. She clicked her nails against the table.

'Now?'

'They're waiting for me,' she looked to a large trimaran at the pier, 'but I wanted to thank you for including me in your wedding. I've missed them all back home.'

'Meet us again.'

'I will.' She frowned at the plate. 'That toast is rubbish and you need something richer with all the sex.' She stood and flung the slabs over the side. The student winked and disappeared into the galley. A clang of pots pulsed from the doors; an expletive was followed by a thick pause.

When the medical student emerged, ruffled with an avocado halved in her hand, she smoothed her hair back into its twist. The cook swayed the doorway, ravenous, hands lingering on her waist. He kissed her feverishly. 'You come back anytime now, you hear? I'll slow cook vegetarian feasts fit for a queen!'

She laughed and placed the avocado on the plate before clicking away on her kitten heels.

§

On the bridge, the engineer spat toast into the trash.

The men then reviewed the work schedule, now divided among their skeleton crew. Over the weeks, several able crewmen balked at the trip to the frozen north, taking jobs on other ships. The work detail from the storm damage trickled, with the arrival of replacement parts parsed out to a couple of times a month. The bo'sun would assist the engineer with a camshaft and an injection valve when the parts came, and the cook would help him install the new stove, when that finally showed up as well. They'd been sitting there for over three months, just as the captain had foreseen.

The captain sat at his desk. Behind him, a crowned lion strode the ancient map; before him, he studied a more contemporary chart—aqua blue and webbed with lines. 'When we're ready, it will take about six weeks to make the trip back to my country. We'll pass your country. Do you want to make contact?'

'What? Why? Too many pirates.' The engineer looked past the captain at a laden elephant on the calfskin.

'We're taking the canal. Think about it.' The captain watched his frown.

'There's nothing to think about.'

'What is it?'

The engineer tapped on his empty coffee cup, eyes glazed. 'When I left, many people I once knew left as well.'

The captain sipped cold coffee. 'Isn't there anyone there?'

The engineer rubbed his neck, his face splintering.

The captain rested his mug on the chart. 'There must be someone.'

'I don't know. Maybe someone at my university.'

'Send a message. See what comes back.'

§

On deck, the old islander had come aboard and stopped when he saw the captain's wife standing in the galley doorway. He mentioned his niece, the doctor's wife, and said, 'Please, tell her to come home. She needs to touch her own sand. She needs her people. She can even bring that witchdoctor with her.' He smiled.

She nodded, thinking she'd ask the captain to send a message.

'And you,' he said. 'You need to go back to your own sand too. Dig that snake out the ground.'

At first she was confused, then sunlight glinted off the rail and struck her eyes. A dark cavern gaped on the other side of the world.

He said it again with his eyes: *Find the snake.* The sun was suddenly blinding; the heat coarse as the old man leaned into the stairs.

She left her dog with the cook and retreated to her cabin, shutting the adjoining door. She knew, in some primordial sense, the man's advice was seismic; the very plates of her person would shift if she did what he asked.

She opened to the middle of the poet's book and read: '...the once great beast, gone hollow, bones frail, shrinks, wails at my breast and is stilled with a touch...'

Outside, clouds crept over water, darkening glass.

When late that afternoon, the captain split the room with light, she blinked.

He went to her, cautious. 'What is it?'

He carried her to bed. 'Tell me.'

She whispered, 'I have to ask something of you.'

'Anything.'

'To go back. I have to go back.'

'Yes.'

And he told her that the old man had told him to plan for a cold winter.

§

In a fully functional galley, the cook dished up bacon, eggs and toast to the locksmith, the bo'sun, the ship's doctor, and the engineer. The captain pulled up chairs. The dog waited for his egg besides her.

'We're ready to head out tomorrow,' the captain said, 'I want to thank you all for your hard work and your patience.'

There was a sigh of relief.

'But I still need everyone to stay sane for the next leg. By the time we get to my country, we'll have missed the short summer and it will be cold, so check supply for warm clothes. After we settle the estate, we'll cross the ocean back to my wife's village.' My wife. It still sounded strange and everyone looked at their food. 'After that, if you're interested, we pick up where we left off. Pay raise for anyone who stays; stellar references for anyone who goes.'

Serpent's Wake

'Stellar references!' the bo'sun laughed, waving a hand to decline toast from the cook. 'No one would believe them!'

The ship's doctor slid eggs onto her plate. 'I'd like to stay on.' She bit into her toast then covertly spit it out, covering it with her spoon.

The engineer smeared a slice of toast with butter. 'You know I am staying.'

The captain turned to the cook who turned his back to the stove with a wave.

The locksmith gave bacon to the dog then told the captain: 'Get off it.'

'This bread is bad! Always bad!' the engineer dropped his slice.

'It thawed and refroze a few times with everything, yeah.' The cook slumped into a chair. 'That's the last of it, I swear.'

In the morning, the ship embarked on a long stretch west over a sea peppered with island nations before their northward turn.

'It will be cold,' the captain told her that night in their bed.

She sank against him. 'I'll keep you warm.'

The ship burned love across the sea.

§

'Coffee, tea, butter…' In the galley, the cook rattled off items that they needed, and she wrote as quickly as she could. 'Potatoes, canned tomatoes, garlic, flour, yeast…'

When he finished, she showed him the list. 'Is this all of it?'

'Yep.' He poured coffee and they stood awhile. 'Well, that's done. I'm bored stupid. You got books, don't you?'

She nodded.

'You know,' he said, remembering the medical student, 'she told me I needed to read.'

'She did?'

The cook looked long at the floor then said, 'Here's the thing…' He told her how delicious it was with the student, except for one thing. 'I found out I'm bull's eye ignorant. She said I'm smart but…'

She stopped him, 'But I never finished second grade.'

'That's the point! Who can tell? Help me out here but,' he looked past her, 'can we keep it, like, real quiet?'

She knew it was the bo'sun he was worried about. She said, 'Can you teach me to cook? I lived on honey and toast before I got here.'

'Toast? Can you bake bread? I hate that job and everybody's whinin about it.'

'Yes.' She suddenly felt her mother, close in that galley.

'You'll have to get your hands dirty.'

'When?'

The cook leaned in, 'I'll start the heavy drinkin if I don't get a project. How's now?'

In her cabin, they sat at her desk. The cook fidgeted.

She opened the box etched with roses and brambles. Inside, she found the sack of yeast.

'What ya got?'

'Yeast.'

His face scrunched. 'Um, how old is that?'

'It was my mother's.'

He shook his head. 'In all this damp? The bread won't rise.'

'It always rises.'

'No, it won't,' he scoffed.

'Always.'

Then she handed him her father's book of mythology. He cussed a few words then closed it. 'Nice pictures but no.'

She stood over the books spread out on the bed. 'My father said if I could understand poetry, I could understand anything.' She lifted the poet's book.

'Never read his stuff. I was afraid I wouldn't like it; or worse, I wouldn't understand it.' He opened the book and a tiny moth flew into the room. It circled the desk lamp.

They read into the afternoon, until the cook said he needed a breather and, 'Why don't we test out your mother's magical yeast?'

In the galley, she stirred the yeast into warm water and added sugar. She poured the last of their flour and kneaded the dough on a wooden board, then rolled it into a fat ball, covered it with a towel in a bowl to rest. Later, the crew had piping hot bread with dinner.

'Finally.' The engineer slathered a slice with gravy and left for the bridge.

The bo'sun groaned with pleasure at the table, saying, 'Just like me nana's.'

The next day, the cook and the new galley hand abandoned their secrecy. 'So what if anybody laughs?' He left books open in the galley and read little rum-boiled incantations over steaming pots. While they worked, a third mug of wine was always left untouched at the table before an empty chair.

When they refreshed their stores and got new flour, she baked loaf after loaf—rye, whole meal, rosemary with sea salt—while he taught her to cook things her mother had never seen. Books lay everywhere, supine, parsley and flour kissing pages.

The cook split a strange orange fruit that looked like a dragon's egg. Round black seeds spilled onto his wrist. 'Pawpaw,' he said, a kitchen rag tied on his head. He sliced off a wedge and held it on the end of his knife.

She smelled sunlight, juice dripping. 'Read this,' she pointed to another page.

'The will spits cinders as I purge the wars of men. Hollowed, hallowed, stars and moon have left me; in this labyrinth, one light dies as another ignites…'

The ship's horn pulsed in sets of three and the engineer's voice called for all hands. She and the cook ran from the galley with the dog. Pirate cages and locks and windows were double-checked; fire hoses manned. The ship spun. Shadows slipped across the deck as the ship changed course.

The engineer's voice rang out over speakers: 'All clear. All clear.' They returned to the galley, the dog trailing, panting.

'Now what?' They cook peeled a clove of garlic.

'Mythology,' she said.

'Naw, those crazy names overshoot the mark. Too scary.'

'You just proved you're ready for pirates. You can't be afraid of this.'

He laughed, chopping. 'That was just a drill.'

'Mythology is just a drill.'

He slid the garlic off his knife with his thumb and turned. 'Right. Bring it to me!'

§

After dinner in their quarters, she took the captain straight to their bed, a trail of clothes on the floor. She had cooked one of his favorites: meatballs and gravy that the captain's mother used to make.

After they collapsed into the sheets, the captain pulled a lock of her hair over his upper lip. The hair drooped like the moustache. 'Tell me,' he attempted to maintain a sense of propriety, 'what is going on between you and our cook?'

'What?' She crawled onto his chest.

'I smell bread baking all the time...'

'You mopped your dinner with it.' She leaned into his ear and kissed him, soft as a moth's feather feet treading on glass.

In the bed of arms and legs, sleep softened them and made them edgeless.

The captain, his voice mere breath, spoke of the poet. 'You know what he told me? He said, "When you truly love, there so much more, not less, of you about."'

§

Continuing west through the subtropics, the ship passed through a strait and entered another empty stretch of ocean. Mid-morning, it veered.

The engineer arrived on the bridge, eyeing the captain's wife and the radio in her hand. He asked the captain, 'What is this?'

The captain didn't answer; a radio crackled. He was fixed on the horizon; the calfskin behind him, a banner.

The engineer took up binoculars. The sea was empty. 'We're straying from the shipping lane. Not good. Not here.'

On the ocean plain, a dot appeared. The captain increased the ship's speed without announcing his actions: another break from protocol.

'Are you fit for the bridge?' the engineer blurted, then glared at the young woman on the bridge. 'Is she a part of this?' Through the binoculars, he saw a dank mirage: a battered fishing vessel creased with barnacles and rust. It looked like it couldn't take another storm.

'An SOS,' the captain said. 'Conditions are perfect to have a look.' On the map behind them, a mermaid shielded her eyes; the hunter looked ready, jaw set.

'Send a message to international maritime if you have to, but let someone else handle this.' Urgency rose in his voice. 'We're not equipped...'

'I spoke with a boy.'

'We can get a hundred ships to report it but we cannot go near that vessel!'

The captain handed a list to the engineer. 'Send these coordinates to the rest of these ships. Get them to message maritime now.'

'What if they have guns? They always have guns!'

She saw sweat appear on the man's brow. His fingers were twitching. She saw he was terrified and felt the danger of his terror.

The captain ignored him. 'The boy said it's just him and his brother and one sick old man. The boss is gone.'

'Lies! They're out of water and they want ours!' The engineer pulled a small ring of keys from inside his shirt. 'This is an alley for pirates! Do you know what these people do?' He turned and said, 'What they will do to your wife?' His gaze was vicious.

'Do your job.'

'This is not my job!' The engineer jammed a key into a steel locker that hung on the wall. Inside, rows of charts and maps were neatly slatted but a dummy rivet moved to reveal another keyhole. A small key opened the back of the locker where high-powered rifles stood in a row.

The captain slowed the ship and pointed toward the chatter at the console. 'What are they saying?'

The engineer read that international maritime was inundated with these coordinates. He said, 'Ships are already on their way. It looks like...' he wiped his forehead with his sleeve, 'like almost every ship you contacted reported this vessel?'

The bo'sun walked onto the bridge. 'I'm not one to judge, but you know what that ship looks like to me?'

Behind him, the locksmith crunched his hat in his hands, eying the open rifle locker. 'What the bloody hell...'

The captain told his crewmen about the call, then grasped the engineer's arm. 'I'll go down. You pilot.'

Part V: Prayer Labyrinth

The bo'sun took a box of shells, loaded a rifle and wrapped it in a fire blanket.

The locksmith slung a rifle over his shoulder and closed the locker. 'I'm on the bridge,' he said. 'We might need the crane.'

As the captain clipped a radio to his pocket, he looked at his wife.

Her heart was pounding and the air on the bridge was thick with the men and worry, but she smiled. She had heard the boy's SOS herself and saw a young wolf in a snare, dangling over the sea.

The captain's eyes softened for only a moment before he left the bridge.

She stood at the window, her hand a visor.

The engineer, sweat-soaked at the helm, swung the stern close to the vessel as the captain's instructions poured over the radio. Beside him, the locksmith rested on the controls for the crane.

The engineer snapped at her, 'Get away from the window.'

She slipped behind a blind to watch two teenage boys, emaciated, appear at the stern of the fishing boat. She saw ribs and collarbones and even from this distance, she recognized herself; she imagined what her mother saw the night she had returned. Her eyes burned.

The boys waved long arms; one flapped a dirty towel. A man appeared, clinging to a rail, frail with a mop of gray hair. He was sick; she could see it as he staggered into the wind. He cradled a distended belly with one hand and hung onto a rail with the other. Staying upright against the ocean chop was weakening him.

Below, the captain opened a section of rail as the boys shouted in one panicked stream. He radioed the bridge, conveying what the bo'sun discerned of their words.

The bo'sun was positioned behind a pillar, aiming the cloaked rifle and holding a radio. The boys were from a string of islands cored by poverty and cyclones, where money from illegal fighting could feed a man's extended family for a year. The bo'sun radioed the bridge: 'Yeah. They're sayin hurry.'

Both boys leapt into the water. The towel slipped away on the waves.

The bo'sun radioed, 'They're committed.'

The captain threw down a ladder and two lifesavers. The bo'sun stowed the rifle within reach: in the gunwale of a lifeboat.

The swimmers lunged, the water sloppy between the ships. One boy went under then tugged himself into a lifesaver. The captain pulled. The other snagged the rope with his hand and pulled the ring over his shoulder. They snatched at the ladder and half-climbed and were half-hoisted on deck. The first boy collapsed against the ship's doctor; the second panted on his knees. Despite their short dip in the sea, they were exhausted, malnourished, filthy; their skin crusted with grime and fish scales.

She ran down the stairs to assist, the engineer hurling abuse at her as the door swung shut.

She arrived to help the ship's doctor, who was throwing towels around both boys and saying 'Good lord, I think they're twins!'

Across the gap, the old man stared at the bo'sun. Swift, broken conversation ensued between a boy, the bo'sun and the captain.

The bo'sun said, 'The old man covers for the boss. Kidnapped lifer. Kids got to the radio because he's sick. He thinks we're gonna gut him but the boss is gonna feed him to the sharks when he finds the boys gone.'

The captain looked out at the man and frowned at the swirling gap between the ships.

The bo'sun said, 'Stuff him. Let him answer to his boss.'

The captain put his radio to his lips and turned from the wind. He waved up to the bridge, motioning to swing closer and lower the crane. He collected a dripping rope and lifesaver. He threaded it through a chain.

The captain said, 'Tell him no one's hurting anyone.'

The bo'sun glowered. 'I don't know how to say that in anybody's language.'

The captain waited for the stern to swing tighter and threw the lifesaver, which slung over the rail beside the man.

The old man assessed the ring as the crane reached over his head. He studied the captain, his head sinking against one shoulder as he clung to the rail. He could barely stand.

The captain stood beside his wife at the open rail. His gaze was steady over the sounds of the sea; he met the eyes of an old man bereft of everything, even his capacity for cruel obedience. In a voice deep as the pounding sunlight and red as coral, the captain shouted in broken bits of a shared language. He asked him to come aboard and said he would be treated honorably.

The man swayed as he looked from the captain to the bo'sun to the young woman at the rail.

The captain muttered, 'I don't know if he has the strength. He could let go.'

She took one of the rings the boys had used and held it up. She stepped into it, pulled it around her hips, and held the rope up with her hands.

The old man smiled crookedly at her demonstration. He staggered and maneuvered the ring under his slight hips. The crane swung the man over the sea right into the captain's arms.

'The infirmary,' the doctor said, a boy coughing raggedly in her arms.

'And the hell outta here,' the bo'sun said as the engineer leaned the engines into full.

§

When she reached the infirmary, the engineer called down to say reports were pouring in, ships were all over the vicinity, and three relief agencies were lined up to receive them. He requested the doctor's presence on the bridge to liaise with them.

The girl offered blankets while the doctor reproached the bo'sun for scowling at the old man. 'He's not long for this world,' she motioned to his distended abdomen. 'It's so advanced, I can smell it. Go find clean clothes in supply.' She held up a camera and took photos of all three of them.

When the bos'un returned with a stack of clothes, t-shirts and shorts, the old man nodded sternly at him.

One boy called out, putting up his fists and motioning toward the old man. 'He saw you fight long time ago! He says you're a killer!'

The bo'sun broke a raucous smile. 'Go on...'

The boy answered for him, 'He was scared to get on your boat!'

The bo'sun laughed as the old man pulled a gummy smile.

The doctor handed washcloths to the girl, 'I need to get to the bridge. Can you start cleaning them up?'

She nodded and filled a basin.

One of the boys took a washcloth from her and spoke to the bo'sun in a mix of languages. She wrote it down for the doctor. He said the big boss was desperate for women and left the old man in charge.

The man shrugged.

The boy said it wasn't hard for them to get on the radio. The boss left their coordinates in pencil and they'd learned SOS from black market movies.

When the bo'sun asked how they ended up on the boat, the boy said they were promised jobs in hotel construction but had been trapped on that boat catching fish for months. They were worried about their families and with the help of the bo'sun, She transcribed their details.

The bos'un handed a clean set of the poet's pajamas to the old man, who touched the burgundy silk to his nose. The bo'sun said to the girl, 'You know whose these are?'

'Just another poem. He left them everywhere.' She spilled a basin of brown water into the sink.

The bo'sun asked the boys, 'Did he beat you?' and pointed to the old man, but the boys laughed.

'Big boss.' One boy made a fist into a gun and raised the other and let the butt come down slowly on his brother's back. She found months of wounds leering back at her; some old, some fresh, all encrusted with fish scales. When the doctor arrived, she took more photos and opened ointment.

The girl sponged the boy's backs and the tiniest of the fish scales drifted into the air as she worked. She rinsed the sponge and scales lit the sink; the curves of the porcelain soon swirled with rainbows. She soaped another washcloth and scrubbed their shoulders. Scales fell to the floor. The boys put their heads in the sink and the doctor doused them with tea tree oil to kill the lice and gave them combs.

'Let's get everyone on a drip.' The doctor prepared three IV bags. Both boys continued to wash while the doctor inserted a cannula into the backs of their hands.

The old man, however, refused to let anyone touch him. He clung to those pajamas, buried his face in them until the doctor sat at the edge of the bed and convinced him to let her inspect his hair.

The girl wrung away dirt as a multitude of tiny fish scales stuck to the walls, the dire smell fading.

When the captain appeared in the doorway, the boys leaned forward, lifting their bowls of broth from their laps with a smile. He saw the old man, clean and in the poet's pajamas, put up a hand, an IV lead trailing. The whole infirmary sparkled, spectral and iridescent with fish scales.

§

When the captain arrived back on the bridge, the engineer was standing at the helm. 'Something came in with the messages,' he said as he hung onto the console. 'I did what you said. I sent a message home. A woman answered. A woman!'

He continued, 'She said my professor retired and she replaced him. She knows who I am. She said that the one who did this...' he touched his arms, 'was found floating in the river three years ago. She invited me to come home.'

'What will you do?'

'I don't know.' The engineer's mouth was visibly parched.

The captain handed him a glass of water. On the map behind him, one man devours a snake, another wearing nothing but a helmet rides a stag.

§

A vessel flying a relief agency's colors met the ship in calm waters at dusk along the shipping lane. The boys left with a stack of sandwiches while the old man didn't lift his head from a stretcher.

That night in bed, the captain held his bride.

He was silent until he said, 'I want to tell you something terrible.'

He told her how his father, five years ago, had crawled to the infirmary when everyone was asleep and shoved a box of morphine into his pajamas. His father had come back to these very quarters and filled a syringe with enough to kill three men but his eyes and hands were so bad, he couldn't find a vein. The captain had found him slumped on the bed tearing at himself, blood everywhere; and when the old man looked up, he broke a glass and threatened to slice his throat if his son left to get the doctor. He shouted and threatened,

Serpent's Wake

his hands shaking blood onto the sheets: 'I'm leaving this goddamned world tonight, you son of a bitch! We can do it messy or we can do it neat!' Until the plunger fell, under the captain's thumb.

She held her husband tightly. And when the room was still, she stroked his temple and said: 'Stay with me.'

§

The ship headed north along a coastline that had exported ivory until it nearly disappeared. They passed railway stations and oil refineries and harbored after the captain negotiated a sandy berth at the edge of an industrial port, intentionally within the engineer's country, and close to his capital city.

Down in the galley, the bo'sun clapped the cook on the back. 'Let's go shoppin.' They headed ashore to procure twenty cases of cigarettes: bribes to smooth all points of the next canal.

The engineer paced the deck. The captain brought him coffee and gave him a job. He said, 'We've been asked to take a few passengers through the canal tomorrow. Lock everything up. Tell the crew.'

When the cook and the bo'sun returned, the engineer asked them to run a security check. He then told the doctor to triple-door any drugs and lock up the infirmary until the ship was clear. He asked the locksmith to triple-check all locks. During his own security checks, he saw that one of the rifles was missing from the bridge cabinet and remembered that the bo'sun had stowed it in the gunwale of the life raft on deck.

He found the gun and left it right where it was.

§

The following morning, the ship sliced up the coast, crossed a lean sea, and met a convoy lining up for a desert canal. She and her dog joined the captain on the bridge. Cartons of cigarettes left the ship and itinerant passengers, taken as a courtesy along the canal, came and went.

It would be hours before they entered the new sea and the captain traced their anticipated route upon the calfskin map. Just off-center on the map, a circular maze comprised the heart of an island: it shone like a bewildered eye.

Part V: Prayer Labyrinth

'We're heading this way,' he gestured, 'hopefully bypassing the labyrinth.'

She remembered one of the poet's lines: 'in this labyrinth, one light dies and another ignites,' and said: 'A labyrinth is just another form of prayer.'

'Not this one.' He looked into the eye. 'It once held a monster that ate kids.'

'Blood sacrifice.' She remembered the story from her father's book. 'A monster—half man, half bull.'

Below, the engineer and bo'sun reported to the bridge by radio. They checked documents, searched for weapons, and kept passengers on deck. The captain watched them all, but it was the engineer who worried him.

Long sleeves covered his arms as the engineer circled a table of five young men from his country, his eyes steely. After a few rebuffed attempts, the men, barely out of their teens, stopped engaging him, finished their coffee and waited for lunch.

'He's troubled,' she said. The captain did not answer. 'Let me go down and help.' She tied up her hair.

'Radio first,' he said.

The cook answered on his handheld and welcomed her help.

She kissed the captain and left the bridge with her dog.

The young men on deck smiled at her as she cleared their coffee mugs, a sight after the engineer's scowls. Arms folded, he stood against the rail like a prison guard and clearly disapproved of her appearance on deck.

As she pushed on the heavy galley doors with two fists of odd mugs, she let the dog go first but tripped. The galley doors were usually hooked open but were closed for safety along the canal. Two mugs slipped, hitting the deck. Pieces rolled.

One of the young men stood from his table and stooped to gather the scattered shards. He followed her into the galley and the door swung shut behind them.

The engineer, watching from a corner of the deck, lowered his head. He slipped his arm into the lifeboat, drew out the rifle, and carried it close to his thigh.

She saw this from the window in the galley door, over the shoulder of the passenger. She took the shards from him as she heard the captain call out for the engineer over the radio.

The door swung open and the engineer shadowed the doorway. Past him on deck, the four young men stood.

The rifle leveled upon the passenger.

Stillness. A radio crackled. The captain's voice again.

She took the last of the broken ceramic from the passenger and pulled him behind her, saying, 'I broke a couple of mugs,' but she saw in the engineer's eyes that he couldn't hear a word.

She and the passenger slowly sank to the floor, hands up.

The cook grabbed his handheld radio and shouted.

That's when the dog looked up and saw the gun. He leapt upon the engineer. The man fell backwards, finger on the trigger.

The dog hit the floor and returned, teeth bared, aiming for the engineer's arm.

A shot rang.

The dog hit the galley floor hard, tail wagging furiously. She crawled to him. He lay on his side, each breath heaved; all four legs stiff as arrows. A pool of blood grew under his chin. She searched for the wound but found his lashes quivering. He didn't make a sound but he was leaving.

She found the crush on the hidden side of his once beautiful face and planted a hand over the flow but there was no stemming it. Red ran through her fingers quickly soaking her clothes, the floor, but that tail kept wagging and wagging and wagging. She hugged the dog tightly. The tail slowed, then stopped.

She slipped the dog from her lap and stood over the engineer, clear as a demon. She wrenched the rifle from his hands.

The bo'sun heaved the engineer to his feet by a shoulder and dragged him through the galley doors. The four young men took in the scene, terrified, but relieved when they saw their friend.

Radio static.

The captain's voice called. The cook reached for his handheld: 'The kid just wanted to help! The poor dog, man, the poor dog!'

She pushed through the door, ran onto the deck and hurled the weapon overboard.

§

'You drugged him?' the captain asked the doctor. His engineer dozed, one wrist handcuffed to a bedrail.

'Protocol,' she said over her report, 'plus I always wanted to.'

'How is he?'

'A mess. He's getting a full psych eval when things cool down. I recommend counseling sessions with a colleague of mine. I've already contacted him.'

The captain rubbed his face. 'How?'

'By radio. Right here from the infirmary.'

'And you've got the dog?'

She tilted her head toward the cool storage. 'I'm just glad no one else is in there.'

The captain closed the curtain around the engineer, creating the suggestion of privacy. The engineer opened his eyes to slits.

The captain sat.

The engineer pushed his head back into the pillow. 'I am so sorry.'

'You could have killed someone.'

The engineer covered his face with the elbow.

'You know that rifle should have gone back to the bridge during the security check.'

'I hate this canal. Drifters. Always drifters. Anyone could be on board.'

'We told them you were fresh from combat.' The captain squeezed the balloon on a blood pressure monitor. 'We're lucky they believed us.'

'I need time. Don't rush me. There is a terror that touches a man... one he cannot control.'

'He will.'

The engineer looked at the ceiling. 'I will be so good in my head if no one rushes me.'

'What rushed you?'

'You did. Making me send messages. Women asking me to come home. Taking me so close to home like you did.'

'I understand my part now and I'm sorry. But you're unstable. A liability.'

'I know.'

'That's a start. You're confined to the infirmary, on report and under full medical supervision. We'll both decide if you stay or go.'

Serpent's Wake

'Are you going to shoot me in the arse?'
'That's only for bullshit. This is real.'

§

The ship berthed under darkness at the captain's home village. It was late summer in the northern hemisphere, but it looked and felt like winter. The crew gathered on the bridge to watch the heavens roll in chartreuse fits.

The ship's doctor said, 'I've never been this far north. Why would you ever leave this?'

'Because it's always freezing.' The captain smoothed his beard.

The following day, the captain and the engineer left to meet the poet's estate manager. A driver took them to the office where they discussed the poet's will. The captain, clearly uncomfortable despite the warmth of the lawyer's reception and hot tea, asked, 'He left funds for an annual scholarship? How on earth will we choose a poet for that each year?'

'Wait for the letters,' the lawyer said. 'Death ends nothing for poets.'

'Who should read them?'

'Do you have a bookish type on board?' the lawyer asked.

The engineer nudged the captain, 'His wife.'

Back in the galley, the captain and the engineer approached her with their proposal. The cook sliced potatoes. She listened to the captain as she cut little crosses into the hard skin of chestnuts. She wiped her hands.

The captain said, 'You know he would have chosen you.'

'Both of us,' she said, as she stood beside the cook and took off her apron.

The cook laughed. 'What the hell do I know?'

'Both of us.'

The captain agreed.

Later when the galley was quiet, she pulled a tray of roasted chestnuts from the oven. Burning her fingers, she peeled a chestnut, the steam rolling like fronds, and handed it to the cook.

He said, 'I see what you're doing.'

'What am I doing?'

Part V: Prayer Labyrinth

'Making me use the booksmarts you gave me.'
'I didn't give you anything. You did this all yourself.'

§

The ship stayed a few weeks in the cold, with the backdrop of a churned sea. After a trip to the attorney, she and her husband bought thick coats and boots and gloves lined with fleece for the remaining crew. She picked out a few things for the locksmith, since everything he wore was older than memory and suited to warmer climes. In recent weeks, he buried himself in cotton layers, his old bones protesting as he moved. She found a knitted sweater patterned around the neck and a pair of lined woolen trousers.

On the way back to the ship, they walked through the old birch forest and found the graveyard where his mother's headstone stood. In the silence of light snowfall, the wood held them.

When they returned to the ship, she left the new clothes beside the locksmith's door, under the sign that read: DANGER—KEEP OUT in four languages. She was halfway down the corridor when he called out: 'What's this, ay, missy? Come in! Come in!'

She'd never been in his quarters.

'Get these for me, did ya?' He squeezed the sweater with both hands as an involuntary tear fell from one eye. He ignored it.

'Have a seat.' He pointed to a chair in his tidy cabin. He opened a drawer, hugging the sweater as he searched. 'You know the medical students we get? Look what one of them gave me.' He pulled a bundle wrapped in tattered tissue from the drawer. 'Bookmarks. Real lace. Made them herself. People don't know how to make lace anymore.'

She noticed how tenderly he rewrapped the bookmarks and how he hadn't any books.

'This tea,' he rifled to the back of a cupboard and wiped a box with his sleeve. 'This is pretty posh.' The box was still sealed.

He pulled the sweater over his head. 'It's so warm!'

'Good,' she said. 'The crossing is going to be freezing.'

'Aye, missy. Big ocean ahead.'

The next morning, they set sail down the coast then across the great ocean for the next twelve days.

§

She pulled scones from the oven. The cook and the bo'sun sat at the table, pancakes and eggs before them. She piled the scones onto a plate with jam and a dollop of cream.

The locksmith sat in his new clothes. 'I'll have to let out me new trousers if you keep pushin these!' She regretted not purchasing a second pair of pants.

'We get in late tomorrow,' the engineer said in the galley. He was still under the ship doctor's strict observation and restricted to the light duties but took breakfast with the crew.

He stirred his coffee. 'We're all to stay on board as your port's gone sour.' He explained that only the captain was taking her inland. 'Winter came early for them, so it will be much like the climate we just left. The whole region has fallen into depression and religious fanaticism. Feels like home.'

The cook had to ask, 'Did you just make a joke?'

She left the table and cleaned the sink.

The cook stood beside her. 'You're from strong people. They'll come good again. It's the way of the world.'

The bo'sun snorted, 'Who brought the philosopher?' but the cook ignored him.

Through the window, she saw the color of the sea, gray as wet slate.

§

Darkness.

Crushing weight.

A rippling force grappled her abdomen and she saw that fearful face locked upon her. Her fingers searched for a hold. She gouged at the gleam of its eyes. Her legs kicked in its gullet. Its mouth full, the serpent dislocated its jaw to draw her further inside and as it wrangled its lips, its words unhinged across her hips: 'My love...'

She kicked harder; thrashing now.

It spoke again: a rumble, a greedy contortion of the captain. 'My love...'

And she found herself at their cabin door, sheets about her legs, clawing for the handle.

The captain's arms encircled her. His beard brushed her cheek as she let herself be taken back to bed.

§

The ship berthed as sunrise threw rose gold across a frigid sea. On deck, she buried her nose into her coat and saw the old man in the lighthouse extinguish the lamp. Almost home.

That morning, the captain paid double what he should have to rent a truck from an ancient sailor with one gray eye. As the sailor limped ahead to push the snow off the hood with a broom, she glanced at scorched women hiking the wharves. A train whistle screamed.

The cook loaded the dog's body into the back of the truck as its engine turned over with a splutter. He leaned on the window and said, 'Good luck, darlin. We'll be waitin for you. Don't look so sad. Lots of ports go bad this time of year.'

The captain turned up the heater, which just blew cold.

She took off her gloves as they rounded the corner where the mariner's pub stood charred, a cage of broken rafters.

The captain pulled off a glove and squeezed her hand. The truck creaked along like everything was loose. They followed the mountain road, most of the time in silence.

When the doctor and his wife came out to greet them, the smell of breakfast—apple crumble and chicory—flooded the cold air. The doctor shouted: 'Welcome, welcome!' just as the curtains of the village pub across the street were drawn.

He said, 'Winter hit us harsh and early. Come in!'

The doctor's wife took her by the arm and led her into the kitchen where she put her hands on her shoulders. 'Oh!' The woman's eyes flashed. 'Now there's a surprise!' and the young woman assumed it was the honeymoon blush.

After breakfast, the captain unrolled a map in the sitting room and determined to head out the following morning. A fire crackled and the windows were etched with frost.

Well into the afternoon, the men consulted the map and queried her as the doctor produced his notes from the night of her return. She conversed with the crows of memory and the path of the winter sun. The men sketched her passage: her river crossing, her encounter with the trapper, her movement across the frozen lake, and the hunter's camp. She felt the hunger of dogs and snow beneath bare feet. Darkness fell as her journey swept over paper. A heaviness grew in her chest and her mouth began to water. Quickly, she excused herself for the bathroom.

When she opened the door, the doctor's wife handed her a glass of water. 'You're pregnant, dear.'

'No...' She hadn't considered it. 'Just telling this story...'

'I say you're four to six weeks.' She reached out to smooth a strand of indigo hair. 'Are you up for this?'

'No one's ever asked that. Not once.'

'Well, you're pregnant. My grandmother and my mother could tell. It runs in the family.'

She reached for the woman. 'Please don't say anything.'

'Dear girl. I held my beautiful little secrets for months. My husband, a doctor no less, had no idea. But then, I didn't go leaping into caves.'

She led her to the kitchen where the kettle was boiling an arch into the air. The men's voices drifted from the sitting room.

'Take our truck,' she said. 'That thing you hired will die out there. Please. Especially since you're both insisting on doing this on your own.'

The doctor's wife opened her cupboards and filled a satchel. 'Tea for nausea. Enriched flatbread. Try it.' She snapped off a corner. 'Nibble. And you'll need protein. Trust your cravings. There's dried meat in here too—I know—but I made it myself. From a good farmer: my son. I taught him to give them a little whiskey before he takes them home. Don't eat to live anymore. You're making a person.' The woman tore off a strip and gave it to the girl who put it to her lips and handed it back, shaking her head.

'Maybe later. And when you get back, recover here. And of course, this.' She pulled a sheathed blade from her apron and slid it into the bag. 'My uncle—I believe you two have met—dispatched a saltwater crocodile that killed three children on my island with this. It's blessed by a holy man.'

That's when the girl remembered. 'I have something for you too.' She found her bag and held up one of the necklaces from her wedding.

'They want you to come home.'

She lifted the string over the woman's head and draped it around her neck, shells rattling; her eyes lost to the hot trade winds of her island. She held the woman's hand. 'Why didn't you tell me they were your people?'

'I wanted to go where there were no snakes.' The woman cradled the shells, touching them to her cheek.

§

As the captain and his wife lay in a guest bed at the doctor's house that night, she nuzzled him but he felt clammy.

'What?' she asked.

'Landsick. Can't remember the last time I slept in a bed that didn't move.'

She gave him the ginger tea that the doctor's wife had made for her.

Propped on one elbow in the bed, he said, 'You're challenging me. I see it with every step. You're growing me,' before he fell asleep.

In the morning, the men packed provisions into the doctor's truck while she pulled on her boots and touched a hand to her belly. She looked up to find the doctor's wife wearing the necklace from her island.

'Listen,' she said, 'we're taking your dog to the farm for you. Please, be careful.'

The necklace shuddered with a distant tide as they embraced.

Departing the village, they traced a frozen dirt track, then an ice fishing trail where the snow was dry and churned like dust under the tires.

The captain revved the engine, tires clawing across snow. He breathed: 'This is a good truck.'

By the afternoon, they made camp on the other side of the frozen lake. A greedy fire melted a circle in the snow. The captain studied the map. 'I say it's around here.' He pointed to a ridge in the distance, 'But there's a lot of ground to cover...'

Darkness fell and she nibbled flatbread. It was a cloudless night with a haloed moon, nearly full. Far away, wolves howled and she recognized each voice.

Serpent's Wake

By the fire, the captain wrapped his arms around her. He watched her reach absently for a strip of dried meat. She pulled at it with her teeth, engrossed by the flames until together, they made up a bed in the back of the truck.

At dawn, she wiped the frost from the window and saw a white wolf standing at the edge of the camp. She pulled on some boots and slipped out the door, wrapped in a blanket.

The wolf sniffed the air. He limped toward the ridge the captain had pointed out the night before and looked at her again.

She turned to see her husband watching from the truck. She motioned: 'Let's go.'

The truck followed wolf prints along a forest clearing and veered toward the mountains. An eagle soared, a circling speck.

She put her hand to the cold glass. 'We're close,' she said, hoping with a quiet dread that she could find her way, that she could trust her memory and wouldn't get lost, or worse. When the trees parted, she saw the solitary oak. Beyond the tree, a curved horizon lay before them: a woman lying on her back contemplating eternity. A belly of snowy pines, a breast of stone, a chin and a face rose in snowy, rounded peaks.

The great mountain woman turned her head. Snow slid down her cheek.

'Here,' she said, opening the door to the oak. She slipped off the seat and stepped across roots awash with wolf prints.

In the distance, the mountain resumed her repose.

She traversed the clearing to find the tumble of stone cloaked in a wall of snow. She pulled her hands from her heavy coat and pushed at the drift until it collapsed.

'Gloves!' the captain put her hands to his mouth. 'Too cold, my love.' His words hung in the air where an entrance expanded.

And so with ropes and torches and two rifles from the ship, they crept into the cavern, into the cold, cold earth and began their descent. She led, a sphere of light trembling ahead of them.

'How far?' the captain murmured, crouching behind her.

'Far.'

'It should be asleep,' he said. 'Snakes can't do cold.'

'Snakes can't do what it did to me.' She paused.

With the light from the entrance fading behind them, she shined her torch on a stony wall and found four streaks from four dirty fingers: the grimy ripple of a snake.

He touched a gloved finger. 'You did that.'

'Yes.'

'Are you all right?'

'No,' she laughed a little, shivering, and he held her in his warmth.

'You don't have to do this,' he said. 'Let me go ahead and come back. I'll tell you what I see.'

She kissed his mouth and led the way.

They were forced to their knees in the dim light, shuffling along the descent. Moths fluttered in torchlight as the passage tightened. They moved onto their bellies and elbows as they scooted through spider webs down, down, down into the earth.

The captain cursed in his language then said to her heels, 'Now I understand…what happened…on the stairs of the cathedral.'

'This is the easy part,' she said.

Occasionally, they paused to rest. He placed his hands on her calves for a moment then they resumed their crawl until there it was, the dull gape of the cavern before her. An opening dawned in the lamplight.

She whispered under her arm, 'Here,' and struggled for calm, acutely aware of both the presence in the cave and the one in her belly.

'It's different this time,' he whispered. 'I'm with you.'

One after the other, they entered the cavern and knelt side by side, sweating now.

She shined her jittering torch, carefully unfolding the underworld in segments. The walls were seamed with streaks of milky turquoise blue.

'Looks like an old mine,' he whispered. 'That's copper ore.'

She searched. The space compounded. She saw that it was actually beautiful in the light with its rivers of deep blue cutting across stone here and there but her beam swept deliberately until it came to rest on the farthest wall of the cavern.

Her breath halted.

There, at the edge of the torchlight, was the serpent: coil upon coil, like fat seams in stone casting voluptuous shadows. A thick, flat face rested on its curves, black scales dim under a thick layer of dust: its eyes set straight upon them.

Serpent's Wake

The captain aimed his rifle.

She steeled herself, every muscle taut, her heart skipped as her rifle pointed at the place between its eyes. She waited for that great black fork to slide across its heavy lips.

But it didn't.

The captain moved into a crouch. Slowly, he approached the beast, rifle steady.

For the girl watching, panic rose to creative heights as she imagined him struck, felled, dragged across the ground with an unforgettable look on his face. She opened her mouth but her words had gone.

His back was to her, obscuring the face of the serpent now. The rifle shifted in her arms.

In the tricky light, was there movement?

Did a shadow inflate?

She scrambled in tremors to her feet.

She hit her head on the stony ceiling.

A handful of shells rattled in her pocket.

The captain, close now, lowered his weapon.

He wiped a gloved hand across a coil.

She threw up a hand to stop him.

She choked: her mouth a dry well.

The captain, inches from the beast's sunken eyes, turned to her. He removed a glove. 'It's dead.' He touched its lips and pulled.

She craned, wobbling.

'Your hair,' he marveled in the light. He pulled and pulled and pulled. 'So much of your hair. Look. Maybe…you killed it?'

She couldn't speak.

He pulled more hair from its lips. Strands hung from his palm.

She couldn't hear or see the captain anymore.

She yanked off her gloves.

She pulled the knife from her satchel and unsheathed a serrated blade: the one blessed by a holy man; the one that killed a child-eating crocodile.

She touched the serpent: cold leather.

She traced her fingers along its face to the base of its skull. With all of her strength, she drove the knife straight into its hide. She braced for a reflex, a movement of any kind, a protest.

Nothing.

She began to saw through flesh, using her whole body to rock the blade back and forth; a fierce, rending sound that echoed through the cavern.

Eyes stinging now, she felt the captain's beside her, offering the handle of his father's axe. She took it from him. With three smart strikes, the serpent's head fell from its resting place: a dry thunderclap.

He drew a large hessian sack from his pack, cut it and wrapped as much of the head as would fit. He bound it round and round and round with rope, and tied a hitch.

When he looked up, he found her aiming a torch into the animal's gullet. She reached an arm into the darkness.

He saw something shining and bent to the ground. She took a silver bell hewn by her father, silenced with dirt and turned it between her fingers. Reaching deep inside the cavernous gullet, she placed the bell against the swell of a rib. She rested her forehead on the snake's flesh and finally, she blessed it.

§

Early that evening, when the truck stopped in front of the doctor's home, she saw faces in the pub windows. The door swung open and the barmaid ran into the cold; apron around her hips, arms hugging her body to keep warm.

The captain muttered, 'What's the plan?'

The barmaid crossed the street.

They stepped out of the truck, and the captain opened the back door.

The barmaid took in the full height of the captain. 'Find it? Whole town knows you went to go get it.'

The captain pulled on the ropes until the hessian let go and the serpent's face appeared, nearly filling the back of the truck.

The barmaid put her knuckles to her teeth. 'I always believed you. Everyone's going to want to buy that off you.'

The doctor and his wife hurried down the steps, pulling on their coats.

The doctor said, 'It's prehistoric!'

His wife frowned. 'Where is it going?'

The pub doors banged. The hunter appeared in his black woolen coat, hair and beard longer now. Under his arm, he held a large gray form. In the light wind, it expanded. He moved slowly, considering the captain.

The captain cloaked his words in his language, asking, *What shall I do with him?* His gloves squeaked around fists.

She touched his arm.

The snakeskin whipped along behind the hunter, inflated to full length along the street. Passersby stopped to stare over their scarves. As the snakeskin whipped, it splintered, pieces filling the air like snow.

The hunter stopped at the back of the truck. He handed the mouth of the skin to her and looked casually into the truck. 'Didn't you just go and get that bastard...' He reached a bare hand and she watched his mottled fingers touch the vast scales of its face.

The barmaid shivered. 'Set your price. People are gonna come from all over to see that.' She jogged back to the pub and watched from the pub.

The captain rolled up the skin and handed it to the doctor. His wife shrank from it.

'Where's the rest of it?' the hunter said.

The captain dropped a hand on his shoulder, a bear paw. 'There are miles of it if you want to see for yourself. Looked like an abandoned mine.' He tapped an X on their map and handed it to the hunter. 'It's way, way down. You have to get on your knees.'

The hunter examined the map with an uncomfortable groan. 'Right.' He shifted away from the captain's touch and turned to her. 'I thought you made it all up. I called you a liar.'

'You called me worse than that,' she said. 'It's yours.'

The captain looked sharply at her.

The doctor's wife looked relieved. 'Oh thank goodness.'

'Mine?' The hunter raised his hands in protest.

'I'm sorry about your fingers,' she took hold of his hand. He jerked his fingers but she held on. 'You showed them the skin. Please take them the head.'

§

From the window, she watched steam veil the pub windows. She studied the faces that came and went; even old people with canes and children in mittens.

The captain asked, 'Are you coming to bed?'

'Soon.' She recognized the priest and the trapper, scarves flapping, as they swung the pub door and noise flew out again. She kissed her captain, asleep now, ran downstairs and across the snowy street barefoot. Her feet stung.

She opened the pub door. A hush fell and a sea of faces turned. The pub owner popped up from behind the bar, cheeks flushed, hair a peaked fright. On the wall, right over the hunter's concave shoulders at the bar, the serpent's great head hung.

An old woman sat at a table and broke the silence, her yawning grandchild perched in her lap. 'What a horrible thing,' she smiled. 'Wouldn't miss this for all the world!'

The priest and the trapper stood beside the hunter. The trapper was pink-eyed and pallid. The priest said: 'God does love an abomination.'

The trapper called out, 'Where are your shoes?'

She approached him.

The pub owner slowed a beer tap to listen. The barmaid placed a tray of dirty glasses onto the bar.

The trapper crunched his hat in his hands. 'Tell me what good this is.' He took hold of her arm and pulled her behind the bar, just under the creature's face.

She looked at the knuckles of his grip.

'It's filthy. What are we supposed to do with this?'

She saw the sleepy child resting her cheek on her grandmother, watching everything.

'Why would you bring it here?' The trapper shook her. 'It's a devil!'

The hunter stirred. 'Oh shut up.' He leaned on a fist. 'Devils never hand over their heads.'

She gently placed her hand around his.

'Look at that little girl over there.' The trapper squeezed harder. 'How do we know you didn't just bring it with you? How do we know it's not some trick?'

The hunter chimed in: 'The rest sits in an abandoned mine past the lake. I'll show you, if you're game to get on your knees.'

Serpent's Wake

The pub door opened with an icy gust and the mayor whipped off his gloves, the police chief beside him. With a backward glance, the hunter swayed on his barstool.

The mayor rubbed his hands in the warmth and looked casually at the serpent's head. 'It's all over now. We can finally lay this to rest. We have our friends and neighbors to thank…'

While the mayor worked the room, she whispered to the trapper: 'The world has its monsters. We were just children when we met ours.'

'We should burn it!'

'Turning it into ash won't erase it.' She peeled his fingers from her arm. 'Take away all the fear. Take away all the mess it made and everything it stole and what's left? We are. Let everyone see that. Darkness dies. We don't.'

The trapper frowned, clenching his fists. 'You and your wolves. Your blue hair! Your bare feet! Maybe you're the monster! I'm telling the chief of police to detain you!'

'Wolves do what they want. You must know that by now. And my hair,' she held up a shining tress, 'seems to be staying this way. My feet are freezing and the police already spoke to me.'

'They did?'

'Listen.'

The mayor congratulated the village for their enduring spirit. He informed them that a team just located the rest of the snake's monstrous body in a cavern, an abandoned copper mine, mysteriously absent from any town records.

Just then, she heard a soft sound: a stirring from behind the trapper, from where the serpent's great face rested on the fire-warmed stone wall. She heard it; only she and it came from within the serpent's head.

From the serpent's nostril, a small, button-eyed face emerged, just above the trapper. Trailing a slender body patterned in rust red and ochre, one of the local farm snakes woke from the frost and drifted toward the open collar of the trapper's neck.

She watched.

The trapper was listening to the mayor. The hunter focused and the priest gasped.

With animal swiftness, she pinched the snake behind its head and tugged the rest of it effortlessly from the nostril; its tongue flicked with surrender.

The trapper took one look and staggered toward the priest.

The hunter roared with laughter.

The pub owner leapt across the bar, 'Any more in there? Give it a shake!'

The room thundered over the mayor's voice. The grandmother cried: 'It's just a corn snake! Don't kill it!'

The door opened and the pub again swirled with cold. The captain.

She held up the sleepy corn snake, wrapped round her wrist like a bracelet, its nose touching its tail.

§

In the morning, they buried the dog at the farm. The doctor's son used a small jack hammer to open the frozen ground and he and the captain shoveled the chunks of soil back into place. A pair of horses watched. They hung their chins over a bright new fence, nostrils smoking in the cold.

She looked around the farm. The roof was re-shingled. A fresh trail of dark slate stones framed by snow led to new wooden steps.

When the captain went inside to make coffee, she reached for the doctor's son and said, 'Everywhere I look, it's beautiful. You've worked miracles.'

'So have you.' He took her hand and looked to her belly. 'Does he know yet?'

'Did your mother tell you?'

'She wouldn't do that,' he laughed. 'It runs in the family, didn't she tell you? We know things.'

'She did,' she said, 'but she didn't mention your talents.'

'Well? Does he know?'

She shook her head.

'Lucky man,' he sighed. 'I admit, it was hard to let you go but I knew. I knew he'd steal you from me. That's why I had to kiss you before you left.'

He let go of her hand.

§

Serpent's Wake

Three months later, with a little belly and her husband beside her, she sat at the mouth of the cave where the poet studied all those years ago. Mist blanketed the valley. The mountains—their plummets of stone and gnarled pines—grew more distinct with the rising light. The rice willed to the monks had been shifted into the temple stores the afternoon before, and the captain and his wife were invited to stay.

At first light, the couple had walked along the mountain path to find the place where the poet cradled his life into poetry. The bee hives he once tended stood, still asleep beneath a stand of budding ginkgo trees, wooden legs tangled in low fog. They watched the light change, shoulders touching; air ripe with moss and water.

It was then that they heard the cranes cooing. Like spirits arriving caped in new light, the cranes materialized from the mist. Long legs stepped along grass, regal and gold with the rising sun; white wings opened and dripped with black mountainscapes: each an invitation to lovemaking. Their necks dipped and beaks pointed from glistening earth to the bluing heavens, their breath visible and ascending. As the cranes danced morning upon the mountain, she took the captain's hand and placed it upon her belly.

The baby kicked.

§

A baby boy arrived late autumn; the doctor and his wife on board to catch him. And when she held her infant son, it would surprise her again and again that such life sprang from hers. In the boy's piercing gaze, she surrendered to amazement.

And sometimes when she dreamt she was trapped and woke gasping, all she had to do was look to see that she was free.

She was free.

She was free.

She would see the dark cabin and the captain asleep beside her and she would rise from their bed. She would walk to the cradle and touch her sleeping son with her glance alone. She would pass through the galley, her books stowed behind a rail the locksmith built especially for her, and drift onto the deck.

On particular nights—on the darkest, moonless ones—she gazed out at the black waters and unfolded within herself the darkness in which she learned to see. Under the bend of a sky salted with stars, she stood in a nightdress, fingers and toes splayed in the cool air, and reminded herself of where she had been and held it all, unafraid.

And from that place alone could she be with her whole self until everything scattered and rose from her at the edge of dawn: sea eagles on the wind, serpents evolved to take flight.

§

I know you are brave.
Or you wouldn't have come this far.
The story has peeled away to its heart, and grown whole again in your hands.
It's ready now, bright as dark feathers shining over a mountain peak; ready, like you, to fly into the sun.

Made in the USA
Middletown, DE
12 August 2024